Remigiusz Mróz

NEVER FOUND

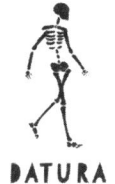

DATURA

DATURA BOOKS
An imprint of Watkins Media Ltd

Unit 11, Shepperton House
89-93 Shepperton Road
London N1 3DF
UK

daturabooks.com
Picture Of You

A Datura Books paperback original, 2026

Cover by Sarah O'Flaherty
Set in Meridien

ISBN 978 1 91741 520 0
Ebook ISBN 978 1 91741 521 7

Printed and bound in the United Kingdom by CPI Group (UK) Ltd, Croydon CR0 4YY

The manufacturer's authorised representative in the EU for product safety is eucomply OÜ – Pärnu mnt 139b-14, 11317 Tallinn, Estonia, hello@eucompliancepartner.com; www.eucompliancepartner.com

9 8 7 6 5 4 3 2 1

MIX
Paper | Supporting responsible forestry
FSC® C013604
www.fsc.org

For those who know that silence is the loudest scream.

There are two kinds of males – men who stand up for women's rights and cowards. The choice is yours.

Abaida Mahmood

CHAPTER 1

1

If I had proposed to her a moment earlier, it would never have happened. We wouldn't have been assaulted, I wouldn't have ended up in a hospital and she wouldn't be gone from my life forever.

Thirty seconds, maybe even less, would have been enough. Sometimes, however, it only takes one moment to wreck someone's whole life. And to make whatever remains of it a mere attempt at oblivion.

An attempt at which I was unsuccessful. I turned that event over in my head, over and over again, and considered what would have happened if we'd drunk one fewer beer, left the pub earlier or had a smoke by the river for a while. Psychologists call this counterfactual thinking – creating alternative scenarios of events that have already taken place. It is neither a rare phenomenon nor a completely negative one. It allows us to avoid making the same mistakes in the future, often raises our spirits and gives us a sense of control over our own destiny. In my case, though, it had the opposite effect, making me even more depressed, amplifying my guilt and my sense of having no agency whatsoever in the world around me. I kept saying to myself that all it would have taken was for me to have pulled that ring out a mere few seconds earlier – but I hadn't. On that unlucky day, every step and every decision, no matter how small or trivial, had led to what had happened.

That Saturday night, ten years ago, began as usual. Ewa and I went to the Highlander, our favourite pub in Opole's Old Town. It was located in a small alley, right by the river.

We'd been regulars there long before we could legally drink alcohol. At that time, we would also often go to the Sneering Lodge, a place on the bank of the Młynówka River. You had to climb down the narrow stairs behind the pub to get to it. I don't know how it got its name, which had been written in spray paint on a small wall a good decade earlier and stuck for good.

As we went downstairs, Ewa could already sense something. However, this had nothing to do with the group of men who were just finishing their beers at the Highlander. She knew me very well and she must have noted how nervous I'd been all evening.

We'd been an item for as long as we could remember. Circumstances brought us together already in the eighties, when we both hung around the estate on Spychalskiego Street in Zaodrze, carefree and unaware of what life would bring.

We quickly became inseparable. We were in the same class in elementary school, and first kissed each other at the age of ten on the stairs leading to the locker room. At the beginning of high school, on a school trip, we slept together for the first time. Before graduation, everyone kept telling us that we would split up – Ewa got accepted to the polytechnic and I went to university. According to our friends, we were supposed to pay for our earlier inseparability, but that never happened.

We rented a flat together and started planning our future. It seemed natural to me that I should propose. And maybe that day Ewa knew I was going to do it.

I chose the Sneering Lodge because it was probably the only place in Opole where we spent so much time. We smoked loads of cigarettes there, drank pints of cheap wine and had a joint for the first time.

There used to be nothing romantic about the place. It was a littered stretch of riverbank, hiding under the frail branches of a lonely old tree. When I proposed, however, it was different – the place became part of the Opole Venice, a newly developed waterfront, of which the most distinctive was a row of colourfully illuminated buildings, almost touching the water.

The Sneering Lodge, I thought, would do.

I went to one knee and would probably have felt like a complete moron if not for the fact that I was well sloshed. Ewa raised her hand to her mouth theatrically, making me realize with that gesture that she had known all along what was coming.

I slipped the ring on her finger, kissed her, held her tightly and then stayed silent for a moment. We were so close that in our relationship silence was more of a bond than an ever-growing gap that separates some people. We were both drunk with happiness, feeling blessed and carefree. I put my arm around Ewa and then we moved up the stairs towards the pub and a small car park.

Just as we were about to pass the Highlander's doorway, five men came out, pissed out of their minds, talking loudly and pushing one another. At first, we weren't bothered because that was by no means a rare sight on a Saturday night on Opole's market square, but after a moment things took a different turn.

One of them looked at Ewa and went silent. It seemed as if he'd suddenly found himself in the eye of a cyclone. His mates shoved him, shouting something, but he stood motionless, never taking his eyes off my fiancée.

"Oh, fuck," he said.

I keep going back to that moment, to the sight and the voice of that man. They're just as blurry for me now as when I embraced Ewa and decided to walk faster.

The one who spoke stood in our way. His friends looked at him uncertainly for a moment and then joined him.

"Something wrong?" Ewa asked them.

Now I know that I should have said something, should have drawn their attention to myself. Maybe it would have made things different.

Or maybe not.

"Well..." Only one of them spoke. The others calmed down and got serious, everyone suddenly focused on Ewa, and I looked around nervously, hoping to see another passerby, but the riverbank was empty.

Ewa mumbled, "Sorry," and tried to go past them, but none of the men even moved. We stopped closer to them and I felt that my heart was about to burst out of my chest.

"What's the matter?" I asked.

"You left something downstairs," answered the largest of them, pointing to the stairway.

The others weren't that muscular, but it didn't matter. There were five of them, and I was on my own. Even if I'd been an MMA fighter, I couldn't have taken them all.

The first blow, which almost knocked me to the ground, made me realize that very clearly. It was a sloppy, street-style punch, but unexpected enough to nearly knock me out.

It was the large one that had hit me. I heard Ewa screaming something, but my head was ringing so loud I couldn't make out the words. Then the gang grabbed us by our lapels and pushed us towards the Sneering Lodge.

By the time I realized where we were going, we were back at the riverbank. I tried to get away, but one of the group held me down and the big one hit me again, then three or four more times. I fell to the ground next to the tree under which we'd once smoked our first joint. I felt no pain, but there was a metallic aftertaste in my mouth and blood was spilling from it freely, almost in spurts. Everything went blurry, but I could see clearly when they threw Ewa on the ground a little bit further down.

They said something, laughed. Ewa screamed. To this day, I can't get her words out of my mind.

I tried to get up, but they quickly knocked me back down. One well-aimed blow was enough. I fell, but immediately started crawling towards Ewa. One of them had already torn off her blouse, and the bigger one started to squeeze her breasts brutally. I screamed silently, or at least I thought I did, trying in vain to get close to her.

At some point, they noticed my pathetic attempts, and one of them hit me in the head, then gave me a swift kick, and things went dark for a moment. When I could see again, another one was taking off Ewa's trousers.

The world became unreal. I felt like I was being suffocated with something heavy, like my fiancée must have felt when one of her attackers covered her mouth. I threatened them, cursed them, and then begged them to stop. Eventually, I started begging to God to intervene, promising Him I would do anything to save Ewa.

Then I saw her red lace underwear she had bought some time ago – for a special occasion, she had said at the time.

With a roar of laughter, the aggressors tore off her panties. The first one dropped his pants and lay down on top of Ewa. Another man stood behind me, lifting my head so that I was forced to watch what was happening.

Every time I tried to get away, I got hit in the back of the head. I screamed, still desperately trying to get to my fiancée. I dug my fingers into the ground, but by the time the rapist was finished I hadn't got even a foot closer.

Then another one dropped on top of her. He was very forceful, like he was trying to crush her. I heard her wail and cry, saw her trying to push her attackers back. She didn't stand a chance.

I managed to get a little closer before the others noticed me again. One of them came up to me, said something and then raised his leg. Before his heavy boot fell on me, I looked at Ewa. Her expression of suffering, pain and humiliation burned into my memory forever.

It was the last time I saw her.

At least until I found her picture on Facebook ten years later.

2

The identity of the attackers was never determined. Neither they nor my fiancée were ever found. She disappeared without a trace, as did the life I was planning.

It wasn't just that I was forced to live without Ewa. My life changed in every other aspect, too.

After graduation, I could have applied to study economics in Wrocław, Poznań or Kraków, and almost any university would have accepted me with open arms. I had chosen to study management at Opole University only to stay with Ewa, who insisted she didn't want to leave the city.

She hadn't had to work hard to convince me. She was all that mattered, and besides, with good grades, I had expected to land a well-paid job in Opole after graduating. Not an exciting one, perhaps, but enough for a decent life. That was all I cared about.

But I never graduated. After that horrible night, I was never the same.

For the first few months I was constantly on the move, frantically trying to find any trace of my fiancée. I followed up on every lead, every opportunity, and involved all the services, organizations and associations that could have helped in any way.

Nothing. It was like Ewa had fallen into a black hole. Our attackers had apparently been just passing through Opole. At first, I was convinced they'd come from one of the villages near the city, but after several months I realized that if they had, someone would have recognized them by then. Meanwhile, they remained unidentified, and soon their faces, blurred and disturbing, seemed to exist only in my memory.

After a few intense months, I was exhausted. I gave up my studies, hid in our apartment and spent most of the time immersed in growing lethargy. I drank more and more and had less and less interest in the outside world. After a while, all that mattered was opening the next beer and killing the time however I could, mostly by playing video games. *Dead Space*, *Left 4 Dead*, *GTA IV* and *Fallout 3* replaced reality. Or maybe they helped me survive somehow – "somehow" being the key word. Before I knew it, it was too late to go back to the plans I'd once had. I'd have had to retake too many classes at university, I would have to lie on my CV, and I would have to give up everything that had kept me alive for so many months.

About a year after the events at Sneering Lodge, I went back to the area and got a job at the Highlander as a bartender. I worked a lot of shifts, enough to know every scratch on the counter and all the customers. But Ewa's tormentors never came back, and I didn't even know if I'd ever really counted on it.

I moved from pub to pub, never staying in one place for long, not establishing any closer relations with anyone. In a city of a hundred and twenty thousand, everyone knew my face, and I became known as something of a weirdo. No great surprise, really.

After almost ten years, I got a job as a waiter in SpiceX, a new Indian restaurant on the market square, near the monument that we nicknamed the Wench on a Bull. It was the only Indian place in Opole, and the location was good, so my salary and tips were enough to pay for my flat, alcohol and broadband – my only expenses.

During my leaner years, I was helped by Adam Blicki, whom we'd called Blitz ever since elementary school, and who was my only friend. In a way, at least. We didn't hang out – I never went over to his place, and he never came to see me. Not after he'd knocked at my door a dozen or so times and I'd pretended I wasn't home. Instead, he came regularly to all the places I worked, as if they were his favourite hangouts. He kept that up for almost ten years, and I think it suited both of us. He would usually show up with good news, as if he'd made it a point of honour to constantly try to raise my spirits.

But one day, he came to SpiceX with a laptop under his arm, looked around nervously, then sat at a table by the window and called me over with a gesture.

"Werner!"

I approached him slowly because the stuff he usually got excited about was of no interest to me. I stood at his table and opened my mouth, but he wouldn't let me say anything.

"You have to see this," he blurted, opening his laptop. "Sit down. Sit."

It was early in the morning. There was only one customer in the restaurant, and I'd just brought him mango lassi, so I didn't have to worry about getting a dressing-down from my boss for chatting with a friend. I sat next to Blitz and looked at the monitor.

"It's her, right?" Adam said.

"What are you talking about?"

"Look," he said, pointing at the screen.

The system woke up and a Facebook post popped up on the screen. The photo was slightly blurry, but not so much that I couldn't recognize who it was.

I felt as if the air around me crackled with electricity, heralding a storm. But instead of a distant rumble, I was hit by lightning.

Ewa.

She'd changed the way people usually do over ten years. Her wrinkles had grown more pronounced, she'd gained a little weight, dyed her hair a little, maybe gotten a nose job, but I had no doubt that I was looking at her picture.

"How do you–" I broke off. I couldn't get anything else out.

Blitz, whom we also called Blitzer or Blitzkrieg, usually reacted to everything immediately, ever faithful to his nickname, but this time he was silent. Meanwhile, I felt like the world was becoming increasingly unreal. Just like ten years earlier on the riverbank. I tried to swallow, but my throat was stuffed with dry cotton wool.

"How is that possible?" I blurted.

"I don't know."

"What kind of fan page is this?" The question was symptomatic of our time. Once, I would have started by asking Blitzer how he'd found the photo, where it was taken, and so on. Now, of course, I didn't have to; his answer could actually tell me everything.

"*Spotted: Wrocław.*"

I shook my head and only then realized that it was really happening. I rubbed my neck and looked around nervously. I felt like an animal in a dark, impenetrable forest, stalked by a whole host of hunters.

"It's really her, Werner."

I forced myself to nod a fraction.

"And she was less than fifty miles away."

I leaned back over the laptop, trying to get a grip on myself. After years of searching, I finally had a lead. There was a glimmer of hope that I would finally get answers to all the questions that had been buzzing in my head for a decade.

What happened to her after the rape? Why did she disappear without a trace? Where was she all that time? Did she know our attackers? All those unanswered questions roared back like an echo of an artillery volley that had once razed my whole world to the ground.

I looked at the picture, which showed Ewa during some kind of an outdoor concert. It was late in the evening, and the image was full of luridly coloured lights. She wasn't looking into the lens, and maybe hadn't even been aware that someone was taking her photo. She was laughing, raising one hand towards the stage. There was a man standing next to her, holding her by the arm, as if he wanted to get her attention or draw her to himself. He was standing with his back to the camera, so his face was hidden, and was wearing a grey hoodie-type Foo Fighters sweatshirt emblazoned with a winged bomb motif and the inscription *there is nothing left to lose*.

Foo Fighters – Blitz's favourite band since 1995. He'd been listening to them while others had been trying to impress their friends with their collection of hip-hop records while secretly listening to the *Toy Story* soundtrack.

"It's…" I began, pointing to the sweatshirt. "Was that their concert? Were you there?"

"I was."

"For fuck's sake, Blitz! Did you see her?" I felt like grabbing his shoulders and shaking him, but managed to stop myself in time. My heart was hammering and a wave of heat washed through my body. My mind veered between understanding what was happening and losing all touch with reality.

"No," said Blitzer. "I only saw her in that picture half an hour ago, when–"

"How did you find it? And who took it?" I broke in, then realized I needed to get a grip on my emotions or I'd shoot out a whole cannonade of further questions. I closed my eyes, straightened up and stayed still for a while.

"If you let me get a word in edgewise," he said, "I'll tell you everything."

"Go ahead."

"It was yesterday, that concert. Foo Fighters played at the City Stadium."

"Yesterday?"

"Take it easy."

I took a gulp of air and held it in my lungs. "You didn't tell me you were going."

"Since when do we talk about that kind of thing?" He shrugged. "You don't give a shit, and I don't feel like I need to share it. Like when I meet a proper marten."

Only Blitzer could call a woman that. Normally I would have said something, but now it didn't even cross my mind.

"Like this time, for instance," he added, not taking his eyes off the photo. "Unfortunately, I scared her away and she disappeared into the crowd, so I started looking for her first thing in the morning. And that's how I came across this *Spotted* page, and this photo."

By now we were both staring at the photo like it was a religious icon. In it, Ewa was wearing a T-shirt with a different band logo. All I could see was a fragment of their name: Gutierrez Y Angelo. The title of the album or the single was *Better Days*. I'd never heard of it.

The silence dragged on. I didn't notice that the other customer had finished his mango lassi and was looking around impatiently.

"Maybe..." I started, and then paused. "Maybe I was too quick to think it was her."

"What?"

"It's impossible. After ten years, why would she suddenly show up now?"

"Why not?"

The question was as good as any. Maybe I let myself get carried away and hastily assumed it was Ewa. Or maybe not. Maybe it was really her.

"Christ," I moaned, then shook my head. "She looks happy," I added.

"She *is* at a Foo Fighters gig."

"Still."

"You've assumed someone had kept her locked up in a basement for ten years?"

"I don't know what I assumed." I couldn't have said a more real thing. There were too many theories swirling around her disappearance, some of which I'd come up with myself, others that I'd taken from journalists and anonymous internet users commenting on local articles that each year reminded everyone Ewa was still gone. These kinds of articles would crop up every year, with a photo and a suggestion that the most probable scenario was that the girl had fallen into the river, though the authors emphasized that the body had never been found.

Then there were a couple of more sensational articles. One even ran with the headline, "NEW FACTS IN THE CASE. DAMIAN WERNER INTERROGATED". In truth, about halfway through the statute of limitations, I was indeed questioned, but only as a witness, one of the investigators wanting to make sure that the case was rightly dropped for lack of evidence. That was one of the "new facts" mentioned in the article's headline. Just clickbait.

What I had in front of me now wasn't clickbait.

"Is anybody looking for her?" I asked.

"The guy who uploaded the picture, Phil Braddy."

I looked at the thumbnail of the photo and read the post. "American?"

"British," said Blitzer. "Apparently, he came all the way from London for the gig. And he liked the girl he met by chance. He writes here that they chatted briefly, had a laugh together, and then he left to find his friends. When he came back, she was gone. Now he's looking for her."

I'd have to write to him right away, to find out what Ewa said, as if it meant anything.

"I sent him a message before I left home," added Blitz.

I nodded my thanks. The customer sitting a bit further away grunted pointedly, but I ignored him.

"Anyone write back?" I asked.

"A dozen or so people. Say what you want, but this picture stands out."

Blitzkrieg was right. Slightly fuzzy stroboscopes in the background, a big party and focus on a laughing, pretty girl. The picture was definitely eye-catching.

"Anybody write anything specific?" I asked uncertainly.

"No, just a bunch of bullshit comments you don't want to read."

I didn't mean to, but I was sure I would as soon as I got home. But before I did, I had another place to visit first. I've watched too many films and TV shows not to know that failing to inform the police immediately upon finding new evidence is a big mistake.

I thanked Blitz, went to the back room, called my boss and told him I was coming down with something. Working around food had the advantage that pub owners took such things seriously, especially if they wanted their customers to come back.

My replacement arrived quite quickly, but before he did I managed to serve another customer a plate of poppadoms and scrutinize the photo of Ewa until I knew every minute detail by heart. By the time I arrived at the station at Powolnego Street, I could have described it from memory to the officer in charge, but I didn't have to. We went on Facebook and I showed him the picture. He looked at it for a long time, his brows drawn. Deputy Commissioner Prokocki had been in charge of the case ten years ago, and I expected to see a flash in his eyes that would finally make me believe that what I saw was real, but he looked as if I was showing him a picture of some random person.

"It's quite normal, you know," he said at last.

"What?"

"That you're looking for a missing fiancée in other women."

I opened my mouth but couldn't get a word out. The absolute certainty in his voice baffled me. Prokocki took his eyes off the monitor, took deep breath and looked at me with compassion. "You haven't had a relationship with anyone since then, have you?" he asked.

"No, I have not. But what does that have to do with anything?"

"You're still missing her, so it's only natural that–"

"You've got to be kidding."

"These things happen."

I pointed my finger at the monitor as if in accusation. "Do you see what I see?"

"I see a girl who looks like Ewa, Mr Werner. That's it. That's all there is to it."

I stamped my foot and looked around helplessly, as if I could expect anyone to come to my aid here. "It's her, damn it!" I said sharply. "Don't you see?"

He took a breath. "Unfortunately, I can't agree with you," he said officiously. "Yes, there is a resemblance, but–"

"I know what my own fiancée looks like."

He stood up slowly, as if afraid he'd offend me if he didn't, then put his hand on my shoulder and slowly started to explain that I knew what she looked like ten years ago, and that my mind was now playing tricks on me. He continued in this vein for several minutes and I listened to him with less and less focus, becoming increasingly upset by his smooth confidence, the utter certainty in his voice and his unwillingness to admit that it *could* be her.

"Of course, we'll check it out," he assured me, guiding me to the exit. "Don't worry about that."

But I was worried. Something was undoubtedly very wrong here.

3

I was sure that coming home would give me at least partial relief. It happened every day when I closed the door behind me and then turned its three sturdy locks. If I knew I didn't have to go out anymore, I would feel almost ecstatic, but if I knew I'd have to leave again later, I would feel anxious and uneasy.

That day, my home-sweet-home was supposed to have a calming effect on me, but I felt like a stranger in my own flat. I filled it with the sounds of Rainbow because, unlike Blitz, I liked bands you didn't hear about anymore.

My hands were shaking and I felt like I had a fever. Only then did I realize how sweaty I was. The cool fabric of my

T-shirt stuck to my back, and there was no trace of the wave of heat I'd felt earlier. Standing in front of the mirror, I almost didn't recognize my reflection. I was deathly pale, and the shadows under my eyes were even more pronounced than usual. My hair, usually dishevelled anyway, looked like a tangle of wires.

I rinsed my face with cold water, then opened a beer and sat down in front of my PC. I had assembled it myself, saving a pretty penny. I turned on the latest *Elder Scrolls* game, then reached for my phone, intending to turn it off. I felt the need to disappear from the world, right now, before I completely lost my mind. There was no point in torturing myself by refreshing the same Facebook post or waiting for Phil Braddy to reply. I'd been waiting ten years; I could wait a little longer. But I had to calm down.

Blitzer didn't give me a chance, though. As soon as I touched my smartphone, his laughing face popped on the screen – a selfie he had taken years ago, when I was still working at the Highlander – and the default ringtone sounded. Yes, I'm one of those people who moves all their photos to their new phone. Nowadays it's not much of a hassle, but in the past transitioning from the first Ericsson Sony cameraphone to the new Nokia wasn't that easy.

I paused the game and swiped my finger on the screen. "Not a good time," I told him.

"Have you seen it?" he blurted nervously and coughed.

"No, you haven't, otherwise you wouldn't have said that."

"Have I seen what?"

"The new post."

I turned off the game like my life depended on it, then booted up my browser and refreshed the page. Yes, there was a new post from Phil Braddy.

"Maybe someone will recognize her in this photo," he'd written in English, and attached a link to the previous post.

I stared at a picture but it felt as if I was looking directly into a portal leading to an alternative reality. I knew the picture very well. It was special to me.

"Are you there?" Blitzer asked.

I tried to say something, but the words stuck in my throat.

"Werner!"

"I... Yeah, I'm here."

"It's definitely her," he said. "She's standing somewhere on Krakowska Street, not far from the Wench on a Bull. And she's a good few years younger."

"Ten," I groaned.

"What?"

"I took this picture myself."

"What do you mean? When? Where?"

"A few days before she went missing. But Blitz..."

"What?"

"I've never shown it to anyone. I've never uploaded it. I've never even told anyone I had it."

"What? Why?"

"I don't know," I said, rubbing my forehead. "I guess I just wanted to have something for myself, something for me, just for me, because–"

"Never mind," he cut in. "Where did the Brit get this picture?"

"I have no idea." I couldn't imagine how Phil Braddy could have gotten his hands on the photo. This photo. My photo. All possible explanations were utterly absurd. Even if he had talked to Ewa longer than the first post suggested, she didn't have the photo. I hadn't even had time to show it to her, and I'd remembered it only after she'd disappeared.

I reached for my beer and drained it in one gulp. My stomach complained.

I realized that what I had was a lot more than just a flimsy lead. The fact that Braddy had this photograph proved he had to be involved in the case.

"Did he write back to you?" I asked.

"Yeah, right after he uploaded the picture."

I felt shivers down my spine. "And?"

"Says he doesn't know her, not really. Never seen her before or after, and just wants to get in touch with her. He asked me if I knew her."

"Tell him that..."

I stopped mid-sentence, figuring I shouldn't rely solely on Blitz anymore. I pulled up Phil Braddy's profile and looked at a face I already knew by heart from staring at it for hours. Then I sent him a message: "I know the girl you're looking for. Where'd you get the other picture?"

Blitzkrieg said something into the headset, but his voice seemed to fade somewhere on the line. I kept staring at the computer screen, feeling like the room was getting hotter and hotter. Finally, the blue icon next to the message I'd sent to Braddy lit up, indicating he'd read it. But there was no indication that he was replying to me.

I pushed the chair back, leaned forward and started to hit my thighs with my hands. Looking at the monitor, I felt like I had just issued a challenge.

A challenge that had yet to be answered.

"He's not writing back," I said.

"Huh?" Blitzer grunted. "Did you write to him?"

"Yes, but–"

"You were supposed to leave it to me."

I didn't remember us ever agreeing to that, but maybe Blitzer assumed that, since it had all started with him, he had some historical responsibility to bring the matter to a conclusion.

"He's still not answering," I said. "Although he did read the message."

"Hold on a sec."

"That's all I've been doing, Blitz," I murmured. "For the last ten years."

Every second seemed to drag on slower and slower, and I was losing patience. I felt like I had answers at my fingertips. All I had to do was push Braddy.

"The whole thing about looking for a girl from the gig is bullshit," I said. "It's about something else."

"About what?"

"I don't know. But I'm going to find out."

"On your own?"

"With your help," I replied, and suddenly realized that it was probably the nicest thing I'd ever said to him. Actually, for the first time, I'd treated him the way I should have treated him all along: like a friend I could rely on.

"Well, duh," he said. "But that may not be enough."

"I'll go to the police first thing in the morning."

"You haven't talked to them yet?"

"I have, but they sent me away." I gave him an overview of my conversation with DC Prokocki, and he went quiet for a long time. I kept looking at the monitor as if I could force Phil Braddy to reveal his secrets. No such luck – my inbox stayed stubbornly empty. It became clear he wasn't going to write back. He never responded to Blitz, either.

I went to get another beer, knowing already that I would make some bad decisions today and then wake up the next morning with a hell of the headache.

"Hasn't he taken any interest in the case at all?" Blitzer finally said.

"Nope. And not only was he not interested, he tried to dismiss my concerns."

"That is weird."

"That's what I thought at first, too."

"And then you changed your mind?"

"Yup," I confirmed. "Every day in Poland some fifty people disappear without a trace. Prokocki probably gets reports about the miraculous appearance of one of them on a daily basis."

"But he saw the picture. He had to recognize her. He'd been looking for her for months."

"Maybe he did," I suggested, "and he just didn't want to give me false hope." This was the most convenient explanation, one that would justify downplaying new evidence. The other versions that I was considering boiled down to uniquely gloomy scenarios.

However, all that was no longer relevant. Now, when the very same photo I had in my phone popped up on the internet, I could use it as an undeniable proof. Prokocki would take the opportunity to follow up on this fresh lead while there was still time, until the statute of limitations ran out. He wouldn't want to have an unsolved case in his files.

And maybe not just in the files. Maybe, despite the fact that to all intents and purposes he seemed to underestimate the report, he immediately threw himself into the investigation. I could imagine it, although it required an injection of liquid optimism from two more beers.

* * *

The next morning, as I suspected, I woke up hung over. I'd fallen asleep on the couch, the laptop still open on the coffee table. There was no reply from Braddy. He'd ignored Blitzer, too.

I took a quick shower, if only to avoid looking like I confused the police station with a drunk tank when I got there.

When I arrived at the station, I had to wait a while until Prokocki could see me, which was okay; I hadn't expected him to see me immediately. I'm sure he thought I'd come to harass him for no particular reason.

When he finally invited me to his office, I showed him another photo and then that Facebook post. The users gradually began to chime in with comments to the Brit looking for a Polish woman – they identified the location in Opole, informed him that it wasn't far from Wrocław and that it was probably there that he should look for her. But no one recognized Ewa.

Neither did Prokocki.

"Is that her?" he asked.

I needed a few moments to get over the fact that he'd really asked me that question. Then I shook my head and started explaining to him once again that I had taken this photograph myself. Finally, I showed it to him on my phone.

He stared at it for a long time and then looked at me as if I was a criminal, not someone looking for a missing fiancée.

"Did you drink anything this morning?" The question was rhetorical. I was breathing quickly and the office smelled like a distillery.

"Why, what does it matter?" I retorted.

"Nothing. It's your life."

"It's more like a substitute of one," I mumbled under my breath, and then pointed to the phone's display. "Because that's all that's left of it after she disappeared. Do you understand?"

"Of course…"

"And you can see that it's an identical photograph, can't you?"

"That is beyond any doubt."

"So what's with all that reticence?"

He sighed deeply. "It's just professional restraint. You have to understand that I've worked on some similar cases before."

I kept silent, fearing that otherwise I would say something that I would later regret.

"You can rely on my experience."

"I do," I declared, though I no longer had any confidence in him at this stage.

"In that case, please leave it to us. I promise you that we will do everything in our power to examine all the circumstances."

"I don't doubt it."

I'd been expecting more than that – a promise that they would contact the British, or that they'd try to track down Phil Braddy. Anything. Then Prokocki rose from behind his desk and reached out to me. I thought he wanted to shake my hand.

"I'm afraid you'll have to leave your phone with us."

"Excuse me?"

"It may prove to be an important piece of evidence."

"But–"

"Mr Werner, trust me, please. We'll do everything we can to find your fiancée."

I looked at my mobile phone and felt like I was going to say goodbye to something much more important than just a phone. Although I didn't use it very often, I felt like I didn't have a reason to hand it over. Plus it had a picture of her in it. My only copy.

"I'd rather not."

"Don't you want to find her?" the deputy commissioner interrupted me.

I nodded.

"In that case, you'll have to trust us. We know what we're doing."

He kept his hand out until I gave him my mobile. Maybe I would have objected if not for the hangover, and if everything that happened hadn't made me feel completely confused.

"So you're going to reopen the case?" I asked him as he led me towards the door.

"If anything new pops up, of course."

"If?"

"We'll be in touch," Prokocki assured me.

I didn't tell him that might not be so easy now he'd taken my phone away.

But it wasn't the only thing I lost that day.

I came home with the intention of downloading the photo from Facebook as soon as possible. I had to have it; in a way it was more important to me than the memories of Ewa.

But the photograph had disappeared. Just like the previous post.

Along with Phil Braddy's account.

4

Finding somewhere to eat that was open before noon wasn't easy in Opole, at least not where you could eat well, but

SpiceX was the exception. The boss opened in the morning and we worked until midday, then he closed for some time and in the afternoon we opened again, working full tilt. In the Mediterranean, or in India for that matter, that kind of schedule may have worked, but here I figured it would end in bankruptcy sooner or later. However, I wasn't about to share that opinion with the owner.

Blitzer showed up before eleven AM, with his laptop. He didn't look much better than I did, and apparently he hadn't got much sleep either. He must have finally dozed off in the morning, because when I talked to him on Skype after visiting the station, I was under the impression that I'd just woken him up. I summarized everything he needed to know.

It felt strange sharing what was happening in my life with someone. This made me realize that for ten years, that life had been closed to the outside world. Even when I visited my parents in their small apartment on Grottgera Street, we talked about anything but what had happened to Ewa.

Blitz sat down at the same table as before and beckoned me over.

"I still can't get over it," he said. "The posts are just gone."

"Did you write to the admin?"

"Right after we talked."

I had to rely on him this time. I would have liked to take a leave of absence, not only because I was terribly hungover, but I knew I would have problems with my boss afterwards, and I couldn't afford to see my only livelihood disappear now. I figured I'd be needing the money soon.

"They said they didn't delete any entries," Blitzkrieg continued. "And I know they say nothing disappears on the internet, but I couldn't find any trace of them."

"No trace of Braddy, either."

"None," Blitz confirmed, lost in thought, turning over the menu on the table.

Then he froze, and slowly turned his eyes to look at me. He didn't have to say anything; we both knew how shady the whole thing might prove to be.

From time to time there were reports in the media about police officers whose sins came to light only years later. Recently, several had been accused of misconduct in the murder of a young girl some fifteen years earlier. They'd been charged with failure to comply with the law, exceeding their authority and obstruction of justice. It turned out that for years they'd been deliberately confusing clues and concealing the truth. Together, they conspired to cover up for one another and the perpetrators. Was that also the case with Ewa? Or was I starting to dream up conspiracy theories?

But even if I assumed the police were involved, how did they remove all traces from Facebook? And so fast?

And how did Braddy get my photograph?

There were more and more questions, but I was convinced that I would find an answer. All I had to do was find something specific, something to get me on the right track.

"I told you my help wasn't enough," said Blitzer.

"Yeah, you said. And you see where that led us."

"I wasn't talking about the police."

"Then what?"

"A private investigator."

I looked at him in disbelief. I associated such agencies with either cheap media theatrics or spying on cheating spouses.

"It's a real thing," he added, turning the laptop towards me.

I looked around to check I wasn't being observed by any other customers, then leaned over the table. In spite of myself, I started reading the website of a company called Reimann Investigations.

"The owner is former law enforcement," said Blitzer. "They're officially licensed and everything."

I looked at the general information on the website.

"They're also members of the WAPI," he went on.

"The what?"

"World Association of Professional Investigators," he explained. "Plus they're members of the WAD, which brings together agencies from all over the world, ever since 1925. These are some credentials."

I leaned even further and clicked on the price list, mainly to get an idea of what they were doing.

The hourly rate was a hundred zlotys, and for the whole eight-hour working day they charged eleven hundred. A business background check was a bit more expensive, while tracking down a witness was cheaper. They also provided services for law firms, carried out financial investigations, found lost property and, of course, searched for missing persons.

This last position in the price list was the most expensive. Prices started from forty-seven hundred zlotys.

"Look at the team," Blitz said.

I opened another page, which featured information about the company's headquarters and the people who work there.

"Rewal?" I asked. "It's by the sea, about six hundred kilometres away, Blitz."

"It doesn't matter."

"Maybe for someone who's got money. I can't afford the commute."

"They mostly work from the office."

I found a chair and sat down in front of his laptop.

"PIs no longer have to run after someone with a zoom lens to keep an eye on them," Blitz continued. "All they need to know is how to do the same thing on the internet. And these people apparently do know."

I went over the list of employees. There weren't many of them, and all had their faces covered for obvious reasons. The owner was Robert Reimann, a former customs officer. He was the recipient of a number of awards and had won several Man of the Year titles for the entire province. The main investigator was his wife, Kasandra Reimann, which in a way added credibility to the company. If someone was planning scams, they probably wouldn't involve their family, I reasoned. Or maybe I was just deluding myself.

The team consisted of several more people. One of them was a graduate of AGH University of Science and Technology, another had studied at Łódź Technical University and the third was an alumnus of Technische Universitat Kaiserslautern. Everyone apparently had experience in the IT industry, but no details were given.

"Looks good," I said. "But, uh…"

"You need these people, Werner."

"Maybe," I said. "But I also need money to hire them."

"I'll lend you some."

"And how am I going to pay you back?"

"We'll think of something," he said, dismissing the issue with the wave of his hand. "The important thing now is to get to the truth quickly before they cover their tracks."

I raised my eyebrows in disbelief and looked at him closely. "'They' who?"

"I don't know," he admitted. "And that's probably the worst part of it all."

At first, I was ready to agree with him, but then I realized that the worst part was that somebody had concealed the truth from me.

No, not someone – she had. Either Ewa or the people who had hurt her that night had done everything to keep me from finding out what really happened after that ill-fated night.

"All right," I said.

Blitz wrinkled his brow, looking at me.

"If you vouch for the Reimanns, I'll hire them."

"They look like solid players," Blitz replied. "I did a little background check."

"What do you mean?"

"I Googled them."

"That's not research. It's the internet equivalent of looking around."

"Don't underestimate the power of Google. Some people live because of it."

"I don't," I said.

"Take computer scientists," he went on. "In ninety-nine cases out of a hundred, their advantage over ordinary mortals lies in the fact that they know how to quickly check stuff on Google."

Blitz was still dwelling on the historical importance of the company founded by two Stanford PhD students. I tuned him out, more or less, when he claimed that a non-functional search engine was the only universal and undeniable proof that the internet wasn't working, and that we had reached a point in history when it's hard to believe that Page and Brin did indeed develop Google... without Googling it first. As he talked himself blue in the face, which might have been his way of coping with his emotions, I reviewed more documentation and evidence that Reimann Investigations really knew what they were doing. I tuned back in when he'd run out of steam.

"Anyway, take a look at the results yourself," he muttered, noting my lack of interest. "They've made a name for themselves in Pomerania. They give a lot to charity, support local businesses and bankroll two animal shelters."

"Sounds suspicious, if you ask me."

Blitz rolled his eyes. "If you suspect those who help you, I don't want to know what the world looks like from your perspective."

"Like a place that a few motherfuckers want to destroy at all costs."

"It's not that bad, actually."

"No," I confessed, massaging my shoulders. "It is just that everyone else looks at them with curiosity and waits to see what's going to happen instead of stopping them."

"That sounds more like you."

"Mm-hmm," I murmured, not wanting to go even deeper into the pessimism that threatened to envelop me. "Anything else you found out about the Reimanns?"

"Only that they anonymously support some NGOs."

"They must be very anonymous indeed, if you're telling me about it."

He sighed, as if uncomfortable with the idea that he was playing devil's advocate. "Some local journalists found out. It's all unofficial."

"Anyway, it sounds suspicious," I repeated and raised my hand, silencing his objections. "I mean, apparently they made a small fortune, and–"

"Yeah, they are pretty comfortable," he agreed.

"In the private investigation business?"

"No, Robert Reimann left the service because he inherited a local company made up of several marinas, restaurants and holiday farms. His wife also has a flourishing real estate business." Blitzkrieg did indeed come well prepared, handing me a potential solution to my problem and even offering to pay for it himself.

I decided not to hesitate any longer. "Okay," I said. "If you're willing to lend me the money, let's do it."

"Great. Especially since they've already agreed on a flat rate."

"I beg your pardon?"

"I've already discussed the costs with Kasandra. Exceptionally nice marten."

"No doubt." I pictured a typical businesswoman, a proud wife of a wealthy local tycoon. Although, according to Blitz, they valued privacy and rarely appeared in public, I pictured them looking like a typical Hollywood couple.

"The payment will be made in advance, because they can more or less estimate how much effort it will take to carry out this investigation."

"And? How much do they want?"

Blitzer dismissed the subject with a wave of his hand, but I assumed that the price was much steeper than the one on the website.

"You must know they don't take all cases."

"Just the ones that can get coverage in the media?"

"No. They're not after publicity, I told you."

Did they really work in the shadows? Actually, from the PR point of view, it was an appropriate strategy for a PI firm, and gave them a certain enigmatic appeal. Maybe they really were the antithesis of all those detectives I saw on TV every day. It turned out they attracted the most desperate clients – and I sighed when I realized I was one. It just went to show how pathetic my situation was. But if the police didn't want to help me and the evidence disappeared quicker than it was found, what else was there for me to do?

"I have one condition," said Blitz.

"What's that?"

"You're coming by tonight."

"What? Where?"

"Fuck, Werner, that's not what people say when they invite someone to their house," he whined. "You're really not very good at socializing, are you?"

I didn't have to answer that question. Ten years ago I was no different from the average graduate of any university – I'd spent five years partying hard and had a healthy social life – but now I'd reached a point where I even avoided virtual multiplayer games in favour of single-mode entertainment.

"You come by, we'll have a beer, we'll talk about everything."

"Today? Actually, I was planning to–"

"What?" he cut in. "Get shit-faced?"

I was still hungover from yesterday, but such a thought had indeed crossed my mind, truth be told. In the end, though, I had no choice but to accept Blitzer's invitation. Besides, I thought it might do me some good, and that maybe we could put everything together into a coherent whole between the two of us.

By the end of the evening, we were completely hammered.

For the first hour or two, we did indeed drink beer, but it was only an innocent prelude to stronger spirits that Blitz had in the fridge. The deadliest poison was gin and tonic, but I suppose that given what we had brewing in our stomachs by then, even a non-alcoholic beer would have knocked us out.

The next morning, I woke up feeling pretty good, so there was only one conclusion: I was still drunk, and the worst was yet to come.

I dragged myself out of bed in the guest bedroom and walked into the living room. It looked like a post-apocalyptic battlefield, strewn with empty bottles and cans, open packets of crisps and overflowing ashtrays. My stomach lurched.

I vaguely remembered that after the first or second beer we contacted Reimann Investigations. I was a little concerned about their methods because they were extremely secretive. To talk to the person in charge of our case, we were sent a text message with a single-use access code and then entered it together with our login and password on a dedicated website with no domain, only an IP address. We were also told that it wasn't indexed in any search engine. I thought that it was all a publicity spiel to make a dilettante client feel as if they were dealing with real IT experts, maybe even with a group of hackers who couldn't reveal their identities.

We gave Reimann all the key information we had, set the time for a conference call the following day and then proceeded to sample every type of booze Blitz had in his apartment. At some point, we might have gone to the off-licence for more, and now, on evaluating the chaos in the living room, I thought we must have cleared out the whole alcohol section at Tesco's.

I gathered up my things, then shuffled towards the door. I didn't want to wake Blitzer up; for all his commitment to the cause, he needed his beauty sleep.

When I got to the door leading to the stairwell, I noticed that it was open. I felt anxious, but figured in my hungover state that we'd we been too drunk to lock it when we'd got back from the shops last night.

I swallowed down a thick glob of alcohol-flavoured saliva and turned around. After a moment's hesitation, I headed for Blitzer's bedroom. I was a little dizzy when I opened the door.

But it was nothing compared to the feeling that struck me as soon as I saw Blitz.

He was lying on the bed on his back, one hand falling to the floor. The bedding was soaked with blood, and Blitzer was staring at the ceiling with empty eyes. His mouth was open unnaturally wide, frozen in a macabre scream.

I stood there, motionless. I don't know for how long.

Finally, I stumbled over to the bed and pressed my fingers to his carotid artery, but I knew there was no point in checking if my friend was alive.

5

It took me a while to decide to whom I should assign the case of the girl from Opole. There were actually two people I had in mind; the rest were busy with other projects. I didn't intend to consult Robert about it – he treated Reimann Investigations as a side hustle. At first, it was a hobby for him, and by now it had become just one of his many former interests, one which he didn't even seem to remember.

Eventually, I decided to go with Jola Kliza, a graduate of the University of Kaiserslautern, specifically because of that particular entry in her CV. She was a skinny, clearly insecure girl, but by no means timid – if anything, she seemed rather brusque, but I knew that this was because she felt uncomfortable, not because she was obnoxious by nature. When we took her in, Robert's eyes didn't linger on her even for a moment, and he was one of those men who appreciated female beauty.

We met in one of Robert's restaurants in Grunwaldzka Street in Pobierowo. During the peak season, Baltic Pipe was under constant siege, but at this time of year I often used the small café to do agency business.

Contrary to what our clients thought, we had no headquarters. Although the address of our house on the quayside was entered in the National Court Register, this was only because such was the official requirement.

It seemed reasonable to me, since we were largely active online. Our team consisted of people such as Kliza, who surfed the internet with the ease of the best windsurfers around here.

I gave her all the necessary information and Jola made contact with the client that evening. Formally, it was Adam Blicki, but when we negotiated the terms, he emphasized that we should treat Damian Werner as the principal.

For the first time ever, Kliza was late for our meeting. I thought she'd spent all night collecting information. When we hired her, we expected a competent researcher, but what we got was a dedicated workaholic. From our point of view, it couldn't have been better.

"Kasandra, I'm terribly sorry," said Jola quietly as she took her seat at the table.

I insisted that our employees call me by my first name. Robert agreed, although I knew he was reluctant. I assumed, however, that since most of our conversations took place via instant messaging anyway, there was no point in insisting on official forms of address.

"Don't worry about it," I replied, handing her a menu.

She shook her head as if to object and then tried to smooth out her dishevelled hair.

"You're not going to make me drink alone, are you?" I asked, pointing to a glass of Prosecco.

"It's only just past noon," she observed.

"All the more reason for you to join me."

I looked at the room with all its industrial décor, nodded at the waiter and then pointed to the glass. He got the message.

I didn't drink much, at least not all at once. However, I'd been sipping Prosecco all day long for at least seven years. It started right after the pregnancy, when I gave birth to Wojtek and had to reward myself for a long abstinence.

I didn't wonder if I was an addict, just as the ancient Greeks or Romans didn't. They would start the day with a glass of wine, just as we would with a cup of coffee. I was just observing ancient customs.

"Thanks, but I have some work to do," Jola replied, putting her tablet on the table and turning it on. We paid her enough to be able to afford the latest iPad, but she said she preferred hardware that she could adapt to her own needs. "You gave me an interesting case," she continued.

"Apparently," I replied with a slight smile.

She raised her eyes at me and furrowed her brows. Her swollen eyelids became even more pronounced.

"You obviously didn't get much sleep last night," I observed.

"Not everyone can look like you."

"Thank God," I answered, lifting the glass in a salute. "Otherwise, we would have to deal with hordes of snobbish, nouveau-riche women who think they're aristocrats."

Jola opened her mouth, but before she could reply, the waiter put a sparkling wine in front of me.

"That's not what I meant," she said.

"All right, I don't take myself too seriously. It's the Prosecco talking."

"But I guess… You don't really see yourself that way, do you?"

I shrugged.

Kliza looked around and said, "For many you are… I don't know, almost an icon. Certainly a role model."

"When it comes to hunting rich husbands?"

"More in terms of style, elegance and class."

I smiled because her social awkwardness made it impossible to get across even the most obvious jokes. "Don't count on a raise," I said. "At least not until I hear a few more compliments like that."

"I'll try to do better," she replied, pointing to the tablet.

We both grew serious. Time to get down to business.

"Good for you," I said, "because it might be a big case."

"I thought we didn't care about publicity?"

"Not in the sense of the investigation itself. But the results are a different matter."

I pushed the glass back and crossed my hands on the table. I was sitting ramrod straight. An expensive jacket and a light blue shirt made of almost a hundred per cent cotton would fit me well anyway, but after years of training I took that position reflexively.

"What have you established?" I asked.

"That our boy was suspected at first."

"Damian Werner?"

She nodded. "And that the preliminary findings indicated a murder."

"But the body wasn't found?'

"No, although the investigators thought the boy threw it in the river. They searched it, but not until days after Werner reported her missing. By that time, the body could have been in a completely different location."

"Why did they suspect him?" I thought it was a fair question, even though law enforcement usually took interest in the vic's partners. They're the ones who turned out to be the perpetrators in eighty per cent of cases, committing unplanned, emotionally motivated crimes, and police statistics proved that it usually took only forty-eight hours for the truth to come to light.

Of course, there were also those who hid their spouse's body in the basement for twenty years and told everyone they'd gone missing or left on their own.

"No one saw this alleged argument in front of the pub," said Kliza.

"So Werner's injuries could have been self-inflicted?"

"They assumed the fiancée would have tried to defend herself."

"It's a pretty twisted version," I said. "Did they really consider it as a real possibility?"

"Yeah."

"The boy proposes, then rapes his fiancée, kills her and throws her in the river? They have some imagination."

"Or experience."

Good point, I thought. Investigators certainly weren't strangers to such things.

"So there were no witnesses?" I asked.

"None. The clients mentioned only the group of men who left the pub at approximately the time indicated by Werner, but everything else was based on his testimony, so..." She shrugged.

"And the DNA?"

"Samples were taken from the table where the men sat. They were checked, but there were no matching records in the system."

"And the one at the scene? At that... Scorners' Congregation?

"The Sneering Lodge," she corrected, and I nodded. "They had real mitochondrial soup there, so much material they would keep all the labs in Poland busy."

"Traces of semen?"

"None found."

"Sweat? Other secretions?"

"Everything in abundance," said Jola, never taking her eyes off the tablet. "But it's apparently quite a busy place in Opole, at least it was at the time. Now it's a terrace of the nearby pub here, and most of the area has been developed."

I took a deep breath, drained my glass and ordered a non-alcoholic drink for Jola. The waiter bent to his task, but I knew he was listening to our conversation and he didn't take his eyes off us.

"CCTV footage?" I asked.

"No cameras there. The nearest one was a few hundred metres away, but didn't record any group of men at that time. All those that passed through there were identified and interrogated. They were nowhere near the Młynówka area that night.

"The what?"

"The old riverbed of the Oder River," Kliza explained with a wave of her hand. "It doesn't matter, anyway."

"There are no sluices in there?"

"There are, on both sides."

"So..."

"If the boy had thrown the body into the water, it would have stopped at one for sure, but by the time the search began, the gates had been opened several times. You have to remember that at first they treated it as a missing person case. They only decided later to start looking for a body."

"But they eventually eliminated our client as a suspect?"

"Technically, yes."

"And informally?"

"It seems that the chief investigator, Tomasz Prokocki, now a deputy commissioner, wasn't sure if that was a wise decision."

"Because?"

"Werner seemed suspicious to him. There must be more details in the report, but I don't have access to it."

"Not yet."

Kliza understood the thinly veiled allusion and nodded. I knew she was able to access any information, as long as she was given enough time. And provided she didn't have to interact with other people.

It took a long time to make her feel comfortable with me so that she could speak in full sentences. I couldn't imagine what it must have cost her to overcome such difficulties at Kaiserslautern. Or maybe she never did. Maybe she locked herself in her room, lost in study, hence her impressive grades.

I spent a good half hour listening to her telling me what she had established. None of the evidence pointed to Damian Werner, so in the end it was decided that the fiancé had nothing to do with it. It seemed that it took the police more time to reach that conclusion than pure logic would dictate.

I shared that thought with Jola and she pursed her mouth in response. "I guess they were just being thorough, at least as far as he was concerned," she said. "Anyway, I think something else seems suspicious."

"What?"

"They took biological samples from his body and his clothes. He also had traceological evidence on his face, which indicates how he was treated by his attackers."

I raised my eyebrows.

"I mean shoe prints."

"Yes, I know what traceology is," I replied with a smile and reached for my Prosecco. "What's so suspicious about that?"

"Just that the investigators didn't match the prints to the sample from the pub. They could create a consistent profile, with a bit of luck, including cheiloscopic traces and fingerprints found on beer mugs." This time she refrained from explaining that the former meant regarding the lip. "They could have had a lot more, but for some reason they didn't bother looking."

"Someone on the police force had something to hide?"

"Maybe."

For a moment, we were both silent. The waiter kept looking at us as attentively as a butler in an aristocratic manor house. I saw that it made Jola uncomfortable, but there was little I could do; Robert gave orders to the staff that even I couldn't overrule.

"So the girl disappears ten years ago, and then suddenly she shows up at a concert Werner's friend happens to be attending," I concluded.

"Not just his friend but his best friend. His only friend, in fact, as far as I've been able to establish."

"Plus, there's a picture on the web that only Werner had on his phone."

"Yes," Kliza confirmed.

"And finally, as soon as they start digging into the case, everything vanishes off the face of the earth, along with the Facebook account of the one who posted the photographs, like a stone dropped into water."

Jola winced as if that last remark meant something unpleasant. "Worse than that," she said, "because I could have tracked a stone, and I can't find this Braddy fellow."

It was probably the first time I'd heard such a declaration from her. She always said that if was true that nothing was lost in nature, it was even more true on the internet. Everyone left a trail online, even the greatest virtuosos in masking their virtual tracks.

I kept silent, waiting for her to continue, but apparently she was done.

"You said it was easier to hide in a desert than on the internet," I said. "You must have found some trace?"

"I did," she replied with a heavy sigh. "Google archived those entries, but all I got was... an afterimage of Phil Braddy's presence on Facebook. I could only check the IP, and all that led me to determine was that he was using Tor."

Tor – the onion router, a multilayered network enabling encryption of internet traffic. With Tor, more people were successfully hiding from law enforcement agencies than there were jihadists in Afghan caves at the peak of the al-Qaeda era.

"There were really a lot of routers," Jola continued, "most of them in Britain, and maybe one on Braddy's computer, too. I can't figure it out now."

"So he went to a lot of trouble before he uploaded the picture."

"Certainly more than the average spotter."

I saw a flash in her eyes and I wasn't surprised the case kept her awake. In her place, I would probably have spent the night trying to solve even the tiniest fragment of the mystery, too.

"Okay," I said. "What are you going to do now?"

"I'll follow up on the second photo. If the only copy was on Werner's phone, I need to see if anyone had access to it."

"How about this friend of his?"

"He does seem like a prime suspect," she admitted. "Especially since he was in Wrocław. And he found that picture on the *Spotted* profile in the first place."

"And yet it was him who paid our bill."

"That could have been just to keep up appearances."

I looked out the window and kept silent for a while. The empty streets, which would fill with a steady stream of tourists in a few months, had a soothing effect on me.

"The basic question is, can it really be her?" I mused.

"All evidence points to that."

"Didn't she have a missing twin sister? A doppelganger?"

"No twin, nor a clone or another version of herself from alternative reality, no."

"Then what's been happening to her all these years? And why did she disappear?" I asked, shaking my head. "Somebody held her against her will?"

Jola looked at me uncertainly, as if she wondered whether I was asking myself or her. "In the picture from the gig, she doesn't look like she's being forced to do anything," she said.

"Maybe it was staged?"

"Maybe," admitted Kliza. "The man standing in the back certainly doesn't look friendly."

There were many possibilities. I told Jola to narrow them down as soon as possible and got up from the table. I noticed that Robert drove up to Baltic Pipe in his silver BMW 4 Series. The Gran Coupe stood out on the street and it was hard to miss, although even with my eyes closed I'd have known it was my husband who drove up. We had an appointment, and he was never late.

I said goodbye to Kliza, suggesting she should have a Prosecco on the company, then got in Robert's car. It smelled new, even though it was over a year old. I glanced at him when he gave the waiter standing by the window a long look. The waiter nodded and walked away.

My husband cleared his throat. "Listen, Kas..."

"There's nothing to talk about," I assured him. "Bygones are bygones."

"Are you sure?"

I was sure, but of something completely different. What Robert did would have profound consequences. He would destroy his life, and change mine completely, even though he didn't realize it yet.

When he thought that silence on my part was enough, he turned back and headed towards our villa on the waterfront.

"How was the meeting?" he asked.

"Kliza is the right person to handle it."

He nodded in silence, staring at the road ahead of us. Then he looked at me in a way I knew all too well.

"For God's sake, Robert," I moaned. "I didn't tell her anything. What do you suspect me of?"

He didn't say a word.

6

I ran into my parents' flat at Grottgera Street sweaty, panting and utterly confused. In fact, I didn't even know what I was doing. Maybe some biological mechanism was at work that made me seek help from my parents in a crisis.

I had no doubt I'd find them home. It was the middle of the week, but they'd both been retired for several years. They spent most of their time rereading all the books they already knew well. I rarely managed to persuade them to do anything new.

My mother opened the door, but before she could speak I rushed past her and came inside. I didn't miss the expression of horror on her face.

"Damian?" she asked, her voice shaking. "What's the matter? What's happened?"

Breathing hard, I slammed the door behind me and leaned against it. I bent my head and closed my eyes. *Good question*, I thought. What *had* happened?

Before I'd run out of Blitz's place, I'd noticed a bloody knife in the bedroom. I'd only seen one wound to the body, right under the ribs. The blood, which covered almost the entire bed, suggested that it took some time for Blitzer to die, perhaps that he'd tried to find help as he lay dying, or fought his attacker for his own life.

I winced.

It couldn't have been a coincidence. I had no doubts about that. It hadn't looked as if anything had been taken, and Blitz had no enemies that I knew of. Everyone liked him, he never fell out with anyone, and the women he slept with and then promptly abandoned didn't even know where he lived.

He had to have been murdered by whoever was behind Ewa's disappearance.

"What's happened?" my mother repeated.

I opened my eyes and looked at her the moment my father came into the room, wrinkling his forehead. "Son?" he said in his deep, low voice.

He always called me that, I don't think he's ever used my name. Initially, it was his personal protest against my mother's choice of the name Damian, which he did not like at all. Then it became a habit.

They were both kind, decent people – and I would have said that about them even if they hadn't raised me. Sometimes I thought that the concept of pure evil, so well understood by many, seemed completely abstract to them.

It made it all the harder to describe what had happened.

I needed a good hour to get it out of my system. We were sitting in their small, cluttered living room, theoretically drinking cups of tea, though they had long cooled before we'd taken our first sip.

At first my parents didn't believe me when I told them what had happened, and then they went into the denial stage, but in the end they accepted the truth faster than many other people would have. I knew where such ready acceptance came from. We were by no means strangers to tragedy. After Ewa disappeared, we were ready for anything.

She was like a daughter to them, especially after her parents died in a car accident less than a year before the attack on Młynówka. Earlier, they had been a bit distant, maybe because Mum and Dad didn't really get along with my would-be in-laws. They came from different worlds – my parents grew up in simple, working-class families and had never known wealth. Ewa's parents, on the other hand, had almost too much of it.

Fate had taken Ewa's mother and father away from her just when she had grown closer to them. I used to think that we were all made tougher by that accident, but as soon as I finished recounting recent events, I found out that at least one of us wasn't tough at all. I felt sick, close to vomiting in fact.

"You're all pale," my mother said.

Could I have expected another comment? She looked at me with fearful eyes, while my father stared vacantly at the wall. For a few moments none of us spoke.

"Jesus, Mary and Joseph," she said with a sigh, shaking her head, and then rose abruptly. "Wait, I'll make you something to eat. You must... You haven't had anything to eat, have you?"

"I haven't, but..."

She went to the kitchen and I shared a short but meaningful look with my father. It gradually dawned on both of us how bad my situation was.

"Did you call the police?" he asked.

I shook my head.

"Maybe you should. They better find out from you."

"How would that help?"

"It would make a better impression than them finding out another way."

"Oh, I think the impression they'll get is quite clear," I told him. "My fingerprints are all over the place."

"That's what I'm talking about, son. You have to prove that you had nothing to do with that as soon as possible."

Thanks to our shared trauma, which had been nothing but a burden for us for years, we were now able to think with cool heads. Still, I couldn't come up with a single scenario that would be good for me.

"I can't work miracles," I said, slouching in the chair. "Besides, somebody must have alerted them already. Maybe they're even taking fingerprints as we speak. They're going to run them through the database today, and then they're going to come after me."

"You don't know that."

"Don't I?" I said with a snort – out of helplessness, I guess. I closed my eyes and tilted my head backwards, and for a moment it all seemed like an alcohol-induced hallucination.

"You saw a knife in there, didn't you?"

"I think so, yes." My memories were hazy, but I didn't delude myself that they would stay that way for long. It would happen just as it had with my memories from Młynówka. At first they would be blurry, as if obscured by a gauzy curtain. Then, as the brain threw up nightmares and images from the deepest recesses of my mind, they would grow clearer and clearer, until eventually they would become as clear as the present.

"Your fingerprints aren't on the knife," Dad pointed out. "That should be enough."

"They'll say I could have worn gloves."

"Were there any gloves there?"

"Dad..."

"These are all legitimate questions."

I shook my head helplessly. "For you, but not for the police. They'll assume that I took the gloves with me, and then just got rid of them."

As soon as I said it, I realized that leaving the flat was the worst I could have done. I should have stayed there and informed the authorities immediately, then waited for them without touching anything.

The smell of eggs wafted from the kitchen. My mother made the best scrambled eggs in the world, but right then I was getting queasy just thinking about food.

I bent down and hid my face in my hands. What the hell was going on here? Who would kill Blitzer, and why? And in such a way that everything pointed to–

I stopped thinking, suddenly flushed with heat. My hands were dripping wet and the nausea intensified. I slowly lowered my hands, looking at my father with empty eyes.

"What is it?" he asked.

"That knife."

Dad raised his eyebrows and the long wrinkles on his forehead seemed to travel up to his thinning grey hairline.

"Oh, shit," I moaned.

"What's going on, son?"

"I used that knife last night," I replied, rubbing my neck nervously. "I used it to open a wine bottle, cut the foil on the bottleneck."

"Are you sure it's the same knife?"

I nodded. I wasn't one hundred per cent sure, no, but it seemed logical. The killer entered the flat, saw a knife lying on the kitchen counter and decided to use it. Blitz couldn't have put up much of a fight; he'd been as drunk as I was, maybe even more so. Against my will, I imagined him waking up from a drunken dream only to die in a matter of moments. I shuddered.

For a while, we didn't speak, stirring from our inertia only when my mother entered the room bearing plates of scrambled eggs. She gave us each a plate, but she must have realized that, given the fate of the untouched tea, breakfast would follow suit. However, she needed to know that she had done something, somehow tried to take care of us.

She sat down on the couch next to my father and looked at me with deep concern. "What are we going to do?" she asked.

"Nothing for now," I replied. I was afraid Dad would try to convince me to contact the police, but he didn't say a word. It was only after a while that I realized he had decided to convey his objections in a different way.

He fixed me with a stare that I knew all too well.

"It doesn't make any sense," I cried.

"I'm not saying anything, son."

"You don't have to. I see it on your face. You're still insisting I should call the police."

"I'm not insisting anything."

"That's good," I said a little too harshly, but my emotions were starting to rise. "Because I think I'm being framed. And whoever's behind it is somehow manipulating the cops."

He sighed and my mother refused to look at me. This was an all-too-familiar tune to them, one that I'd sung over and over again for some time after Ewa's disappearance. I'd gone through all the stages of grief then, blaming anyone I could think of.

For a while, I'd been convinced that it was the investigators who had been covering up the evidence and were involved in what had happened. At one point, I'd even come up with the idea that the attackers were off-duty police officers who'd decided to have a bit of fun. Eventually, I'd rejected conspiracy theories and all other absurd scenarios, but now I had to reconsider them once again. Everything was possible at this stage.

"It's not the communist police anymore," said Dad. "Now they've got the equipment, they've got the technology... they're going to figure out what really happened there."

What happened was that I was alive and Blitz wasn't.

There could be only one reason for that. The killer intended not only to get rid of my friend and send me a message, but also to frame me. But why? Wouldn't it have been easier to kill me too?

I got even hotter when I thought about how close I'd been to death. Only a moment. One man's decision.

"They'll only see evidence that points to me," I murmured under my breath. "Whoever did this took care of that."

Before any of them could respond, there was a sound that made us all jump. It took me some time to understand it was coming from Blitz's mobile. I must have taken it with me without realizing it in my panic, needing to have contact with the outside world with my own phone being confiscated. I took the phone out of my pocket and saw one unread message.

The machine from Reimann Investigations had sent out an access code. I put the phone on the backrest of the chair, but then frowned and looked at the fading display.

I got up and moved to my old room, which was now my father's office. Some time ago I'd given my old computer to my parents because they'd insisted they wanted to keep up with the times and enjoy all the benefits the internet offered, but their old PC wasn't up to the challenge. I couldn't persuade them to buy a new computer.

In one of the cabinets there was also an old ASUS, my first laptop, which frankly should have been in a museum. Still, it was better than the clunky old PC.

I turned it on, booted up the website and entered the code.

A small window popped up with a list of two users, identified only by strings of random numbers and characters.

The script that was running on the site was supposed to have decent security features, but I didn't know how much of that was true and how much was the usual advertising spiel that RI employees had given Blitzer to encourage him to use their services. They claimed that all their data was encrypted with military-grade protocol AES-256-CTR, and that was supposedly even before it was sent from the client's computer. That meant the company's server received the encrypted version – impossible to read without the code that I was supposed to receive by text message. Additional security was provided by the fact that the messages were stored for no longer than ten seconds on drives owned by Reimann Investigations.

I looked at the black screen and waited. Finally, a question popped up:

[xc97it] Are you okay?

I didn't have to think for long about how to answer.

[w0p6z1] No, I'm not okay. Nothing is okay.
[xc97it] I'm talking to Werner, aren't I?
[w0p6z1] Yes. Who are you?
[xc97it] My name is Jola.

I watched the lines of text appear and then disappear. The name didn't tell me anything. I didn't even know if it was a girl on the other side.

[xc97it] We talked yesterday.
[w0p6z1] I don't remember much.

There was a long pause, at least from my point of view. It felt like several minutes had passed before the next message appeared.

[xc97it] What happened out there?

Now I remembered that the person we had contacted yesterday introduced herself as Jola Kliza. She was the one who was supposed to be in charge of Ewa's case, and Blitz claimed that we couldn't have done better – mainly because he imagined Kliza as a long-legged blonde with an hourglass figure.

I looked around the room and saw that my parents had left a lot of things here from my childhood. Some gifts from Ewa, I think from the time we were in elementary school. Among other things, there were some Spider-Man action figures, a superhero I was obsessed with at the time, to the point that Ewa started calling me Tiger, the same pet name Mary Jane gave to Peter Parker. Normally it would be a bit embarrassing, but with all my love for Spider-Man I was happy to accept that. There was also a road sign that me and Blitzer had stolen together when we wcre in hlgh school.

Suddenly I was crushed under the weight of all that had happened. But I knew there would be time for grief later. For now, I had to make sure my life wouldn't come tumbling down in a matter of seconds. I might have been paranoid, but I thought I could guess what would happen otherwise. The police would take me in, the prosecution would charge me, I would be arrested, then put on remand, where I would await trial. Then they would send me straight to prison.

There would be no question of discovering any clue from Ewa. I would never find her. This time, she really would be gone forever.

I was looking at the monitor with unseeing eyes, my thoughts taking me further and further away. I only woke up when the same question came up again.

[xc97it] What happened out there?

Realizing that Jola was the only person who could help me at the moment, I described to her what I remembered. I didn't go into the details, figuring they weren't the most important thing right now. After a while the text disappeared and I was staring at an empty black window again. The white cursor blinked alarmingly.

[xc97it] Do you have anything to write on?

I searched the drawers and found a block of yellow Post-it notes in one, then wrote down the number that appeared on the screen.

[xc97it] Buy a pre-paid card and a used mobile. Then send a text message to the number I gave you: b4lt1cp1p1.

I wrote down the code.

[w0p6z1] Then what?
[xc97it] I'll tell you what to do, but for now you have to get rid of the phone.
[w0p6z1] You want me to run away?

The cursor blinked again like an eye of a feral animal in the dark. I swallowed.

Finally, there was a response.

[xc97it] Yeah.

Then suddenly I was logged out and the window closed. I sat stunned for a while, before I realized that Kliza must have had access to information I didn't.

Maybe she knew more than I did.

I had a couple of options, but they were all pretty much hopeless. I finally chose the one that seemed the best, figuring that if Blitz had trusted the girl, for whatever reason, maybe I should too.

I didn't think for a moment that it might have been her who'd gotten him killed.

7

I had bouquets of white irises waiting for me at home, one in each room, which in total made quite an impressive number. Robert knew perfectly well that they were my favourite flowers and bought them for me at every opportunity. I was happy to see that, although I saw a certain absurdity in it – after all, white symbolized innocence, and that was hardly something my husband could boast.

On the way home, he made sure several more times that I wasn't angry with him, and I kept repeating that no, I wasn't. When we entered the spacious hallway, he watched me closely to see my reaction, so I did everything I could to convince him that an apology was not necessary.

We hugged, kissed, and then he took me by the hand to the dining room. It was located on the ground floor, on the north side. The south side overlooked a forest, but the living room windows gave onto a view of the boundless Baltic Sea. The villa was located on a small slope, so you could easily look at the distant horizon. When the weather was good, we could see the outlines of giant ships on the open sea, which from our perspective looked like tiny dots against the sky.

The food was ready when we got there. We used the Amica IN app to control most of our household appliances remotely. Robert had put the food in the oven before leaving, and on the way home he'd turned it on via his phone.

He served me Vietnamese duck. I knew that he missed cooking – it was one of his passions, for which he had no time. The spicy taste and clear aniseed notes didn't surprise me; Robert always prepared this dish like that. Actually, I wasn't surprised by anything he did. Everything was a constant element of the pattern we both knew.

"What did you talk about with Jola?" he asked, pouring us a New Zealand pinot noir. He claimed that no other wine went so well with a duck.

"Just about the case."

"You didn't mention…"

"I already told you I didn't."

He poured me a third of a glass, then sat across from me. "There's one thing I didn't say," he said.

"What's that?"

"I'm sorry."

I looked at him and sighed. Indeed, until now, he'd only tried to make sure I didn't hold anything against him, but he'd never actually apologized. Sooner or later he would, as always, but before then he had to prepare the ground for himself. It was a dance that we both decided to do in order for our love to survive, hence the white irises, cooking for me, waiting on me hand and foot as if I were a queen and he was a servant. It was all a beautiful illusion.

And it only happened during the day.

"You're welcome," I said.

He dropped his eyes and appeared deeply embarrassed – but was he really? Although we fell in love almost as soon as we met at university, it seemed to me that I never really knew my husband.

"Try the wine," he said.

"I've just been drinking Prosecco. I don't want to mix it."

He didn't insist, and I didn't have to say anything more. He knew that if I got tipsy now, then I would blame myself later – there was still a lot of the evening left, and I still had a lot of bubbly to drink. All high-functioning alcoholics know that in order to be able to drink, they have to keep things in check. The key is not to cross the line under any circumstances.

Robert ate a piece of duck and then slowly placed his cutlery on the plate, still not raising his eyes.

"It will never happen again," he said.

"I know it won't."

"I had too much to drink, Kas. I was completely out of my mind."

"I've told you already that–"

"That there's nothing to worry about, yes," he interrupted me, shaking his head. "But it's not true."

He got up and walked up to me, squatting down by my chair. He took my hand and looked me in the eye for a long time. I saw grief in his eyes, shame and deep sadness. It wasn't a fake feeling; there was a real emotion there. He was a man of contradictions, maybe just as much as I was.

"We can't simply get over it," he said.

"Oh, come on."

"I hit you, Kas."

Not for the first time, I thought, *and probably not for the last.* Not only that but each subsequent time, he seemed to get worse and worse. No, not "seemed"; he *was* getting worse.

It started innocently, as far as any act of violence can. One night Robert screamed abuse at me for not taking care of a trivial matter related to one of the restaurants by the beach, some bullshit I don't even remember. At first it was only words, but one day he went a step further. He slapped me and then pushed me. He quickly sobered up, as if breaking out of lethargy – he apologized, even begged for forgiveness and swore that it would never happen again.

I believed him then because I wanted to. I felt humiliated, weak and threatened, but he was still the only man I could rely on. If you've never experienced violence from a loved one yourself, you can't possibly understand. It's something that defies rational thinking and logic.

It wasn't long after that he hit me with his fist. Sometimes he would yell at me as he punched me, and I prayed for only two things: that he wouldn't go any further and that little Wojtek wouldn't hear anything. My pleas for the former remained unanswered, but as for the latter I think I eventually managed to convince some higher power to help me.

The previous night, though, Robert had gone too far. He'd pulled my hair, screamed in my face and then hit me in the belly several times. I decided that I wouldn't take it anymore.

Today was supposed to be the day I would remember as the first step towards a new life.

But that was why Robert had asked me what I was doing and who I was talking to. And that was why he'd instructed one of his employees to keep an eye on me. He knew he'd crossed another line, and I wouldn't let him so much as come near to it again.

I looked at the bouquets of white irises. I was fooling myself into thinking I still loved those flowers. In fact, I'd hated them for some time. They were a tangible proof of how hopeless my situation was.

"Let's not leave it like that," he said quietly.

"What do you mean?"

"You should let a doctor examine you."

"What?"

"I'll take you to Kamień Pomorski. We'll go to the hospital and–"

"Are you crazy?"

"Then you'll have proof."

I moved the chair back and turned to him. He leaned down and laid his head on my thighs. We stayed like that for some time in silence, with me gently brushing his hair.

He wanted to have the Sword of Damocles hanging over him? Proof of what he did to me?

It couldn't have been anything else. I even assumed his motives were sincere. I saw that he was trying to change. He even managed to restrain himself several times, before he hit me.

However, these were just exceptions that confirmed the rule.

"Do you think this is going to change anything?" I asked.

"I'll know that at any time you could…"

"What? Go to the police?"

He raised his head and gazed at me, his eyes glassy, looking nothing at all like the man who yesterday had yelled at me, pushed me and beaten me.

"Would I let them put you in jail?" I continued. "So that Wojtek would be left without a father? And we would have to do without you?"

"Don't say that."

"But it's true, Robert. How could you think that?"

For as long as I can remember, we'd always been direct with each other. It seemed to me that in any other relationship the situation would have been vastly different. Either the woman would be afraid or violence would become a taboo subject.

We didn't have any taboo subjects. We talked about everything and never fooled each other, never lied to each other – except for him keeping quiet about having an abusive nature, of course.

He came closer, and then embraced my waist. "How can you be with such a bastard?" he asked.

"I have no idea," I said, and forced myself to smile.

"If I were you, I'd at least key his fucking Grand Coupe cock extension."

"Oh, don't worry, I'm going to take a spray can to it tonight."

"Good idea."

He looked at me again and I kissed him, pressing my hands firmly against his cheeks. Again I thought that we were different from other couples, who in such a situation would probably go straight to the bedroom, but we rarely slept together. Ever since the violence started, the sex had become less and less frequent. I even had the impression that Robert reached sexual satisfaction when he beat me up, that he was driven to it by wild, unbridled emotions, an animal urge he couldn't stop. But at the same time, he was careful to hit me where it wouldn't leave a mark. That was what bothered me the most, because it made me think that somewhere there was a cool, reasoning mind behind it all.

I closed my eyes and focused on the touch of his mouth. For God's sake, was that really all it took for me to lose courage? Until a few hours ago, when I'd gotten into his BMW at the restaurant, I was sure I wouldn't give up, that I wouldn't let him treat me like that anymore.

How little did it take to change my mind? And had I really changed it? I couldn't answer those questions. All I knew was that love was the most dangerous toxin nature ever created.

Robert went back to his seat and took a gulp of wine. He looked at the duck uncertainly. "Either I messed up, or I feel so disgusted with myself that it translates into taste."

"Or both."

"You may be right," he replied, pushing the plate away. He looked almost as pale as Jola Kliza, who never went outdoors, except to go from one building to another. Her complexion was almost spectral, and her black, waist-length hair only emphasized that. She always seemed to have her head slightly inclined so her tresses fell on her cheeks.

I wondered if she'd made any progress on Ewa. It was a good train of thought to break away from what happened at night. I decided to share it with Robert.

"I told you about that missing girl, didn't I?" I said.

He put the glass away and watched me closely for a moment, as if he was wondering if changing the subject was a good idea. "Only that she had been raped by the river, and then disappeared without a trace," he said. "And her assailants, too."

"Until those pictures popped up."

"Oh, yes. It was in Opole, was it?"

I confirmed with a nod.

"I think I heard something about that. How long ago was it?"

"Ten years."

"And do you really think that after all this time she would just resurface?"

"It seems so. But at the same time, it looks like somebody's made sure the trail vanishes again."

"Maybe it's her doing?" Robert asked, and I went back to the duck. "Maybe she doesn't want to be found?"

"Hard to say," I replied, chewing a small piece of meat. The dish was too hot for my taste, but I wasn't going to say anything. After all, he made it as an apology and preparing it took a lot of time that Robert never had.

"Maybe after the rape she decided to start all over again," he noted.

"And she'd just leave her fiancé behind? I doubt it."

"Did you talk to her family? Friends? Maybe somebody knows something? Maybe somebody was in contact with her?"

"There is no family," I said, and decided to drink some wine after all. "Parents died in a car accident less than a year before the rape."

"Bad luck."

"*C'est la vie*," I replied, shrugging.

We didn't go into the subject because I saw that Robert wasn't too interested in it. When we'd started Reimann

Investigations, he was absorbed in what we could achieve. He acted like a little boy who'd finally got the toy he wanted, but over time his enthusiasm had waned.

So had mine, of course. We were approached mainly by people who wanted us to spy on their spouses or track down debtors that suddenly disappeared with their creditors' money. We were waiting for a case like the one involving Ewa's disappearance. I thought taking it on would give Robert his old sparkle back, but apparently I was wrong.

We ate without talking about anything important, and when I stood up from the table, I got a little dizzy. Prosecco and red wine did not make a good combination, especially if the day started with the former.

And if it was going to end with that, too.

There had been days when I'd convinced myself this wouldn't happen, but this certainly wasn't one of them. I'd already known that emphatically when Jola's text message came in.

Robert was about to pick up Wojtek from primary school. I didn't like the fact that he drove there in his BMW, which created a gap between our son and other pupils. And knowing the children's propensity for bullying, I suspected that it happened, and not just between classes.

I also objected to him driving with half a bottle of wine in him, but I kept quiet, knowing there was no point in protesting, Robert would still get behind the wheel, and the only thing that my objections would bring was yet another argument.

He didn't have to be afraid of the police. Even if he was detained by a law enforcement officer, they'd rather give a ticket to themselves than to him. Formally, the Rewal commune had a reeve, and each of its villages had a leader, but in reality people like Robert – local moguls of the tourism and catering industries, which supported many families – ruled the place.

"What's wrong?" Robert asked, standing up from the table.

I looked up from my mobile. "I got a text from Kliza."

"What does she say? Any progress?"

"No, just problems," I answered harshly. "She says she needs to talk to me as soon as possible because the situation is complicated."

"Do you want me to drop you off at Baltic Pipe?"

"No, I'll do it on the phone."

He collected the dishes, then rinsed them briskly and put them in the dishwasher. I tried to explain to him that he shouldn't do that because the detergent doesn't have anything to penetrate and just floats around the dishwasher pointlessly, but he dismissed me.

He kissed me goodbye, even though he was supposed to be back in a little over a quarter of an hour. Then I heard the silent murmur of his BMW's engine.

I took a deep breath and dialled Jola's number. She answered immediately, as if she'd been waiting for the call.

"Blicki's dead," she blurted out, never one to mince her words.

Her news threw me off and for a moment I didn't know what to say. Nothing seemed right.

"He was found dead in his apartment," she added in the emotionless tone of TV anchor.

I got up and walked up to the fridge. It seemed that today was the day I would violate the sacred principles of high-functioning alcoholism.

"Do you have any details?" I asked.

"No. The police never give out any details about the case, for the good of the investigation."

"What about off the record?"

"Looks like Werner spent the night at his place."

I froze with a glass in my hand. "You don't mean to say that–"

"No," she interrupted me. "Why would he go after his friend?"

I took a sip and felt a little better.

"It doesn't make any sense," Kliza continued. "Blicki wasn't just his only friend; he was the only person willing to help him. Besides, Werner's smart enough to plan something more sophisticated."

"So somebody's trying to frame him?"

"Worst-case scenario, yes. Best case, it's just a coincidence."

I didn't believe in coincidence. It's just an empty word we use when we don't know the actual cause of something.

"Anyway, there's certainly enough of his biological material on the scene for him to be charged."

"Are you sure?" I asked.

"Not entirely, no. Like I said, I don't have any first-hand information. But they'll definitely treat him as the prime suspect."

"Then you need him to–"

"Go into hiding, I know," she cut in. "I've already taken care of it."

So why did you call me? I thought, frowning. Yes, I've told her many times that I want to be kept informed about what was going on, but only if there were any significant issues to be resolved. In this case, she'd already made her own decision.

I put the glass down and perched on the kitchen countertop, looking out of the large windows to the coast.

"Make sure he didn't do it," I said. "I don't want any mud to stick to us later."

"I will," Jola assured me. "But first, I have to make sure they don't lock him up or we'll lose contact."

"Yeah," I muttered. "It's obvious, but that's not why you're calling me."

"No, not for that."

"So what's the matter?"

"I went through all the evidence again." There was a clear, almost childish excitement to her voice. "This girl tried to send a message."

"What's that?" I exclaimed. "What message? To whom?" The questions sounded like cannon fire in my head.

"I don't know yet," Kliza replied. "But I'm going to find out."

8

I bought a second-hand mobile from the first shop I found, and then picked up a SIM card from a roadside kiosk. I had no intention of wasting time and immediately sent a message to the number I got from the girl from Reimann Investigations. She called me back almost immediately.

"All right," she said. "Now we can talk in peace."

"I'm a little short of peace."

"No wonder."

I scrubbed at my hair nervously, looking around. It felt like every passerby was staring at me. Everyone seemed to know that I was targeted by the police.

"How did this happen?" I mumbled. "How did this all happen?"

"We'll get to that eventually, but for now–"

"No," I interrupted her. "I need to know what's going on. Who did this and why?"

A man passing by gave me a suspicious, accusatory look. I looked over my shoulder at him, but I saw only his back slipping away. I felt like I was being paranoid, but I suppose I should have expected that.

"Why would anyone kill him?" I pressed.

"We'll find out everything."

"Who's working against me? The police?"

"Werner, listen to me for a second."

"What do they want?"

"Werner!"

I shook my head and woke up. In fact, Jola Kliza's unfamiliar voice snapped me back to into focus, probably because she sounded like someone who knew me, which made me realize just how unfortunate my situation was. The only person I could trust was a complete stranger.

"You've got to get a grip on yourself," she added. "We'll figure out what happened, but for now the most important thing is to keep you out of custody."

I was nodding my head as if in a trance.

"Are you there?"

"I am."

"Right now, no one's officially after you, so you're going to have to make use of that."

"Officially."

"I mean, you won't break the law, even if you go abroad," she said emphatically, but with a timid note in her voice. "No charges have been brought against you. There's no warrant out for your arrest. You enjoy the same freedoms as any other citizen. And you have to take advantage of it."

"Do you want me to leave the country?"

"No. But I could do a lot more for you if you were in Pomerania."

I stopped at the Piastowski Bridge and looked up at its steel arches. People walked on them so often that the city authorities had to install a comical notice forbidding them to cross that way.

I stood on the right side and leaned against the railings. I looked in the direction of two hotels on Pasieka, a small island surrounded by the waters of the Odra and Młynówka rivers. The Sneering Lodge was on the other side.

"I'm not going anywhere," I said.

"It's not very wise, considering–"

"I have no intention of doing the wise thing," I muttered. "If I did, I'd have reported to the police a long time ago."

"That doesn't sound like a reasonable solution, Wern."

"Wern?

"It suits you," she responded.

"It's either Damian or Werner. Don't call me Wern."

I shifted my eyes towards the boulevards stretching from the amphitheatre. I envied all those people who walked around carefree. They didn't feel the burden of the past that I carried on my shoulders. They weren't in such a hopeless present. And they didn't have such a dark, disturbing future ahead of them.

I was wondering if there was even anything left that was up to me. Whoever was behind what had happened, they seemed ready for anything. If I needed confirmation, all I had to do was close my eyes to see the image of Blitz's bloody body burned into my retinas.

"Maybe I should do it after all," I murmured.

"What?"

"Report to the police."

"No way. That's never a good idea, especially in this situation."

"Why not?" I asked her, turning around and leaning against the railing. "Maybe we're being paranoid. Maybe the police have nothing to do with this."

"Do you want to check it out for yourself?"

"Why not?" I replied with increasing confidence, but only in my voice. "Maybe I'll be safe at the station. There's CCTV, there are people there, and–"

"Like nothing ever happened under such circumstances, Wern."

"Werner."

"I'm just saying, you should be careful. And until anyone charges you formally, you have the right of free movement."

"Theoretically," I answered, lowering my head. "I've fled from the crime scene. The first thing I should do is report to the police."

"You were in shock."

"And now I'm not anymore," I said through clenched teeth. "If this case goes to court, my skipping town will be at least seen as suspicious."

"It doesn't matter."

I snorted. Kliza's self-confidence seemed to contradict all logic. But maybe I shouldn't have been surprised – private investigators rarely got on with the police.

"Speaking of shock," she continued, "did you get rid of the phone?"

"No."

"Why did you even take it from Blicki's place?"

"I don't know."

She kept silent for a moment, but I knew exactly what she was trying to tell me: I had to throw away the only thing

I had left of my friend. Sooner or later, Blitz's mobile would become a burden for me.

I took a deep breath, turned around and, careful not to draw anyone's attention, threw the phone into the Oder River. It sank like a stone in the murky water.

"I know you don't want to hear this," Kliza said, "but you have to–"

"Done," I interrupted her.

"Okay, good."

She was silent for a moment again. I assumed that it was not easy for her not to say anything in a situation when silence was the most telling confirmation of the enormity of my problems. I'm sure she was feverishly wondering how to break it. In the end, she picked the worst possible option.

"You can't trust anyone right now."

"Thanks," I said. "That's exactly what I needed to hear."

She sighed, and I started walking.

"If you're not going to come here, at least stay off the radar."

"How?"

"We will help you with everything," she said. "I'll book you a motel room in the suburbs right now. Do you have anything like that in there?"

I raised my eyes to the sky. "I can't even afford a cheap B&B."

"Don't worry about that right now."

"And who's going to pay for that? You guys? Suddenly you're a loan company?" I knew I would eventually have to let go of my constant suspicions. I might have my reasons not to believe anyone, but I should show at least a modicum of trust to the people Blitzer had relied on.

"Kasandra herself has taken an interest in your case," said Jola, as if that should mean something to me.

"Who?"

"Head of RI."

"I thought Robert Reimann was the owner."

"Yes, but he's long since lost any interest in the agency. It's all up to his wife now, and I'll try to make sure she's just as invested in the case as you are. Anyway, she's already involved and, as the investigation progresses she'll sink her teeth even deeper into it."

"I don't think it's enough to pay for my accommodation."

"Take it easy. These people don't have to count every penny."

Either she was suggesting that she was going to scam her employers or that I was the one who, as a matter of principle, expected others to stoop to such things.

As I headed towards the Old Town, I passed more people who seemed to focus solely on me. Only now have I realized that this was by no means a delusion. It was nothing suspicious, either, because I was attracting their attention myself, looking around as if I was lost.

I took a deep breath, trying to calm down.

"Why are you helping me?" I asked.

"Because your friend, the one who's dead, hired me to do it."

I didn't answer.

"That's not a good enough reason?" she asked. "Or are you offended by my bluntness?"

I had no idea how to answer. "It just seems strange to me," I eventually said.

"I want to find out why he died," she replied. "And I want to help you find your fiancée."

"You have a heart of gold."

"That's my job. And our fee has already been paid."

I decided to let it go. Clearly, there was something wrong with Jola Kliza. At best, she had peculiar interests. At worst, she had psychopathic tendencies.

"As soon as we know what happened to Ewa, we will know everything else," she added.

I wasn't so sure about that at the time.

"Let's start with the picture you had on your phone," she continued. "Can you describe every detail to me?"

"Of course I can. I know every pixel by heart."

Circling aimlessly around the city centre, I described the photo to her, and she mumbled under her breath after every detail. I had no idea why she needed that information. If she wanted to find the photo, she would need to get remote access to my mobile, locked in some safe at the police station.

"Okay, let's get to the other picture. The one from Wrocław."

That one I didn't remember as well, but I'd stared at it for long enough to have memorized the most important things.

"The guy standing in the back had a Foo Fighters sweatshirt that said 'There is Nothing Left to Lose'. There was also a bomb with wings on it – their logo, I think, or the album cover, I'm not sure."

"And Ewa? Was she dressed the same?"

"No, she had a T-shirt with a different logo."

"What was it?"

"Something about good days."

"Specifically, Wern. I need specifics."

I thought for a second. "The Better Days," I said.

"Are you sure?"

"Yeah."

"You don't sound like you are."

She was right: I wasn't. That had been the first time I'd ever come across the band's name. They were some kind of indie-rock band.

I stopped at the back of a small block of flats and put my back against the wall. Only then did I realize that I'd been walking through the city as if in a dream. I didn't even know where I was, exactly. Probably somewhere around Andersa and Waryńskiego streets.

"Maybe without the 'the'," I said. "Just 'Better Days'."

I heard Jola tapping her fingers at the keyboard.

"With or without an exclamation mark?"

"Without."

"So it's not The Bruisers' album. Too bad. They play pretty good punk."

I leaned my head against the wall and felt throbbing in my temples. The adrenaline was slowly fading, but maybe that wasn't such a good thing. It made the hangover come back and say hello.

"What does it matter?" I asked.

"Maybe nothing, maybe something," said Kliza diplomatically. "Do you remember the name of the band?"

"No."

"But it wasn't Foo Fighters?"

"Definitely not. It was some Spanish band."

"What's that?"

"I just told you…"

"Focus, this could really be important."

"Because?"

"Because you usually come to a concert wearing the clothes with the logo of the band that's on stage, right?"

She was right, but I didn't pay much attention to it. Ewa never liked Foo Fighters, saying their music was too chaotic for her. I remembered that clearly, because Blitzer often tried to convince us that we should give their new album a listen.

I reached back to my memories, fishing for the logo on the T-shirt. It looked more like the work of an amateur than a professional album cover. Maybe that's why I immediately thought of indie bands.

"So?" Jola urged. "What was the band's name?"

I rubbed my temples, trying to associate some element with another, to find the right clue or at least one detail that would make something click in my mind. Finally, something dawned on me.

"Wait!" I mumbled. "It made me think of that footballer that used to put on a Spider-Man mask."

"Excuse me?"

"There was an Argentinean player who put on a mask and pretended to shoot a web from his wrists every time he scored a goal."

Kliza was silent.

"I used to be obsessed with Spider-Man in my time," I confessed.

"Right."

"Ewa took it well, even though she wasn't so fixated on anything as a child. Except maybe archaeology. She was particularly interested in the earliest settlements on Polish lands."

Jola grunted quietly.

"To each their own," I added.

She still didn't answer, and it occurred to me that maybe it wasn't by accident that there was a band name on the T-shirt that I associated with my favourite comic-book character.

No, it must have been a coincidence. I'd been looking for hidden meanings where there weren't any. Or maybe not.

"Check it out on–"

"I just Googled it," Jola cut in. "The footballer's name is Jonas Gutierrez."

I snapped my fingers. "Gutierrez," I said. "That's what it said on the shirt."

Jola was quiet again. I was sick and tired of her lapses into silence. Earlier, I could take her reticence as an unspoken comment on my fascination with Spider-Man, but now it was just disturbing.

"Are you there?" I asked.

"Y-yes."

Her voice was weak, as if suddenly all energy left her. I could picture her going pale.

"Something wrong?"

"That name…" She groaned. "Was it Natalia Gutierrez Y Angelo?"

"Could be."

"Oh, my God."

"What's the matter?"

She didn't answer.

"Hello?" I yelled, irritated. "What's going on?"

"More than you could possibly imagine."

9

I didn't think it through.

When Kliza asked if she could come to the villa, instead of telling me everything on the phone, I immediately agreed without taking into account that it would upset Robert. He didn't like it when I made those decisions without consulting him.

This wouldn't have been a problem for other couples – friends sometimes come by unannounced – but for us it was different. If someone was to visit us, everything had to be arranged a few days in advance. Robert had to prepare – and give me time to prepare the house.

He returned with Wojtek before Kliza arrived, so I had the opportunity to keep at least a minimum of appearances that my husband had a say in that.

Wojtek threw his backpack on the floor in the hallway and headed off towards his room.

"Where do you think you're going?" I asked from the doorstep of the living room.

He stopped and looked at me. "Hi, Mum."

"Hi, pest."

He came up and hugged me. He was still at that age when he did it without embarrassment, but I was well aware that it would only last for another three or four more years. One day I would just give him a kiss at school, his friends would see it, and then they would mock him. On that day, he would come home with his head low and all that affection would be over.

I touched his hair and wanted to tell him to take his backpack, but Robert was already bending to pick it up. He was a great father, actually the best I could dream of for Wojtek. Maybe he lacked perspective in some respects, such as when he drove his BMW to pick up his son from school, but in every other respect he was almost perfect.

What he lacked as a husband, he made up for as a father. And maybe that's why I initially tolerated what he was doing to me. Then it became commonplace. The experience of those difficult moments was not accompanied by any reflection. And even if it had been, it would disappear, just as my determination had after the last time.

"How was school?" I asked.

Wojtek looked longingly towards his bedroom. I knew perfectly well that all he wanted was to get to his laptop, even though he had access to the internet on his mobile at school, not to mention that he turned on his tablet as soon as he got in car.

"Nothing interesting," he replied.

I had a daily dance with him, too. It started with "nothing interesting", but I gradually got the details out of him. But that day I didn't have the time, so I let him go to his room, giving Robert a perfunctory smile as he put the backpack on the doorstep. He was still looking at me uncertainly, as if he expected that his crossing another line yesterday would bring hellfire on him. And that I would be the one to set the flames.

I approached him and took his hand.

"Kliza came across something important," I said quietly. "Apparently, this girl sent a message."

"A message?"

"Jola didn't want to give me the details over the phone. She wants to talk face to face."

"Well, maybe I'll give you a lift to Baltic Pipe."

"I said she could come here," I replied quickly. "It won't take long. We'll go to my office upstairs."

Actually, it wasn't upstairs as such, just a converted attic. The room was quite spacious, however, and I loved the slanted ceiling. It was my sanctuary, where I felt best. I wasn't sure why at first, but then I realized that it was one of the few rooms in the villa where Robert almost never came. And one of few where he had never hit me.

So far.

I pushed that thought away, although seeing his gaze, it was difficult for me to do so.

"She's coming here?" he asked, his mouth clenched. Then he shook his head, turned and wordlessly walked into the kitchen, yanking open the fridge door. He shook his head again. I could almost feel the anger welling up inside him.

I also saw how much it cost him to control it.

He pulled out a bottle and poured himself a glass of wine, then emptied the glass in two quick gulps.

"How many times are we going to do this?" he asked.

"She asked, and I just–"

"You know I don't like unexpected guests."

"I know, but it's just business. We'll make it quick in my office."

"Couldn't you meet at the Baltic?" He finally turned around. I saw the resentment burn up his eyes. "What's wrong with there?"

"Nothing, but I didn't want to bother you."

"It's not a bother. Surely less of a bother than having a stranger here."

"She's your employee, Robert."

He took a step towards me, so quickly that I recoiled. Usually, this was a signal that a domestic was about to begin, but this time he stopped himself in time.

"She won't even come in here," I said, looking around the kitchen connected to the living room. "We'll go straight upstairs."

He didn't say a word. He just kept looking at me for a while, and I was afraid that he would suddenly snap and hit me, and then there would be no turning back. In the end, I wasn't worried that it would happen, but that I would have to cancel the meeting. Maybe he'd do it himself by dialling Kliza's number and telling her I wasn't feeling too well. We had been through similar scenarios before.

However, before he took the next step in my direction, there was a buzzing sound announcing that someone was at the gate. We looked at each other in silence.

"I can send her away," I said hesitantly.

"Now?" he said with a snort. "What would you tell her?"

"I don't have to explain myself to her."

"No," he replied coolly. "Let her in."

He opened the gate himself and then took a seat at the end of the couch, so that he couldn't be seen from the hallway. He sat in silence while Jola and I climbed the stairs.

I thought that Kliza would behave exactly like any other visitor who came here for the first time. Usually, there was no end to looking around, nor to compliments and praise. Some guests were captivated by the view from the living room, where almost the whole wall was glazed. Others found the bookshelves installed along the entire staircase particularly impressive.

But Jola went straight into my office as if she hadn't noticed anything. She only spoke once she was inside, seated at a small table under the large skylight. My desk, a couple of chairs and a small bookcase were the only items in the room.

She planted her elbows on the table and rubbed her face anxiously, leaving red marks on her cheeks. Then she glanced at me and I could swear that for a moment she looked like a wraith.

"This is all just impossible," she said. "It's completely fucked up."

I sat down next to her. "What did you find out?"

"Actually, it wasn't me, it was Wern."

I raised my brows.

"I mean Werner," she added under her breath, and then waved her hand. "In fact, we got to the bottom of it together. But it was Ewa who started everything."

"What, exactly?"

Jola set up on the chair and cleared her throat. "In that photo on the *Spotted* profile, which someone has since helpfully taken down, Ewa was wearing a T-shirt that had nothing to do with the Foo Fighters."

"Eh?" I didn't understand.

"It was their gig, but she was wearing a T-shirt with a different band's name on it."

"So what?"

"It caught my attention. Wern had it buried deep in his memory, but I helped him a little and we established that it was Natalia Gutierrez Y Angelo on the T-shirt."

"No idea who they are."

"'Better Days'?" she prompted.

"Doesn't ring a bell."

"Well, it should, because that song was a big deal."

I looked at her a little irritated because I was afraid that any moment Robert would knock on the door, apologize to Jola and say that we had to leave for some reason. He could harness his emotions for a while, but I knew well enough that it wouldn't take long for them to slip free.

"You must have heard of the FARC," Kliza said.

"Sure, I have. Some time ago, they made a controversial peace agreement with the government in Colombia." I only remembered about those revolutionary guerrillas because the peace treaty, signed in 2016 after five decades of bloody civil war, was all over the news at the time. More than two hundred thousand people had lost their lives there during the conflict and five million were forced to resettle. The main architect of the agreement, Santos, won the Nobel Peace Prize. But that's not why I remembered the story.

The Colombian people were supposed to vote for peace in a referendum, but they rejected it by a narrow margin, refusing to accept that some of the war crimes would go unpunished under the terms of the agreement. Their reasoning was irrational, but for some reason I approved.

"Great," Jola said. "Then all I have to do is tell you the most important things."

I made a *hurry up* gesture with my hand while glancing anxiously at the door.

"In 2010, Colombian special forces carried out a series of raids on FARC camps," Kliza went on, straightening up. "One of them intended to take back the hostages who had been held there for almost ten years. However, those hostages had to be informed beforehand."

"Why?"

"Because the FARC had a simple policy of discouraging the government from reclaiming hostages. They shot them as soon as there was a slightest suspicion they could be taken back."

"Okay."

"Colonel Espejo, who was in charge of the operation, had a problem: how to tell the hostages that help was coming and that they should prepare to be rescued. For ten years there had been no contact with them, and any publicly transmitted information, even encrypted, would be intercepted by the guerrillas."

I nodded, hoping that the Kliza would hurry.

"So the military commissioned Juan Carlos Ortiz, a marketing specialist, to develop an innovative method of getting the information to them under the radar."

"And what did he come up with?"

"Morse code."

"That's not very innovative."

"The guerrillas didn't know it very well," Kliza continued, unperturbed. "Unlike the hostages, who used to be in the military. Ortiz assumed they'd recognize it immediately."

"It's still–"

"Of course, they couldn't transmit it directly. The FARC militia didn't have to be able to decode it to know that someone was broadcasting a message and something was happening. Anyway, another problem was how to get the message to the hostages, seeing as they were being held in the jungle, far from civilization. So Ortiz came up with the idea of encoding it in a song that would then be played over and over again on the leading radio stations."

I frowned.

"So they hired two artists and a whole team of songwriters to come up with the right tune. It turned out to be quite simple, and the chorus contained an encrypted message consisting of twenty words. The song itself sounded like a typical pop song, with embedded electronic riffs which were, in fact, Morse code."

"Not a bad idea."

"The song was broadcast mainly in the jungle area, and it was estimated that about three million people must have heard it. But only those it targeted recognized the encrypted message. The hostage rescue turned out to be a success."

"Okay, but what does that have to do with Ewa?"

"The fact that those two unknown artists, who until then had only worked on radio jingles, were called Natalia Gutierrez Y Angelo. And the song with the encoded message was titled–"

"'Better Days'."

Jola ran her fingers through her hair with a satisfied expression. It was the first time I'd ever seen her so happy.

"There were no additional recordings, no commercial releases, let alone T-shirts," she added. "The fact that Ewa was wearing a T-shirt like that at the concert is a message."

"What message?"

"That she was still being held against her will."

I got up from my desk and walked around the office. For a moment I stopped in front of the large windows and watched the clouds glide slowly across the sky. Then I turned to Kliza.

"That would mean that after the rape by the river, those people kidnapped her," I observed.

Jola nodded.

"And that for ten years this girl has been living a nightmare."

"Sadly, that's probably true," admitted Kliza. "But that T-shirt must have been a cry for help. It was no accident that Ewa was at that gig. She was sure Blitzer would be there."

"You think so?"

"She knew he was almost obsessed with Foo Fighters. He wouldn't have missed it, especially since it took place near Opole."

I sat on the dresser and rubbed my neck in thought. "But wasn't she enjoying herself in the picture?" I asked.

"According to Wern, that's what she looked like, yes."

"So that doesn't match the story of her being held against her will."

"Maybe they forced her to act like she was having a good time?"

"Maybe," I admitted. "But why would they even let her go to the gig in the first place? It doesn't make any sense."

"On the contrary."

I looked at Kliza curiously.

"In many cases of kidnapping, hostages are occasionally allowed some limited exposure to the outside world. Their captors want them to feel overwhelmed by it after years of isolation, to see how alien it's become. Then they'd *want* to go back to prison."

"And in your opinion, she outsmarted them."

Jola brushed her fingers through her hair again. This time the movements were familiar, nervous, almost neurotic.

"She must have been preparing for that for a long time," she said. "Just ordering a T-shirt wouldn't have be easy. But apparently, wherever they're holding her, she's got a little freedom. Enough to make a cry for help."

We looked at each other as if we wanted to understand all the implications but, at the same time, didn't.

"Ten years." I said.

"I know, terrible."

"The things she must have been through…"

Kliza shifted her shoulders, but there was no indifference in her gesture. "After the rape, they left Wern on the riverbank, and they had to put her in a car and take her somewhere. I guess they abused her, probably kept doing to her all the things they had done by the river, over and over again, until they broke her. Until they were certain of her submission."

We sat in silence for a while – for far too long. Even a few seconds would be enough for both of us to submerge ourselves in the depressing awareness of what all that meant. I wanted to ask Jola if she'd managed to establish what the message from Ewa was – and if there was anything else we could find out – but then there was a knock on the door. Without waiting for a response, Robert walked in with an apologetic smile. I knew what he was about to say, and sure enough he looked at his watch meaningfully.

"Sorry to interrupt, but we need to get going," he said. "We have a meeting we can't be late for."

Kliza rose from the chair as if it was on fire. "Of course. I'm sorry, Mr. Reimann."

"No problem."

"Listen, Robert..." I started.

"We're really going to be late," he replied and schooled his features into an expression that said he was profoundly sorry that he had to ask Jola to leave.

He was a great actor. And I knew it wasn't going to be a peaceful night.

10

I tried to wring every last detail of that damn T-shirt from my memory – Ewa's stance, her facial expression, anything that might help.

I'm sure there was something. After what Kliza had told me, I had no doubt that it wasn't just a cry for help but something more – a coded message, maybe, or even a clue about where to look for Ewa.

But my memory failed me. The headache, fatigue and recurring images of Blitz's blood-soaked bed didn't help, for sure. Plus, I still had to bear in mind that I was a wanted man, even if not yet officially. The first copper to recognize me wouldn't let me out of their sight.

I knew I had to rest, to refresh my mind a little and let it work.

Kliza called about an hour, maybe an hour and a half after our last conversation. "Where are you?" she asked.

"Back at Zaodrze."

"You should leave the city. As soon as possible."

"I intend to, but–"

"Do you know where Chrząstowice is?"

"Mm-hmm," I confirmed.

"There's a hotel on the road to Częstochowa."

"I know it." Everyone knew it. There were two large tennis complexes near Opole, one in Chrząstowice and the other in Zawada, dating back to the time when nobody in Poland knew the name of Agnieszka Radwańska.

"Stay there for a while," said Kliza. "It's a big place with lots of rooms, so no one should pay any attention to you. Besides, it looks like it's a roadside motel, so there must be a lot of anonymous guests passing through."

"Not exactly," I said. "Just because it's by the motorway–"

"Never mind."

I rolled my eyes and moved my phone away from my face. "Do you have to interrupt me all the time?" I asked.

"I just want to do what's important as soon as possible."

"Then think about another place, because a lot of people from the city go to the restaurant in that hotel."

Jola mumbled something incomprehensible under her breath. I thought it was an expletive.

"Can you move around the hotel without going into a restaurant?" she asked.

"Yes, but–"

"Then you'll check in quickly, and you won't show up there."

I didn't have the energy to protest. Anyway, maybe she was right. I needed a place where I could think about what else was in the photo. I cursed quietly, thinking that I would still have it if we hadn't alarmed Ewa's kidnappers.

But there was one thing I didn't understand.

"Wern? You there?"

By this time, I'd already given up trying to correct her. "I'm thinking about something."

"Don't think about it, just act."

"Is that your motto?"

"No, but maybe it should be yours."

I was silent, watching cars whizz past. The paranoia must have subsided because I no longer felt like everybody was looking at me.

"Who's Phil Braddy?" I asked.

There was no response from Kliza.

"Which side is he on? And what's his interest in all this?"

As the silence on the other side dragged on, I cleared my throat meaningfully.

"What do you want me to tell you?" Jola shot back.

"Anything."

"All I've established is that after he deleted the account, he didn't reopen it. There's no sign of him."

I shuddered at the idea that he might have met the same fate as Blitzer. No, that was impossible. Whoever had kidnapped Ewa wouldn't be able to get to someone in Britain, surely?

I hoped I was right.

"Can you get to this hotel by public transport?" Kliza asked.

I shook my head as if waking up from a bad dream. "There's a bus stop at the allotment gardens," I said.

"That makes no sense."

"I'll walk from there."

"As long as you don't stand out."

"I won't," I assured her, feeling like I'd wandered into some strange, surreal world. I didn't know how I'd found myself there, or whether I really would be able to stay out of sight.

I headed for the nearest bus stop, thinking about the uncertain future that awaited me. "What's next?" I asked.

"I'll pick you up."

Actually, that didn't solve anything, but somehow it raised my spirits.

"You'll stay with me for a while, in hiding."

"Are you sure?" I asked.

"I wouldn't have offered otherwise. Then we'll figure out what to do next."

"I'd rather think about it now," I said. "We don't have the picture, we don't have a clue. All we know is that that Ewa needs help. And since these people have removed everything from Facebook, they've obviously caught on to the situation. Do you understand what this could mean?"

I assumed that her silence this time wasn't due to her ignorance.

"She's survived ten years, she'll survive a little longer," Kliza said after a while. "Apparently, she can take care of herself."

I had no doubt about that, but I didn't even want to think about what she'd have to do to keep herself safe. The kidnappers must have been mad when they found out she was trying to contact me.

Only now did it occur to me that she really had been. After ten long years, Ewa had finally managed to tell me something: that she was alive. She'd tried to act, and fought for her freedom. That was the most important thing.

"She needs our help," I said when I got to the bus stop. "And as soon as possible."

"We'll do what we need to do, Wern."

"Which is what?"

"We'll examine everything carefully. You'll get some rest, which will help you remember the details of that photo."

"Even if that's true, I won't remember all of them. We need more than that."

I swiped my finger through the timetables, looking for bus number seventeen. I knew it started its run at Dambonia and went to the allotments on Częstochowska Street. From there, I'd have to walk about five, maybe six kilometres to the hotel. But I wasn't convinced that was the right direction to go.

"What are you suggesting?" Jola asked.

"I'm going back to Blitz's apartment."

"Are you *crazy?*"

"Maybe he took some kind of screenshot. Maybe somewhere on his laptop there's something that–"

"Oh, you're definitely crazy," Kliza interrupted. "You'll get picked up by the police as soon as they spot you, and you won't find anything anyway. Can't you see how meticulous these people are?"

I wasn't going to argue with her, because deep down I knew she was right. Maybe I even wanted her to talk me out of the idea.

"Do as I say, Wern. It'll do you good."

"Nothing's ever going to do me good." I glanced at my watch. I had about fifteen minutes before the bus arrived. I sat on the bench and hung my head. "Least of all passivity," I added. "That's why I'm going to act."

"How?"

"By using that *Spotted* profile. But not to look for a specific person. I'm going to be looking for pictures from that concert."

Jola sighed down the line. "I've already scoured the internet," she snapped. "You can't see Ewa in any of the photos. Either they took care to remove them, or they made sure that no one would have any record of her. The one you saw must have been the only one that slipped through."

"Because they paid attention mainly to camera lenses, not smartphones?"

"I suppose so."

"So there may be more photos, but no one's published them."

She didn't have to confirm the obvious. Such events were documented by people not in their memories, but on their mobile phones. Rather than focusing on the main event, they looked at the screen of the device recording it.

"It's not a good idea, Wern."

"Do you have a better one?"

"Not only could you get yourself in trouble but her too. If the kidnappers see you looking for more photos, you'll make her situation worse."

"Why?" I asked. "They'll assume I'm just desperately looking for anything that could help me find her." I wanted to think that was true, that we were dealing with amateurs, but I knew deep down that I was fooling myself. "It's our only chance," I added.

The bus arrived in a cloud of exhaust fumes. I thought I'd managed to convince Kliza, at least partially, but I didn't know if I could do the same for myself.

I'd risked contacting Dad and asked him to meet me at one of the stops en route to the allotments. I needed a laptop, and under the circumstances even my old ASUS would do. I wouldn't have been able to contact him if it hadn't been for the fact that he hadn't changed his number since he bought his first phone, back when people memorized their numbers, just in case. These days, like everyone else, I program new ones into the phone memory and immediately forget them.

When the bus pulled up at the stop and I got off, Dad handed me a small bag containing the laptop as the other passengers flowed past me.

"Your mother put some food in there too," he said.

For the first time in I didn't know how long, I didn't have to force myself to smile. We looked at each other without exchanging another word. When the door closed, I saw him follow the departing bus with his eyes.

It was like going back in time to my childhood, and I felt as I had when I'd leave for a summer camp or a field trip. But I was afraid that analogy was incorrect. Back then, I would leave knowing I'd be back soon. Now I couldn't be sure I would ever return.

I checked into the hotel and thought no one noticed me. I realized the laptop bag could actually support the impression that I was travelling.

In the room, I opened my battered laptop and looked at the keys that were worn out the most: W, A, S and D. Of course, that's how you recognized a gamer's computer.

It took me some time to hook up to the wifi and the PC crawled like it was about to die on me any moment, but in the end I managed to create a new Facebook account, upload a profile photo and then even add a few random people as friends.

Only then did I realize that I didn't have to use the *Spotted* profile. It would be much better to post a request to share photos on the Polish Foo Fighters fan page. If the kidnappers were professionals, they were monitoring that too, but I decided that this way I would have a better chance of finding Ewa.

I refreshed the site every ten seconds, hoping that by some miracle someone would react immediately. I didn't make any specific request; I only wrote that I was looking for pictures from the concert. It occurred to me that I might outsmart the kidnappers, but I quickly pushed that thought aside. They'd already proved they were extremely vigilant.

After an hour, the first photographs appeared, taken on mobile phones, mostly, with friends tagged as if it was a good opportunity to reminisce about the event. I looked through them idly, not expecting to see Ewa anywhere. I had no reason to believe that anything would change in that regard.

And it didn't. I spent all evening trying to get a glimpse of Ewa in the crowd, but in vain. I dozed off for a while, then suddenly woke up at a loud electronic bleep. At first I was confused, but then realized it was a message alert on my new mobile.

I reached for the phone without enthusiasm. Kliza would have called for certain, and I'd told Dad not to contact me at all on this number, fearing he could bring trouble both on himself and on me.

And yet the message was from him.

"Turn on the TV."

That was it, so I had no idea what to expect. I looked around for the remote and did what Dad had suggested. I didn't find anything on TVP1, TVP2 or any leading commercial broadcasters, and it wasn't until I switched to TVN24 that I realized what he meant.

"Body of missing girl found in Opole after ten years," the yellow chyron read.

11

I knew I was safe until sunset. I actually lived two separate lives: one during the day with a loving, caring, romantic husband, the second at night with a completely different person.

I helped Wojtek with his homework, then read a few pages of Stephen King's latest. I liked him, but not for his ability to incite fear in the reader; I already had too much of that. What I appreciated about King was the way he portrayed and exposed the darkest demons lurking in the human psyche. It seemed like he knew and understood my life perfectly.

That night, however, I knew I wouldn't be reading for very long. I realised that as soon as Robert entered the bedroom and closed the door. He did it too slowly, too calmly, like he was trying to show his composure on a theatre stage.

Then he turned to me and sent me a long look.

Did he fight his own demons? Did he still try to fool himself that he would be able to restrain his emotions? Did he battle with his thoughts? Did he do everything he could to avoid giving in to what lurked in the darkness of his psyche?

I didn't know. He certainly gave such an impression, but it was difficult to say whether it was just a façade or the overspill from the real battle he was fighting.

"Did you really have to?" he asked.

I didn't say a word, having long ago learned that this was the best option. If I started to apologize, I would just provoke him further. It felt more and more like he was the master of the situation. The master of me.

If I chose the opposite approach and tried to resist him, at first it would throw him off a bit, but in the end he would beat me harder and longer.

"Couldn't you have waited till tomorrow to meet her?"

He came closer, putting his hands in his jeans pocket. Like that would stop his fists.

"I asked you a question."

"It was urgent."

"Oh, yes?"

He stood by the bed, and I closed the book and put it back on the table. The absurdity of the situation was that I knew exactly what was about to happen, and at the same time I was hoping that something would change at the last minute.

I shouldn't have deluded myself, but every morning Robert made me think that if something like that ever happened again, he would stop in time. I thought – hoped – he believed it himself.

"You fucked up all evening," he snarled.

"We really needed to talk."

"There are phones. There's the internet, for fuck's sake. There are so many ways to get in touch," he hissed. "But no, you had to let her in here. And fuck up my mood." He cocked his head and snorted as if I was really guilty, and he no longer had the energy to endure it.

I knew exactly what he was feeling. He'd been described his feelings to me for years. If something happened that diverted from his schedule even a little, he would become shaken up and think about it obsessively, turning it over and over in his head for hours, growing angrier by the minute.

That was obviously what was happening here.

He looked at me with pure hatred in his eyes and stayed motionless for a moment. Eventually, he suddenly picked up the duvet, cursed under his breath and lay down on his back next to me. He crossed his arms under his head.

That was not what I expected. Maybe tonight was going to be different.

"I am going to fucking kick her out."

"Robert…"

"No, it's over. She's out of RI."

"You just sacked Glazur. We can't afford any more layoffs."

He glanced at the ceiling, and I was grateful to him for that. I knew that if he looked at me, I would feel even more apprehensive. Glazur had to say goodbye to Reimann Investigations also because of me, because I'd met with him once too often at Baltic Pipe. The last time had been on business, as usual, but it had been different because I'd forgotten to tell Robert about it. That was enough for him to sack Glazur the following day. So I had to take my husband's words seriously. He could call the HR department first thing in the morning and recommend that they terminate Jola's contract.

"I don't give a shit," he mumbled. "She's useless anyway."

"She's in charge of an important case–"

"Important, my arse," he barked, cutting me off.

For a moment, he was motionless. Then he sniffed quietly again, as if he wanted to show that he had no more to say to me. He grabbed the duvet, pulled it over his head and turned on his side with his back to me.

I was breathing hard.

"Turn off the light."

I did so without saying a word, then carefully lay on my back. I felt like I was walking on extremely thin ice that had just given a warning crack. I had to make sure it didn't break completely.

I lay there for a quarter of an hour, listening to his restless breathing. I knew he wasn't asleep, that his emotions were still buzzing inside him, but I hoped he'd get them under control.

That turned out to be a false hope.

At some point he got out of bed, went to the bathroom and slammed the door. After a while, I heard him turn on the tap. I imagined him looking at himself in the mirror, splashing his face with cold water over and over again. Fighting his demons.

When he came out, I saw straight away that he'd lost the fight.

"As if that's not enough, I haven't been able to focus on anything all fucking evening, and now I'll be awake half the night because of you," he said as he approached me. "Why do you have to *be* like that?"

"Robert."

He raised his arm and hit me in the face with his open hand. I blinked and turned my head. It was the only reaction I've ever had.

He grabbed me by my pyjamas and pulled me out of bed. He pushed me to the floor and by the time I could move, he was next to me.

"Robert…"

"Shut up."

"Remember what you told me?" I asked him, trying to scramble to my feet. Perhaps it would have been better if I'd stayed still, but the need to escape was stronger than rationality. He immediately grabbed me and pushed me to the floor.

"I fucking remember," he said. "And do you remember that I've been working my ass off all day? So that you have everything you need?"

He shook me. My head hit the floor.

"And what do I ask for in return? Is it that much?"

I opened my mouth, but he slapped me again.

"I asked you a question!"

"Robert."

"I just wanted some peace tonight for a few fucking hours!" he yelled, shaking me harder and harder.

I knew he had already crossed the line in his mind, and that it was only going to get worse.

And it did.

As usual, Robert barked more questions, blaming me for everything, even the most absurd stuff, as if every tiny thing turned out to be the source of all failures and everything that didn't go according to his wishes. He thought up whole scenarios, intertwining them with successive blows, each more and more powerful. He dragged me around the bedroom, punched me in the stomach, then threw me to the floor and kicked me.

He ranted about how Kliza's visit had upset his entire schedule. That he wouldn't be able to sleep because of it. That tomorrow he'd be distracted and business negotiations wouldn't go as well as they should. That we were going to lose out, maybe even have to cut costs. Each subsequent element of his delusions seemed to add more fuel to the fire awakened by his own internal demons – the ones King wrote about.

These tirades usually lasted for some hours – sometimes two, sometimes as long as six. I couldn't sleep a wink afterwards, even though the cycles always ended in the same way – his crying, repentance, attempts to make amends. Most often he beat himself afterwards, and once even smashed the bathroom mirror. Then, as his emotions cooled, as they settled into bruises and cuts on my body, he turned into a completely different person.

That was the case tonight, too. After he left me on the floor, bruised and humiliated, he disappeared into the bathroom, and for a moment the whole villa was utterly silent. Then I heard curses, the sounds of fists hitting flesh, and then, finally, crying.

As always, I was afraid to assess my injuries, to touch my teeth with my tongue, to stand in front of the mirror, or to even move. I thought if I moved, I'd discover all the many places he'd hurt me.

Not just physically.

After a few minutes, he came back into the room. He didn't raise his eyes, just sniffed and hit his temple again and again with an open hand. He knelt beside me, begging for forgiveness, and then he lifted me up and helped me lie down in bed. He pressed his face into my thighs, and I felt his tears soaking my pyjama bottoms.

The adrenaline was fading, and it was replaced by pain.

I stayed in that strange stasis until the morning, which seemed at the same time natural and familiar to me. I disassociated, separating myself from all the thoughts I should have had, totally unreflective. Maybe that was the only reason I'd survived for so long.

In the morning, it was like I was lying next to a completely different person. Robert was half embarrassed, half angry. It was as if someone else had hurt me and he was going to punish him at all costs.

He brought me breakfast, then asked me over and over how I was feeling. Again, there were pleas for forgiveness and promises that next time he would sooner cut off his hand than raise it against me.

He'd go to therapy.

He'd lock himself in another room for the night.

He'd buy me a gun.

It was the same old story. Versions usually differed depending on how far he'd gone each time. This time he was willing to promise me everything, and the worst thing was that I could see in his eyes that he really believed it.

I could have held him to them, but I knew our relationship was like a beehive, and the wellbeing of a family resembled an anthill – all it took was a stick to churn it up and there would be a tragedy. Some things had to stay behind closed doors.

At about ten o'clock, I was drinking Prosecco in the living room, looking out at the coast. Robert drove Wojtek to school while I stayed at home alone, assessing the extent of my physical injuries. The mental ones I preferred not to analyze.

It wasn't bad, at least visually. A few bruises that I could mask easily. I'd learned how. The only thing that worried me was the constant pain in my stomach, as if something had ruptured in my gut.

The bubbly helped, as always. I reached for the tablet and propped it up on the table, then started to browse the news. I read a few articles and then the phone rang.

Kliza.

"Yes?" I answered.

"Have you seen it?" she asked without preamble.

"Seen what?"

"Go to any local news website."

At first I assumed there was something about Rewal, but I quickly realized that wasn't it. Jola lived in a different world now, one where Ewa's case shaped her reality. I went to the Opole subsection of the *Gazeta Wyborcza* website and lost my mind completely.

I could feel the blood draining from my face. I stopped thinking about last night, about my abdominal pain and the fact that I should do something before my husband went one step too far.

"That's... that's impossible," I said.

"And yet there it is."

"When did you see this?"

"This morning."

"And you're only calling me *now?*"

"What good would it do if I'd called earlier? The girl is dead. It's too late for anything. Besides, a few problems have come up."

I didn't ask what kind of problems, because my mind was focused solely on Ewa. I shook my head. "Are they sure it's her?"

"Yes. They ran a DNA test," Jola replied. "It's definitely the girl we were looking for. The one we put in her grave."

"Listen, that's not–"

"It's the truth," Kliza interrupted. "If we hadn't started digging into this case, Ewa would still be alive."

I drained my glass and realized my hand was shaking. I jammed it into my armpit, as if someone could see my nervous reaction.

"It wasn't us who initiated the contact," I pointed out.

"That's what you're going to tell yourself so you don't feel guilty?"

"We have no reason to feel that way. Neither does Werner."

"That's your opinion."

I looked at the bottle. I shouldn't go for another glass right away, but maybe I'd be justified on a day like today? No, I said to myself. If I let myself to do that once, I'd become a full-blown alcoholic, not just a high-functioning one. I'd fall down a hole till I hit rock bottom, then have to stop drinking entirely. It was ridiculous. I could only control myself because I was afraid that if I didn't I'd have to say goodbye to booze forever. The horror of losing my fix kept me in check.

Contradiction. One of many in my life.

"We ended her life," Jola added after a while. I wasn't surprised she was using a euphemism. It was so much easier than saying *We killed her.* "Whatever that life might have been," she mumbled.

"Maybe it didn't have much to do with real life."

"Maybe not," Kliza admitted. "But we could have saved her. There was a chance."

"Not necessarily. The lead was gone, right?"

"You're fooling yourself," she said quietly. "But it's your choice."

"I'm just saying how it looks from my perspective."

"There are many things you can't see from your perspective."

It sounded like an unnecessary reproach about the standard of living I had with Robert. I knew others saw us as the perfect couple, living in a dream villa by the sea, with a few luxury cars in the garage and a healthy child we could both be proud of. We went to exclusive parties, enjoyed a good reputation and the future seemed so bright. It was a beautiful picture, but one drawn in blood, violence, hatred and hypocrisy.

But that's not what Kliza meant. I was allergic to criticism of our lifestyle, alert to it from everywhere, but in this case she really was talking about a completely different perspective.

"You don't know everything," Jola added after a moment of silence.

"What do you mean?"

"Wern's just contacted me."

"And?" I asked cautiously, something in her voice making me think there'd been a breakthrough. But did that even matter now?

"He told me that he'd found something important in one of the photos. He sounded drunk, but..."

"What exactly did he find?"

"I don't know."

"Why not?"

She sighed loudly. "Like I said, I've got my own problems here," Kliza said. "And they're pretty serious."

"What do you mean?" I asked, irritated at having to pull information out of her almost by force like this. But couldn't she also have been a bit more forthcoming?

"The head of HR interrupted my conversation with Wern and he said he needed to talk to me," she explained.

I knew what she was going to say.

"He told me I was fired. With immediate effect."

I got up from the chair, the legs leaving scratch marks on the wooden floor. I took out a bottle of Prosecco from the fridge and put it on the counter, then cursed under my breath and put it back.

Before his usual repentance, Robert must have woken up someone in HR in the middle of the night and ordered them to sack Kliza. I should have expected it, I supposed – he'd stopped beating me for a while and walked out of the room, so he must have done it then, but I'd been too stunned to know what he was doing at the time.

"I shouldn't be surprised," added Jola.

"What?" I asked.

"I'd only just started looking for a girl and they find her dead."

"No, that's not it. Don't worry; I'll take care of that."

"There's nothing to take care of."

"Kliza, it's not like that at all."

"I don't care," she said. "It's actually a good thing."

The certainty in her voice made me think that there was no point in arguing with her, at least not now. From her point of view, continuing to work at Reimann Investigations was the worst option. I had to give her time to cool off. And to convince Robert to change his mind.

But was that even possible? I knew him well enough to fear it wasn't, but I still deluded myself that this would be the one time he would change his mind.

"I'm texting you Wern's number," she added. "And I've sent you an email with instructions for logging into the admin panel in the company contact application. Pass it on to the next person or use it yourself, I don't care anymore."

"You can't just—"

"Can't just what?" She cut me off mid-word. "Ewa's been found dead. That's where my work would end even if I wasn't parting ways with the company. We don't comfort widowers."

Before I could answer, she hung up. So much for working with the best employee we've ever had.

I waited an hour and filled the glass. I took only small sips, but it was very difficult. Sitting in front of a computer in the upstairs office, I clasped my hands behind my neck and stayed still for some time.

Then I decided I had to get to work. The case wasn't finished. Werner had something new and I needed to know what it was. At the same time, I had to be careful not to do anything to upset my husband, and I knew that firing Kliza meant that Robert didn't want the company investigating Ewa's case.

Now I had him against me, too.

This made me realize how little influence I had in the company, as well as how little freedom I had. I knew that Robert often checked my phone records, scrupulously logging every call I made. I also assumed that when he was at work, he was using our home camera system to monitor what I was doing.

I logged into the contact panel and sent Werner a single-use code. Actually, this was necessary only when the customer logged in, but I thought it was a good way to get Damian to this peculiar chat.

I wasn't going to bother worrying about anonymity – the connection was still encrypted and the messages were immediately deleted – so I just changed a few settings via the admin account such as usernames. I thought it would make Werner feel like there was a real person on the other side.

He did not log in for a long time and I waited anxiously, wondering if I was doing the right thing. I felt like I was betraying Robert. Maybe I wasn't, but I was certainly considering it.

It was like meeting a male friend at a hotel bar – nothing wrong with it per se, but you knew where it could lead.

When Werner finally showed up, my hands hovered over the keyboard as I wondered what to write, my mind blank.

There was a question on the monitor:

[Wern] Kasandra?

I wasn't sure how much I should explain to him.

[Wern] The owner of RI?
[Kasandra] Yes.
[Wern] What happened to Kliza?
[Kasandra] She had something else to do. It's complicated.

He didn't reply for a while.

[Wern] She has to come back.
[Kasandra] Impossible right now, but I'll do what I can.

The messages were disappearing one by one, and the cursor was blinking, waiting for one of us to write something. I leaned on my elbows and looked into the monitor. So Damian wasn't sure he could trust me. Okay, he *was* dealing with a stranger, but he was using a secure platform. And he contacted the same company that had been the only one to reach out to him with a helping hand.

[Kasandra] Kliza told me you'd discovered something.

The seconds dragged by, then eventually he responded.

[Wern] I did. More than I thought.
[Kasandra] What do you mean?
[Wern] She's alive.
[Kasandra] What?

[Wern] I know how it sounds. But I have proof.

I reached for the glass without noticing.

[Kasandra] Are you sure about that?
[Wern] Yes.

I nodded, as if he could see it. I wondered whether I should tell him that Ewa's body had been found, but realised there was no point. He must already know.

[Wern] I know what you think. The boyfriend can't accept the loss. He's looking for some absurd explanations and grasps at even the most ridiculous hope. But you have to believe me.

I took a deep breath, still not knowing how I should react. Denying it could alienate him. To trust him too soon would be equally unwise. Eventually, I thought it was best to wait until he wrote something else.

After a while, another line appeared.
[Wern] She's alive. And I have proof.

CHAPTER 2

1

I wasn't so deluded that I thought Kasandra would believe my assertion that Ewa was alive, but I assumed her agency would be committed to fulfilling its obligations and she wouldn't bail on me. Blitzer had paid a lump sum up front, true – the money was already in their account – but I was hoping they were interested in good PR. A disappointed, bitter client would be bad publicity.

Our first RIC call lasted a good half hour. I didn't comment on the fact that Kasandra called me *Wern*, and I didn't ask what RIC meant either. I presumed the C stood for "chat". Not very sophisticated.

It took her some time to convince me not to count on Kliza's return. She assured me that she would do what she could to get her back, but warned me that the chances were very slim. She made it sound like Kliza had decided herself to leave the investigation, which I found hard to believe, but then I realized I didn't know her at all. After finding out the body had been discovered, she could easily have reasoned that her work was finished and moved on.

Yet the fact that Kasandra herself had contacted me now didn't fit in with that version of events. Kliza had indeed tried to spark her interest in my case, but I didn't expect her to actually succeed. I remembered what Blitz had said about the Reimanns being rich, happy, respected and constantly busy, either increasing their wealth or spending it.

But apparently there was something else at stake, since Kasandra told me herself that she was going to help me personally, even though she probably didn't believe my claim that Ewa was alive.

Especially since, despite what I'd told her, I had no evidence.

I wasn't really sure if it existed at all, or indeed about anything at that point. The police statement sounded plausible, but I knew I shouldn't trust anyone.

Well, almost anyone. But it wasn't until my father's phone call that I remembered. I answered it with some hesitation, because if there was a warrant out for my arrest, my parents were certainly targeted, too.

I doubted anyone would be listening in on the conversation, but I knew it was only a matter of time before the investigators would find a clue that would lead them to me. I could have brought problems on my mother and father, and God knew they had enough of them already.

But I still answered Dad's call. I needed to hear a familiar voice, and the last call was already recorded. He asked me where I was right away. At first I thought he must have gone crazy to try to find out at all.

Then I thought I'd have to stop this madness. I was getting paranoid, believing I was being hunted by people who didn't want Ewa found. Then I reasoned that, since her body had allegedly been found, there was no reason for them to continue to persecute me.

I couldn't collect my thoughts. I didn't know what was true and what wasn't, what was a logical, valid hypothesis and what was the product of a tired mind. Another sleepless night certainly didn't help.

So I told Dad where I was. I knew I couldn't handle my situation all on my own, and he and Mum were the only people I could count on.

There were also practical issues to consider. If I was finally going to find answers to the questions I hadn't been able to solve, I needed two things: a car and money.

My parents showed up less than an hour later. We met in the back of the hotel and I led them to my room. I locked the door and leaned my back against it.

"Have you eaten anything?" Mum asked.

I shook my head and looked out of the window. "I don't want to sound paranoid, but did you check to see if anyone was following you?" I asked.

"Yes," Dad promised me.

I slipped down to the floor and raked my fingers through my hair. Before Mum and Dad showed up, I'd planned everything out in my head, deciding that ultimately there was only one thing I could rely on: my own intuition.

And it supplied me with one possible scenario.

"Everything will be okay," Mum said.

"I know."

"Now that they've finally found her, we'll be able to–"

"It wasn't her," I told her.

They looked at me, their worried expressions the same as when I got the flu or some other disease and the first symptoms were becoming evident.

"I'm sure it's not her."

"But, son…"

"I know what they've made public," I said, "but it's all just part of the game they're playing. Why would they kill her? Now, after all these years?" I knew what they were about to say, so I headed them off. "The fact that I'm looking for her doesn't change anything. I've been doing this since she went missing."

They looked at each other.

"I didn't even get close to finding her, so they had no reason to be worried I would. And judging by everything they've done so far, they're not afraid of anything or anyone."

They sat on the bed, still not talking. I wasn't surprised. I probably would have kept quiet too at that point. I pulled my legs up and put my hands on my knees.

"Where was she supposed to have been found?" I asked.

"Don't you know?" Dad said.

I hadn't read the latest news updates, though I should have. It would be wise to know every detail of their plan and see how determined they were. But in a sense it was a form of challenging reality, a rebellion against what happened.

"By the river," Mum said. "Somewhere on Bolko."

A small island in the middle of the city, an enclave of ramblers, cyclists, runners and canoeists, and probably a whole host of people looking for other types of entertainment, from adolescent pissheads to retirees sunbathing on blankets. There were enough surveillance blind spots there to leave a dead body, or to suddenly "discover" it somewhere no one could confirm it hadn't been earlier.

"Why would they dump her corpse there?" I asked.

My use of the word seemed to cause my parents almost physical pain, but I refused to use Ewa's name. If a body had been found, it had nothing to do with her.

"If it was her, surely they'd hide her somewhere no one would ever find her," I added. "It doesn't make any sense."

"Maybe they wanted the search to end," Dad suggested. "Maybe they felt you were getting close to them."

"How?"

He looked at me as if he wanted to say, *We don't know, and we probably never will.* But he didn't have to say anything to make me realize that.

"They've confirmed her identity, son," he said after a while.

"Hmm," I murmured without conviction. "Pretty fast."

"These days, DNA tests are done in a flash. Especially if they already have material to compare."

"But not *that* fast."

I looked away, unable to face the worry I saw on my parents' faces. They were convinced that it wasn't just life that had been kicking me in the arse for years; I'd also been doing it to myself. They probably thought I'd be in denial now until I got to the edge of madness.

I got up and swiped my hand over my shirt. I decided that, if not for my own sake then for Mum and Dad's, I had to put on a mask. I sat down at the small table by the wall and rummaged around in the bag Mum had brought. I smiled a little when I saw my old school lunchbox and pulled out a sandwich.

"Is there one with Nutella?"

Mum smiled wanly.

"DNA testing takes longer than a flash, even in matters of national importance," I added. "There's no way they could analyze it that fast."

"The police never said exactly when the body was discovered," Dad pointed out. "It may have been there for a while."

"I don't think so."

"Honey, it's only natural to hope," said Mum, "but you know they never release any information if they're not sure–"

"The only thing I know is that something stinks about this case," I cut in. I knew I was starting to sound crazy, but I didn't care – at least for me – though I saw my parents' anxiety was growing by the minute.

"How is she supposed to have died? Did they say?" I asked around a mouthful of sandwich.

"There's only talk of one possible cause."

"What?"

"Drowning."

"That's it?"

The question was inappropriate, and there was no good way for Dad to answer it. He shifted nervously and Mum put a calming hand on his knee.

"I mean," I went on, "after ten years, her kidnappers just threw her into the Oder or some kind of pond on Bolko? That's ridiculous."

"No one's saying that. They could have stunned her and then–"

"No," I said firmly and put the sandwich back in the lunchbox.

"How can you be so sure, son? Did you find out anything?"

"More than I expected."

They both raised their eyebrows, almost at the same time. That unanimous reaction was by no means new to me, either – they often mirrored each other's behaviour, although neither was aware of doing so. But they'd spent so many years together that the symbiosis was evident at first glance.

I thought bitterly about the fact that Ewa and I had been on the right track to be able to say the same thing about ourselves in the future.

"There was someone who took a picture of her at that concert," I said.

"Who?"

"I don't know, just some random guy. I found it on the internet." I wasn't going to go into the details, and they didn't ask. Despite joking that they'd be able to use the internet on my old computer, I knew that they hadn't gone online even once. The internet was an alien, terrifying place for them.

For me, though, it was salvation.

"She's barely in the frame," I added. "The face is blurry but a piece of her T-shirt is visible."

"What about it?"

"There was a message for me on it."

"What kind of message?" Dad asked. I could hear the scepticism in his voice, and it didn't surprise me. Briefly, I told them what Kliza had told me. They both seemed to need some time to absorb the information.

"Ewa went to a great deal of trouble to arrange it," I emphasized, "and she was very careful."

Mum cleared her throat. "And that's why you think–"

"That her kidnappers didn't catch on," I finished for her. "And that Ewa is still alive. She's waiting for my help."

"But you have no proof," Dad said simply.

"No, I don't."

Their silence could mean everything. I thought it was better to take up the subject before new doubts sprouted up in their minds. I didn't know why I felt the need to convince them. Maybe on some level I needed their acceptance to go further and follow the trail I had found.

"When I was waiting for you, I compared the design on the shirt with the original that was circulating on the internet."

"There was an original?" Dad asked, doubt clear in his voice. "I thought you said this band was fake?"

"It was. They didn't have a logo, and there was no album cover, but someone uploaded a design concept that quickly spread to other websites, probably for one of the articles describing the case. Ewa must have used it to design the shirt."

I opened my laptop and pulled up the picture. It featured an old radio standing on a table in a tent. There were red and blue fumes hovering over it. The linework was delicate, with no sharp corners. The original depicted figures standing in front of the fence, like the Colombian prisoners in the camp. Not all of them fit on the T-shirt; Ewa probably didn't want to alarm her captors with symbols that might seem significant to them.

I turned the computer towards my parents, then pointed to the picture.

"There was one thing that distinguished this drawing from Ewa's design," I said. "An additional cloud, small but clear. On the right side it had a contour and filling, and on the left side it had equalizer bars."

They looked at me uncomprehendingly.

"A display that changes with the rhythm of the music," I clarified.

"Oh."

This time I knew what their silence meant. "It doesn't mean anything to you. But to me, it made sense."

"How?" Dad asked.

"It's a pretty well-known logo. SoundCloud."

"What cloud?"

"It's a free music-sharing service. Someone obviously uploaded 'Better Days' there with the design I showed you as the cover."

At least in one of the files, I added to myself. There was also a copy, apparently the same version, except for one small detail. In the upper-right corner of the thumbnail there was a small, almost indiscernible SoundCloud logo. When I saw that, I realized it had to be Ewa trying to contact me. After a decade of silence, I finally heard her voice. It was fuzzy, lost somewhere in the noise of all the events, but it was there.

All I had to do was find out what she was saying.

Files on the site could only be uploaded by registered users, so I looked into the uploader's name: PaulFrancis. That didn't tell me anything, other than that was the username Ewa chose to use when she uploaded the file.

For a long time I couldn't get used to that awareness. I'd found something she did herself. Of course, it wasn't anything physical, only virtual – but what did that matter? The intangible funds in the bank account were as real as the banknotes in a wallet.

I looked at the equalizer, a visualization of the SoundCloud player. I knew that since Ewa had chosen "Better Days", the message was waiting for me in the song itself. She'd done exactly what Espejo and Ortiz had done, except that instead of transmitting her message via the radio, she'd posted it on the internet.

When I outlined the situation to my parents, I wasn't sure they wouldn't be too confused by all that internet lingo. Apparently not, however, because they both nodded their heads without asking any questions.

"So she showed you this particular recording..." Dad murmured.

"Yeah."

"Did you listen to it?"

"Of course. And you won't be surprised if I tell you that there's another Morse code between the stanzas." I let myself smile again. This time it wasn't forced.

"What's the message?"

"Webster."

They couldn't know what it was referring to. In fact, no one could.

Except for me.

2

That day was different from any other day. For the first time in a long while, I wasn't afraid of the evening – in fact, I was waiting for it. I knew that I would lock myself in the upstairs office, log on to the RIC and find out what Werner had managed to establish.

He had assured us that he'd found something that proved Ewa was alive, but hadn't yet provided any concrete information. There was no time because I had to finish the conversation quickly, hearing Robert coming home.

He didn't have normal working hours, as his role didn't require him to come to the office regularly, mainly because his actual activity had nothing to do with the appearances he maintained for the residents of Rewal and the surrounding area.

Our lives were a façade, both personally and professionally.

He had come into the living room carrying flowers, which I'd come to expect. This time he had chosen a small, not particularly impressive iris in a pot. He'd said he'd take care of it, that he'd do whatever it took to make it bloom. It wasn't a very adequate analogy of our relationship – thin, bare twigs would have been more appropriate.

I had decided to take advantage of the remorse that seemed to overwhelm Robert. When he finally stopped apologizing and promising to change, I brought up the subject of Kliza's dismissal. I'd thought I couldn't have picked a better time, but I'd made a mistake.

As soon as I questioned his decision, his face had closed off and his eyes had gone completely cool.

"No," he'd said.

The firmness of his voice and the sudden change in his behaviour had made me stop trying, at least for now. Once again I'd found out that, although women were perceived as delicate, there was nothing more sensitive than the male ego.

But it didn't matter. Under the circumstances, Kliza wouldn't be willing to return anyway. She wouldn't believe that Ewa was alive, even if Werner had managed to get hard proof.

I was drinking Prosecco and waiting for tonight. It occurred to me that it would have been better if I'd kept a sober mind, but over the years I'd tried it several times and it never ended well.

Wiktor Osiatyński, probably the best-known anonymous alcoholic in Poland, once said that when he sobered up, he no longer recognized the man he became. I had a similar feeling. I questioned not only all the decisions I made, but also the sense of my whole life, maybe even my entire being. My only anchor was Wojtek; it was only thanks to him that I wasn't carried off by the storm.

The best solution was to stay in calm waters, and the wine helped me with that.

Robert and I spent a few hours on the couch in the living room binge-watching episode after episode of *Fortitude*, a dark crime story set in the faraway, icebound north. Suffice to say it didn't lift my spirits. And yet I drew some degenerate, absurd and self-destructive pleasure from it. I liked being surrounded by sadness. I'd come to understand that some time ago.

When we finished, Robert sat down with his laptop and started doing things that required his direct involvement. There were fewer and fewer of them. He delegated more tasks to his subordinates, so he now had more and more time for me and Wojtek.

I was happy during the day. I had a husband who watched my favourite TV series with me, made me gourmet delicacies and treated me as if I were his whole world.

At night, I'd rather he spent as little time with me as possible.

We'd been operating like that for many years. I'd grown used to a certain harmony of the day.

But now, things had changed. I was nervously waiting for the time when I could lock myself in the office. No, not lock myself in – Robert didn't like it when I did that; he preferred me to leave the door ajar.

I didn't mind. I was going to contact Werner anyway via the RIC, which now felt like my own virtual sanctuary.

I logged in and sent Damian a message with an activation code. He came on at once and his first message popped up almost immediately, as if he'd been waiting with his fingers poised on the keyboard.

[Wern] Finally.

The fact that I wasn't the only one waiting anxiously for a conversation gave me a pleasant feeling. Only after a while did I remember that Werner had a completely different reason for that.

[Wern] Couldn't you have contacted me earlier?
[Kasandra] No.

I thought it was best not to go straight into the details. Damian wasn't supposed to be my confessor, only my distraction. No, more than that: somebody else, a person who, by telling me about his discoveries, would get me out of the nightmare of the everyday life I lived.

[Wern] Did you manage to convince Kliza?
[Kasandra] Unfortunately not.

I felt that my "unfortunately" could be perceived as insincere, so I quickly added:

[Kasandra] I've tried different approaches, but it's not going to work. She's leaving town. She's going to do something else.
[Wern] Fucking hell.
[Kasandra] You'll get all the help you need from me, Wern.

For a moment he didn't reply, and I had the impression that every second stretched to infinity. I looked at the door and listened. The quiet tapping on the keyboard downstairs proved that Robert was still sitting in front of his laptop.

I didn't have much time. But I was planning on making the most of it.

Before I could write the message, he sent his own:

[Wern] Werner.

I raised my eyebrows.

[Wern] Not Wern. Wern sounds like I'm some 19th-century explorer with a penchant for exotic voyages.

[Kasandra] In a way, you are.

[Wern] I wouldn't call it that. It looks more like a series of endless tragedies to me.

I nodded my head because I understood that too well.

[Kasandra] What do you need?

[Wern] A way to send text messages back in time. I'd write to myself that a dingy riverbank is a bad place to propose. And to buy share in Netflix as soon as it hit the market.

I smiled lightly, appreciating that he was trying to bring some lightness into a conversation that had very little humour in it.

[Wern] And perhaps also that Brazil will lose to Germany 7–1 in the 2014 World Cup semi-final. I'd make a fortune at the bookies.

For a while, I didn't know what to write back. I finally decided on the worst possible option.

[Kasandra] :)

Luckily, the emoticon disappeared quickly, although only from the screen. I thought that the stupid character might actually be more ambiguous for Damian than most enigmatic words.

I was briefly comforted by the fleeting thought that ancient Egyptians also used hieroglyphics, and I had a sip of Prosecco.

[Kasandra] Do you need anything else?
[Wern] Not yet. My mother brought me sandwiches.

For a moment, I wondered if this wasn't another attempt at a joke. I guessed it was, so this time I decided not to answer anything.

[Wern] But I may need something soon.
[Kasandra] What?
[Wern] You'll find out in time.

So he didn't trust me. I shouldn't be surprised. Not only had I sprung out on him like a jack-in-the-box, but my perfunctory answers could be seen as a sign of reserve or even reluctance.

[Kasandra] I'd rather find out now.
[Wern] Too bad.

I tapped my fingernails on the glass and took another sip. In spite of my understatement, the conversation seemed to be pleasant for both sides. Or maybe I just wanted it to be that way.

[Kasandra] Okay. Well, let's get to what you've found out.

[Wern] First of all, the user who uploaded the audio file was PaulFrancis.

[Kasandra] Is that some kind of reference to the popes?

[Wern] No. Something else.

[Kasandra] What?

He didn't reply for a second.

[Wern] Actually, I would never have thought about it if it hadn't been for the message encoded in the song's tune.

I ran my fingers through my hair and pulled it back. Then I cocked my head slightly, staring at the monitor. It looked as if my face was flushed. If Robert were to come into the office now, he wouldn't hesitate to question what had provoked so much emotion in me.

I had no doubt if that happened, this would be the last conversation I had with Werner.

I had to be careful.

[Kasandra] What was the message?

[Wern] Webster.

[Kasandra] That means nothing to me. Or at least nothing specific.

[Wern] Because it's not for you or anyone else. Just for me. In combination with PaulFrancis, it gives me a clear indication of what to look for.

[Kasandra] What do you mean?

I started turning the glass on the counter anxiously.

[Wern] Keeping you waiting and on edge, am I?
[Kasandra] A little bit.
[Wern] But you do, too. About yourself.
[Kasandra] I don't understand.
[Wern] I don't know if you're having a laugh about all this with a bunch of good girlfriends. I can picture you all laughing out loud.

I sniggered quietly, as if he could hear me. Me and a bunch of good girlfriends – ha! The last time Robert had let me to go out with just women, I'd regretted it for the following three nights. He'd kept going back to that meeting, spinning absurd fantasies: how we'd supposedly had been talking about him, how I'd been planning to leave him, how my friends had been looking for a new guy for me, and so on. After that, I'd never met with them alone again, and if we ever organized anything with Robert, it was always on double dates with their partners.

I put my hands on the keyboard and thought for a moment. In the end, I decided it would be best if I kept things professional.

[Kasandra] PaulFrancis. Webster. What does that mean?
[Wern] You weren't interested in Spider-Man when you were young, were you?
[Kasandra] No.
[Wern] I was, as it happens. And Ewa knows it.

Present tense. Damian really believed she was alive.

[Kasandra] So what's it about?

[Wern] About an American lyricist who wrote the cult song about Spider-Man. If I sang it to you, you'd probably recognize it right away. Though only because it was featured in four movies. In the first one, by Sam Raimi, the original version. Michael Bublé performs it in the second one, and in the third one it's played during the big street party. It's also in the remake with Andrew Garfield, where Peter has it as his ringtone.

I stared at the screen in disbelief.

[Wern] That's how I know where to look for further clues.

[Kasandra] So don't keep me in the dark.

[Wern] All I had to do was write "Spider-Man theme" on SoundCloud and then find the right file.

I opened a new tab and did what he said. A lot of search results popped up. There was the original version, of course, in multiple versions, and then there were covers, pieces done by Spider-Man fans, and many other files, more or less related to Webster's cult song.

[Kasandra] Well, there's quite a few of them.

[Wern] But if you know what to look for, it doesn't matter.

[Kasandra] Do you know?

[Wern] Of course. Otherwise, Ewa wouldn't have left me that message.

[Kasandra] So which file should I open?

[Wern] The one uploaded by someone called Tiger.

[Kasandra] Tiger?

[Wern] That's what she used to call me sometimes.

[Kasandra] That doesn't sound good.

[Wern] It was our thing. Like racing who'd finish changing bedding first. Or like fooling around at Ikea when we were playing house. Or like building a fort to watch movies, with armchairs and blankets.

[Kasandra] A fort?

[Wern] That was a long time ago. To cover up the TV so it would be like in a movie theatre. It doesn't matter, anyway.

I smiled lightly and nodded.

[Kasandra] There was a Morse code message in that track too?

[Wern] Yes.

I could imagine how he enjoyed drip-feeding me information. I looked at the door uncertainly again. This time I didn't hear any sounds from downstairs and I felt anxious.

[Kasandra] What?

[Wern] A bit.ly address.

[Kasandra] A what?

[Wern] It's used to shorten URLs.

I didn't reply for a moment.

[Wern] A service that translates long addresses of websites into short ones, easy to send.

[Kasandra] Where did it lead?

[Wern] To a website that looks like a copy of SoundCloud.
   The problem is, it's blocked.

[Kasandra] How?

[Wern] We need to enter the password.

[Kasandra] And you don't know it?

[Wern] Not yet.

I nodded my head again as if he could see it.

[Wern] And I don't know what's waiting for me there.
   But one thing's for sure.

[Kasandra] What?

[Wern] That the sneaking around is over. Ewa has a
   specific message for me.

3

Kasandra Reimann was actually what I had imagined her
to be: enigmatic, reticent, cool, maybe even indifferent.
But it was her indifference that made her seem somewhat
attractive.

And to think that I was able to assemble the whole picture
out of the letters appearing on the screen. Though was it
really so weird? Ever since the first books were read, people
had been making images out of words.

Blitzer was by no means a wordsmith, but he once
happened to say something really wise. Music shapes reality.
There was hardly a more accurate saying. And similarly,
words sculpt images of people. After all, language is a tool
for mind control – you just need to be able to use it properly.

I'm sure Kasandra could. She communicated sparingly,
keeping her distance, sometimes seeming as if she wasn't
particularly interested in what we were writing about.

Or was I overreacting? Maybe I'd created a vision of a powerful, cunning and ruthless woman to feel that only the best players were playing on my team.

I wasn't going to think about that now. What mattered was the lead I'd found.

I was sure that after entering the password I would see a message from Ewa. And that she was still alive. Being a fiancé, that's just the kind of thing you know. Even if it had been ten years since I'd proposed.

But what kind of password could it be?

It must have been something that only I knew. Ewa was sure that after seeing the photos from the Foo Fighters concert, after discovering "Better Days" and finding the right file with the Spider-Man theme, I would be the only one to find this page. Now she needed to know that I was the only one who could open the door.

I scratched my head, wondering what the password was. I was sure it couldn't have been mentioned in any of the clues. That would run the risk of someone else discovering it. Ewa needed another verification. The equivalent of a single-use text-message code that could reach one person only.

I was circling the room, trying to figure out what it might be. The problem wasn't that I didn't have an idea. On the contrary, far too many ideas appeared in my head.

The history of our relationship was so rich that I was able to fish everything out of it. Fooling around at Ikea or racing who put the pillowcase on first was just a drop in the ocean.

I stood by the window and looked out. My parents' car was parked in the hotel car park. They'd left it for me and took the bus back to town. The old Skoda Felicia looked like a relic, but it worked. It was also LPG-powered, which would make my job much easier, given the limited resources available to me.

All I had to do was find out where to go.

I leaned against the shutter, deep in thoughts. I could think of random words, a flowing stream of words. I finally decided that one of them had to be the right one.

Maybe the usual, primitive method of trial and error in this case would work best.

I sat down in front of my old ASUS and entered the first word: *AMZBGMAN*. It was one of the cheat codes in the Spider-Man game – the only game I'd been able to convince Ewa to play, and then only on the condition that I entered that cheat. It turned the hero controlled by the player into Bag Man – a character with a bag on his head instead of a mask. I thought it was as good a password as any, and I had to start somewhere.

Asterisks appeared on the screen and when I pressed *Enter*, I felt my heart hammer.

The website refreshed itself.

A black screen with a white skull appeared.

After a moment, a blinking message underneath made me freeze.

"1/3."

I didn't have to think for long to come to the conclusion that I'd just wasted one of three attempts. The method I was going to adopt was no longer an option. I cursed under my breath, thinking I should have expected it. Ewa prepared the whole process so meticulously that such a security measure was no surprise.

I had no doubt that after the third unsuccessful attempt the website would be irretrievably lost. It must have a built-in kill switch, some kind of self-destruct system.

I got up from the chair and walked up to the window again. It was as if I was trying to escape from my realization.

I had two more attempts.

I could only make one more mistake.

I watched people come to restaurants, tennis and badminton courts, and I envied them their lives. The biggest worry for them was probably that there was more time left until the weekend than they would like.

It occurred to me that in my current situation at least I didn't have to worry about that. The owner of SpiceX must have already sacked me, since I'd gone MIA on him. No more serving their speciality chicken dishes. My supervisor claimed that all poultry dishes were absolutely unique because chicken was the only animal we eat both before and after its birth. There *was* something poetic about that, but it didn't help me to solve my problem. I sighed, trying to get my thoughts back on track.

I started circling the room, scratching my neck. I couldn't figure out anything specific.

I finally stopped in front of the laptop and looked at the monitor.

My mind went blank. The skull on the screen had been replaced by a digital clock. I didn't know when the countdown started, but there were less than eight minutes left to go.

A time limit. Ewa made sure that both the number of attempts and the time the person entering the password had to think of it were limited.

I felt like something was counting down seconds until my own demise. I could hardly swallow without taking my eyes off the clock. I sat down at the table and shook my head. Time to get a grip.

But instead of thinking about the password, I started thinking about how to bypass the security. By changing the IP address and MAC address, I would be able to enter the website again, to reset not just the clock but also the attempt count.

No, that wouldn't work.

At the same time, the website wouldn't respond like this with every internet user. The first random person that would accidentally stumble on it would ruin Ewa's whole plan.

But the website was definitely not indexed, and its URL was so complicated that it couldn't be found by chance. The only way to access it was to find the Morse-code-encrypted link in a piece by Paul Francis Webster.

It was all meant for me.

I rubbed my forehead, only now realizing that I was hot. The clock was still counting down valuable seconds and I felt as if someone was tearing out a part of me with every single one of them.

And then the situation took another turn for worse.

When the countdown was just over six minutes away, the white skull moved. A long rope appeared on the screen, with a whole lot of needles on it. The corpse's lips opened and the row of sharp objects began to disappear somewhere in their depths.

The clock accelerated. The countdown from five would take no longer than a few seconds.

I gripped the keyboard, realizing that it was better to enter anything rather than to let the mechanism consider the second attempt a failure.

But I hesitated. And that was enough for the time to run out.

"2/3" appeared on the black screen.

The skull disappeared, and so did the rope with the needles. The digital clock popped up again, this time counting down from fifteen minutes. I assumed that, as before, it would accelerate towards the end.

I sat motionless, as if the slightest vibration would make time run even faster, not even daring to wipe away the sweat drops I felt running down my neck.

What I saw couldn't have been random. It was a clue. A hint intended only for me.

I was a little shaken up.

Needle line. What did I associate that with?

No, not the line itself. It was about swallowing it, with those sharp objects.

Suddenly, it dawned on me: Harry Houdini. It was one of his most famous tricks. He placed between fifty and a hundred needles on a long thread, then swallowed the whole thing and showed the audience his empty mouth. Then he reached into his throat with his hand and pulled out all that had previously disappeared.

I knew of it because the last two films we'd watched together had sparked our interest in illusions. In January 2007, we watched *The Prestige* with Hugh Jackman and Christian Bale, and then in March we saw *The Illusionists* with Edward Norton. Then we watched documentaries about illusions on YouTube. Harry Houdini appeared most often, of course, and the needle trick was one of his most impressive achievements.

Contrary to appearances, it wasn't dangerous. Houdini usually risked his health and even his life while performing his tricks, but not in that case. Before the performance, he hid a line of blunt needles in his mouth and dropped the sharp ones into his sleeve or behind his collar – I didn't remember which. Then all he had to do was cover up the blunt ones when he showed his "empty" mouth to the audience.

Harry Houdini.

There was something relevant about the fact that it was him Ewa chose. She knew I'd find out what the hell was going on right away. And what was the password?

I looked at the countdown. Now it didn't matter anymore. I knew perfectly well that even if the clock sped up, I would have managed to write the right word in time.

It all started with music. Since the Foo Fighters concert.

Everything was connected with music.

And it ended with music.

I smiled, shaking my head. I appreciated the tremendous effort Ewa had made. Especially the fact that she'd found a link that join together all the elements into a single whole.

Apparently, she had the makings of a female, modern incarnation of Houdini. But did she also want to pass this on to me when she decided to make the reference? Was it more than just a clue? A suggestion that she'd made the decision to disappear forever that day on the riverbank?

I didn't want to dig any deeper into that, especially since the answers were waiting for me on the website.

I thought back to Harry Houdini. He became famous not only as a master of illusion, but also as a person who refuted myths. He was particularly sensitive on the subject of talking to spirits. He used his knowledge to reveal the tricks that people who pretended to be psychics used to summon souls from the afterlife during seances. He made a lot of enemies, and even lost the friendship of Arthur Conan Doyle. Yet while he was convinced that contact with the other side was impossible, he also thought that, if anyone could establish it, it would be him.

Eventually, he made a deal with his wife. They agreed that if Houdini found a way to communicate with her after his death...

I broke off that train of thought for a moment. I tried to push away the awareness of how many analogies there were between those two people and myself and Ewa at the moment.

There would be time to explore other hidden messages, but now there was only one thing that mattered.

I thought back to Houdini.

He made an agreement with his wife, Bess, that after his death she would visit all those who might actually be psychics. And she did it for ten years, participating in a number of spiritual seances.

The deal was that if contact was really made, Harry would send Bess a message that only they knew. It was supposed to be: "Rosabelle, believe."

"Rosabelle" was their favourite song. Bess used to sing it to him when they met at Coney Island.

I nodded, entered it in the field where the white cursor blinked, and then pressed *Enter*.

The clock vanished. The website refreshed.

4

I knew that the silence of the keyboard from downstairs was a signal for me to end the conversation with Werner quickly. I closed the RIC, disappointed that I wouldn't learn the answers to my questions this evening.

I'd have to wait till tomorrow. I could try to get in touch with Damian during the day, but even if Robert wasn't monitoring our CCTV at home, I'm sure one of our employees would tell him everything.

Sometimes I felt like we had people for everything – for cleaning, gardening, laundry, ironing and, most importantly, ensuring our safety. Most of them came from the east and probably stayed in Poland without a visa. The advantage of that was that we paid them more than they could have earned legally.

The downside was that I felt constantly under surveillance. At least during the day.

At night, it seemed like we were alone at home. Actually, alone in the world.

I went downstairs and found Robert in the kitchen, standing in front of the open cutlery drawer and shaking his head.

"I've asked you so many fucking times."

I stopped between the living room and the kitchen.

"Is it really so hard to put my knives on the right and yours on the left?"

I knew this was as good a reason as any for him to get mad. We had separate sets of cutlery. Mine came mainly from supermarkets, while he bought his on the internet – Gerlach sets, costing almost a thousand zlotys, which he spent without blinking an eye.

Just as he wouldn't blink when he raised his hand to me.

When he turned around, there was no doubt that it would happen soon.

"Why can't you just do what I ask?"

I didn't say a word. I didn't take my eyes off him. I stayed motionless, trying to look at him without emotion. I thought it wouldn't be bad tonight. It would last an hour, maybe two, and then it would all be over. I'd wake up in the morning, have a Prosecco, hold on till the evening. Then I'd find out what Werner had been able to establish.

"It's so fucking simple."

Robert approached me in one quick step. Before I could react, he grabbed me by the collar and pulled me towards the kitchen. He threw me over the top of the counter like a bag of rubbish. He grabbed me by my neck and then pulled me towards the drawer.

"Look!" he got out of his system. "Mine on the right, yours on the left, for fuck's sake!"

He pulled my head up slightly and for a moment I was afraid that it would hit the even rows of tableware.

Instead, he turned me over, pressed me against the hanging cupboard with one hand and reached for a knife with the other – one of his own Gerlach pieces. It was made of stainless steel and had a mirror-like, glossy sheen.

He approached me with the blade to my face like he was going to gouge out my eye.

"Now do you see? Now do you recognize which one's mine?"

"Robert–"

"Shut the fuck up!"

He let me go, but I didn't even move. I knew it wouldn't end well if I tried to escape. Robert swung and hit me with an open hand. Then he grabbed my blouse again, shook me and pointed the knife at me.

"Do I have to do something for you to finally get it into your stupid head?"

"No."

"And yet I've been telling you this for... since I can fucking remember! And you're *still* doing it. You still don't give a shit."

He threw the knife into the drawer, grabbed me with both hands and then shook me so hard I hit my head against the cabinet. He did that for a while, shouting something at me. Most of the words I didn't understand; they were muffled by the sound of his blows. I prayed – not for him to stop, but for Wojtek not to hear anything, and for him never to experience anything like this at Robert's hands.

That was the main reason why I put up with all this. I had a deep conviction that I was somehow protecting my son. That all the blows Robert was inflicting on me might otherwise have fallen on Wojtek.

I thought that by submitting to this, I was sacrificing myself for my son.

"Someday I will fucking *kill* you, you understand?"

He pushed me to the floor and slammed the drawer shut, then he leaned over, picked me up and dragged me into the bedroom.

When he closed the door behind him, I already knew that the torment wouldn't take an hour or two. It would be a lot longer than that.

The festival of brutality lasted until four in the morning.

Then the violence turned into regret, the terror into begging, into pathetic pleas for forgiveness. And for help.

In the morning I assessed the extent of the damage and once again I couldn't help feeling that I was becoming more and more adept at masking injuries. And yet, at the same time, it required more and more work.

Robert was waiting for me with breakfast, reading a newspaper on his iPad. Wojtek was sitting at the table, also browsing the internet. From time to time they exchanged some remarks and it all looked like a typical breakfast of a loving, happy family.

I stood in front of the cutlery drawer and closed my eyes for a moment. Then I made myself smile. It was meant only for me. I had long discovered that even such a mundane thing could make it much easier to keep up appearances afterwards.

I pulled the drawer back and saw that there wasn't a single knife or fork from the Gerlach set in the drawer. I turned around and raised my eyebrows. Robert didn't look me in the eye.

"I threw it away," he said. "Yours is much better."

"Mine cost less than fifty zlotys."

"Good for you. It's just cutlery. Why spend more on it?"

I shook my head. I didn't like it – and it wasn't about throwing almost a thousand zlotys down the drain. I wanted to have that cutlery here. I wanted it to remind him during the day of who he turned into at night.

"Where is it?"

"I threw it away."

I opened the rubbish bin, but I couldn't find the cutlery there. I closed the door a little too hard, which made Wojtek look at me uncertainly. I sent him a warm smile and let it go. There was no point fighting over a few pieces of steel.

Anyway, sooner or later a decent set would come back. Just like everything else came back.

I sat down at the table and started eating the homemade granola Robert had prepared. I knew he didn't really like breakfast like that. He made it for me as if it could erase the painful memory of what had happened a few hours earlier.

I looked at the prominent shadows under my husband's eyes. He slept longer than I did, always passing out after his own catharsis, but he couldn't conceal what I could easily hide.

He closed the iPad case and looked at me.

Someone once said that love was nothing more than the ability to recognize oneself in the eyes of another person. But what I saw in the eyes of my husband was a complete stranger, someone who was nothing like me.

"I'm thinking about Reimann Investigations," he said.

"What do you mean?"

"Either we have to hire someone to replace Glazur and Kliza, or we have to consider whether we need that business at all."

"Of course we do."

"For what?"

"You know I've been running a few cases." I could hardly swallow my sunflower seeds and almonds. In my head I saw myself lose the only thing that gave me a respite from this reality.

It didn't take much for Robert to take it away from me. He'd done it before. Usually he would give me some freedom from time to time – by agreeing to adapt the attic office for me, for example, or allowing me to take over the management of the company. However, once some time passed, he would change his mind. He would come to the conclusion that I'd become too independent, as if it could threaten him in some way.

It was a clear sign of the paranoia that never left him. All the time he was convinced that if I did one thing or another, I would get away from him. It was worse when I was pregnant.

But I didn't want to go back to that. The most important thing was that after Wojtek was born, he'd treated our son as the glue that bound us together, not as someone who would come between us.

"The case of that girl from Opole is over," he said. "And you'll close the others quickly."

"But…"

"You just have a few business background checks to close and one photo shoot."

Photo shoots were the worst jobs RI took on, requiring us to track spouses and collect dirt on them for the divorce.

"We haven't finished–"

"The vetting of a candidate for the board of directors," he interrupted me. "I know."

Of course he did. He knew everything. He was ardent about control. No, more than that, he was fanatic. He was like a merciless dictator who saw foreign territories solely as his future dominion.

"This can all be closed in a week, two at most. Then we could consider liquidating the company."

I didn't know how to answer in a way that wouldn't unleash the storm in front of Wojtek.

"RI doesn't make any money," Robert added.

It wasn't true, but I couldn't say it. I knew what it would be like to challenge my husband's words. Although he wouldn't raise his hand against me during the day, unless I was going to push him really hard, Wojtek would certainly sense hostility. Children saw much more than their parents were prepared to admit.

"But it doesn't cost much either," I said.

"Not much, but still…"

"Think about it again."

"I will," he promised, and smiled.

A moment later I kissed my son on the cheek and patted him on the back. I felt that we were on the cusp of the moment when Wojtek decided that it was high time to stop such gestures.

I watched them leave, then pulled out a chilled bottle of Prosecco and sat down alone at the table. Outside, the Ukrainian man who took care of the lawn glanced at me again and again, probably on Robert's orders.

I poured myself a glass, but I didn't take a sip. For some time I sat at the table, motionless, looking ahead, unseeing.

Robert would close Reimann Investigations. I couldn't do anything about it. Whenever he made a decision, it was final. No one and nothing could convince him to change his mind.

I had a limited amount of time. And I had to make use of it.

I took my glass and went upstairs. If the cameras were on or the staff really kept an eye on me, Robert would immediately be interested in why I chose to spend time in the office during the day. But under the circumstances, I had to take a chance.

I sent Werner a text message with an activation code, and then I waited.

He finally showed up. And he immediately appreciated the nickname I set for him this time.

[J.Verne] I see you're in a good mood today.
[Kas] Exceptionally good.
[J.Verne] And you obviously like shortening names.
[Kas] Everyone has some perversion.
[J.Verne] Everyone has their own plan, too, until they get a slap in the face.

I raised my eyebrows. He couldn't have known how unfortunately accurate his turn of phrase was.

[J.Verne] It's Mike Tyson. And actually, he was right, with one exception. Ewa secured her plan in every possible way. And she prepared herself for every eventuality.
[Kas] Did you guess the password?
[J.Verne] At the last attempt. Turns out I only had three.

I had a drink and it made me feel better. I didn't know whether it was the booze or the fact that Damian managed to find something specific.

[J.Verne] Houdini would be proud of her.
[Kas] What's that?
[J.Verne] Ewa. She pulled a number like this

He broke off, and his message disappeared after a while.

[J.Verne] Never mind that. What's important is that she contacted me.

I got to the keyboard right away.
I wrote without thinking, feverishly. If I had had a moment to think about it, I would probably have decided on a slightly better phrased reply.

[J.Verne] After logging in, I found another website. At first, I thought that it was the same one, just refreshed, but it wasn't. It redirected me somewhere else.
[Kas] Where?

[J.Verne] To the deep web, of course.

[Kas] What do you mean?

The cursor blinked on the black screen for a moment. There was no reply. I was overwhelmed by a parade of dark thoughts in my head; apparently my earlier optimism was extremely fragile.

I could easily imagine someone tracking Damian down. They would locate him in that hotel and then send people to take care of him, just as they'd done to his friend.

I shuddered. I wasn't the only one in a precarious situation. Werner and I had one thing in common: a real threat to our lives. In his case, it could have come from strangers; in mine... not so much.

However, both threats were just as real.

Finally, his reply popped up on the monitor.

[J.Verne] Where have you been hiding?

[Kas] I don't keep up with the latest technological developments. I have a life.

[J.Verne] The deep web is hardly news.

[Kas] And yet you had to Google things and stuff. It took you a while to answer my question.

[J.Verne] Nope, I had to take a break. Nature called.

[Kas] I doubt it. That was too quick.

[J.Verne] How do you know I'm not sitting on the toilet with the computer in my lap?

I smiled and shook my head.

[Kas] I don't.

[J.Verne] And that's the beauty of internet communication.

No, the beauty of it was that Robert couldn't stop me from doing it, at least not right now. I glanced at the open door, afraid I would hear it open any time now.

[Kas] So what is this deep web?

It seemed to me that Kliza used it a lot. I think she even tried to explain to me what it was all about.

[J.Verne] It's a deep network.
[Kas] Yes, that's all I understand.
[J.Verne] To understand more, you need to know that you can access only about 4% of the internet from your browser.

He began to explain that about four and a half billion pages were indexed. Everything else remained under the surface, impossible to access without knowing exactly where to go.

The deep web consisted of both legal and illegal things, from government documents stored on secure servers, ordinary pages that weren't linked to any websites, to the black market, where you could buy anything. And find anything.

The darknet. That was what Wern called that last level.

[J.Verne] It's all there. You can buy multiple Netflix accounts as well as weapons, fake US passports and drugs. You can have all the porn you want, and you can communicate there safely and securely, without fear of anyone tracing you.
[Kas] Just like the RIC.
[J.Verne] No, we don't use TOR. Although, of course, we're in the deep web... only not in the darknet.

[Kas] Never mind.

[J.Verne] The only thing that matters is that no one could just stumble on that site at random. Ewa could be sure that I was the only one who could get to what she left for me.

[Kas] What did she leave?

[J.Verne] MP3 files.

My fingers tapped the countertop in an anxious staccato. How much longer did I have? Robert didn't have to go to the office; he'd probably come home after driving Wojtek to school. No, he'd stop on his way to buy flowers. And the florists would probably have their bouquets ready by now.

I almost laughed, thinking about how it must look from their perspective. Undoubtedly, they believed Robert to be an exceptionally loving husband, who took care after his wife more that most men did for their mistresses.

[Kas] What's in those files?

[J.Verne] Everything.

[Kas] What do you mean? Enough with the mysteries, Wern.

[J.Verne] Sorry. I'm learning it from you.

For a moment I wondered if it was the right time to become more forthcoming. I decided it wasn't. It didn't matter what Damian thought of me.

[Kas] So?

[J.Verne] The files are recordings. Ewa left them for me.

[Kas] But what's on them?

[J.Verne] Everything. I'm really sorry.

I cursed under my breath.

[Kas] I don't have much time.
[J.Verne] That's not good, because it's going to take
    you a while to listen to the recordings. Ewa describes
    what happened to her in them. Day by day. From the
    moment I lost consciousness on the riverbank.

I felt my heart start to pound and the blood race through my
veins, as if my body had only been half-working up until
now. I reached for the glass and emptied it with one gulp.
The bubbles tickled my throat.

I put my hands on the keyboard and took a deep breath.

But before I could write anything back, I heard the door
open downstairs.

5

I was expecting a barrage of questions, but the blank screen
and the blinking cursor seemed to suggest that Kasandra
wasn't going to ask me anything. I thought she was waiting
for me to send her the link to the first recording, but before
I even mentioned it, RIC switched off.

I looked at the old laptop like it was the one to blame. It
wasn't my fault, after all. It must have been Kas who had
disconnected, and the system had automatically shut down.

I had to admit that fate had provided me with a rather
strange ally. I didn't understand her, but maybe I didn't
have to in order to use her help. The problem was, I didn't
have any way to contact her right now.

I thought, however, that sooner or later I would get
another message with a single-use code. All I had to do was
arm myself with patience.

I closed the RIC tab and looked at the almost empty website again. It was hidden somewhere under the surface of the internet, and had been waiting for me all this time, hiding in the darkness yet within reach. All I'd needed to do was light up the path that led me there.

A mesh of equalizer bars appeared on a white background, reminding me of the cobweb that my favourite comic-book hero wore on his costume. But that was where the positive associations ended.

After listening to the first file, I noticed that the web was also a metaphor. Ewa's life. A life I didn't know, a life she kept from me.

The first file was named "Before I met you". When I pressed the familiar *Play* icon, I felt like I was crossing the line between dreams and reality.

Ewa was coming back to my life.

Except she wasn't the same person I'd spent most of my time with. In fact, it was as if it was only now that she seemed to be showing me her true face, revealing all her secrets. And, finally, what happened to her after that fateful night at the Sneering Lodge.

The bars arranged into a cobweb started moving. Then a voice came out of the speakers, though to me it was as though it came to me from the afterlife.

Before I met you, did you think you'd known me forever? Yeah, me too.

Looking in the mirror, I saw the same person you see every day. But neither of us was aware that it was just a reflection.

I know I should have told you everything before it was too late. But how was I supposed to know when that moment would come? I thought we had a lot of time. I was sure there were happy moments ahead of us, I didn't want to spoil them.

I thought we were safe. A lot of people I trusted assured me we were.

So I put off telling you the truth until later – an unspecified later. It was like putting off a visit to the doctor when deep down you already know you're suffering from a serious illness, but you don't want to hear the diagnosis confirmed.

When you proposed, I knew I couldn't wait any longer. You deserved to know everything before we got married. You needed to know exactly what you were getting into.

But then things happened.

I survived, although after that evening I never even looked like my reflection in the mirror. Years passed before I decided to record this for you. But I need your help, Tiger. And I know that if I can count on anyone, it's only you.

You'll find out one thing at a time. I know you'd like answers to all your questions right away, but before I give them to you, you have to understand me. You need to know this story from the start. Otherwise, you'll never understand why I made this decision. Why I disappeared from your life. And why you haven't heard from me for so many years.

I'll start over.

Looking for the scroll bar? Sorry, my player doesn't have one. You won't be able to download the file to your hard drive, either – I took care of that. You're going to have listen to this story on my terms. Because this is my life I want to tell you.

Listen, then…

My parents never got along with yours – that was no secret for us. Usually we would laugh at them, joke about them and come up with absurd fantasies of their reconciliation. And if it came to a serious conversation, we were all to blame for the fact that they came from two different worlds.

My parents got a new car every year or two, always the latest, poshest make. Yours could just about afford a Skoda Felicia and never even dreamt about owning anything else.

It seemed logical that they wouldn't get along. But the reason wasn't what you thought it was. It wasn't about money, career or even priorities.

The point was, your parents are good people.

Mine weren't.

Yes, they took care of me, provided me with everything I needed and at the same time made sure I wasn't too flashy. They were also restrained, although that might be hard for you to believe.

They had enough money to change cars not just every few months, but every few days.

You thought my father had an ordinary law firm, but you were wrong. It provided service and twenty-four-hour help to those who paid the most. He had no moral qualms and, as befits a true lawyer, he had no respect for the law.

Years later, I even think he was specifically looking for clients who did illegal stuff. He knew that was where the honeypot was. And all his existence was reduced to amassing as much money as he could.

It was a perfect confirmation of the principle that the more you own, the more you need. Money became his obsession, even though he couldn't spend it without attracting the attention of the tax office. If my mother had had a different value system, she might have slowed him down at some point, but she hadn't. In that respect, they were made for each other. Both were driven by an unhealthy need to accumulate money. They both forgot that money at best is only a tool to achieve a goal, not an end in itself. They were convinced that wealth means you could afford to buy everything. Not when you own things that can't be bought.

For many years, I shared their understanding of the world – after all, I was their daughter. You didn't know about that aspect of me, because I kept it from you, but in reality I was still deeply worried that by following the path we had chosen, we would eventually find ourselves in a place where we would run out of money.

At times, it was an obsessive fear.

But then I realized that my greatest fear was something completely different: that you would see me as I saw myself.

It reminded me that you were the most important thing. And that I had to start working on myself.

I did my best to reject the upbringing based on the love of money, not the love of another person. And I finally made it, thanks to you, because you showed me what's really important.

It's a shame my parents never found such a person.

Maybe that would have prevented the tragedy that happened less than a year before you proposed to me.

A car accident? No, their deaths weren't accidental. They did not die by chance. They were murdered.

I'll tell you about it in the next recording. All you need

to know for now is that it all started with the deaths of
my parents. This triggered a spiral of events that I fell
into. And I dragged you into it, too.

I'm as guilty as they are.

I meant well, but instead I only brought sadness and
suffering on us. I want you to understand why that
happened. I want you to know what kind of family I
grew up in. What corrupt company my parents kept. And
what kind of people I was around myself because of them.

I grew up in completely different conditions than you. I
made mistakes that I kept from you, knowing I shouldn't
have committed them. The shock only came when my
parents died.

Think about all of this.

And then, when you're ready, go to Wrocław.

In the place where you first got so drunk I had to hold
you upright, there's a flash drive with another recording
waiting for you. It's protected with the same password
that opened this file for you.

Sorry to keep you waiting, but I need to make sure
that those recordings fall into only your hands. Only a
physical verification, only your presence there, can give
me that certainty.

Who knows? Maybe you'll find me somewhere there.

The recording was over, and I realized that I'd been holding
my breath once again. None of what I heard made any
sense. Ewa had had a comfortable life, but I would never
have called it lavish. However, if her father had really feared
unwarranted attention from the state, it seemed logical.

I rubbed my temples, trying to push everything I heard
away from myself. Listening to the recording, I felt as if Ewa

wasn't far from here, that she was waiting for me, that she was fine.

But I didn't know when she'd recorded the message. I didn't know what had happened to her afterwards.

I didn't know if the body found by the police really belonged to someone else.

Now that she hinted at her family's links to the criminal world, I could really expect anything. And my tired mind eagerly took advantage of it, spinning the most pessimistic, gloomy fantasies.

I decided to set off immediately, as if I could leave all my doubts and fears behind me. I packed my laptop, and then I stood by the window and glanced at my watch. My father should be here by now. He was supposed to bring me some clothes, a travel bag and some cash. I thought it might be a long time before I could return to Opole, so I had to be prepared.

But there was no sign of Dad, which worried me because he was never late, even if he had an appointment for an insignificant meeting.

My throat went dry when I thought that someone might have realized that I'd found another clue.

No, that was impossible. Whoever was behind all this couldn't find out about my discoveries in the virtual world. Ewa made sure that everything remained beyond the reach of random people. She'd hidden us in the deep web.

I leaned against the window frame and looked out at the fields in the distance. I thought about what might have happened to my fiancée. And about whether I could still call her that.

This thought was like a catalyst for an extremely dangerous chemical reaction. Actually, it triggered a thermonuclear explosion in my mind, throwing up questions like a mushroom cloud, obscuring my rationality.

What happened after the rape? Why did Ewa disappear for so many years?

Who was Phil Braddy? Why did Blitzer die? Who murdered him?

What had Ewa been hiding from me when we'd been together?

I felt like a drug addict who, after a long stint in a rehab, gets his drug taken out of his hands just as he was about to take it.

The chaos in my mind affected my body, too, and I realized my hands were shaking. I closed my eyes for a moment, took a deep breath and rubbed my temples. When I opened my eyes again, I saw a taxi pulling into the hotel car park.

My father paid the driver and, by the looks of it, asked him to wait. He got out of the car and I turned around, reaching for my bag. I was ready to go. But before I opened the door, I looked out of the window.

Then I saw a black Opel Vectra parked a little further away. I didn't know the licence plate numbers of unmarked police cars as some people did, but I did know that officers often used that make.

I saw two men inside. They didn't get out of the car. And they focused all their attention on my father.

I realized then that I had a problem.

6

I ate in silence, mainly because Robert and Wojtek were busy doing homework together. I wasn't much of a math genius so I didn't interfere with their efforts.

The school was overdoing it with homework, and if I needed any confirmation of that, I just had to look at my husband and son. Even at dinner, they had to spend their time on it.

Research showed that spending seventy minutes a day on homework is destructive to the child's psyche. Other scientific findings confirmed that such activity leads to chronic depressive states.

What appealed to me most, however, was what Harris Cooper, the homework-research guru at Duke University, said. He proved that there is no evidence that this form of education had a positive impact on students.

And yet we held on to it as if it was the only guarantee our children absorbed the appropriate amount of knowledge. I looked at Wojtek and tried to focus on him, not Robert.

But my thoughts drifted away from homework and how it affected my son to the influence his father had on him.

Would Wojtek, as an adult, become like his father? Was that evil I knew so well lurking somewhere deep inside him? And would something trigger it at some point?

I drank my Prosecco as if it would give me answers. When I put the glass away, I saw my smartphone's screen flash. I had muted the ringtone and turned off the vibration, not wanting anyone to interrupt us at the table.

Anyway, I wasn't expecting any phone calls.

Especially not from Kliza.

I frowned, reached for the phone and got up from the table, looking down at my husband, who was so preoccupied with the task that he barely noticed me leaving.

"So you did change your mind?" I asked Jola.

"No. But that doesn't mean I don't give a shit."

I stood in front of the French door leading to the terrace and looked out towards the sea. The sky was overcast, and the weather showed no signs of improving. The wind was strong and the foam-flecked waves in the distance filled me with anxiety.

Actually, I was satisfied with Kliza's answer. If she had told me that she wanted to come back to Reimann Investigations after considering the matter, I would have been faced with a difficult choice: try to save the company and hire her back, thus angering my husband, or avoid confronting him and just let him carry out his plans?

Luckily, I didn't have to look for the answer. Deep down, maybe I knew it anyway.

"So why are you calling me?" I asked.

"As you know, I've been in contact with the locals."

"Locals?"

"Several people from Opole who provided me with information…"

"You talk about them like they're some African tribe."

"Whatever," she mumbled under her breath. "They're all strangers to me."

I smiled a little, but I didn't say a word.

"One of them just called me," she said.

"Who?

"MPIS."

"Excuse me?

"My Personal Information Source."

"Kliza…"

"I can't tell you who I'm working with," she replied. "Especially now that you might want to use those contacts."

It sounded partly infantile and partly hostile, but I wasn't surprised. I'd gotten to know Kliza a little bit, and I knew that she was unable to grasp many interpersonal nuances that allowed me to maintain good relations with others.

"It's about an MPIS from the provincial police headquarters. That's all I can tell you."

"Some officer?"

"No. They don't like me very much–"

"Never mind," I interrupted. "Did you find out anything about Ewa?"

"Not exactly. It's about Wern."

"Specifically?"

"No charges have been brought against him."

I looked at my husband over my shoulder. He seemed absorbed in the calculations, but I knew he hadn't missed any of my words. The control freak didn't even spare a glance at me, though.

"I guess it's good news," I said.

"That's what you'd think," Jola answered. "But if so, why are uniforms looking for him? Because they are – and pretty frantically, if you believe my MPIS."

"Why?"

"I don't know. He doesn't know that either."

"Maybe they just want Werner to give a statement?"

"It doesn't look like that to me. The fuzz act more like they're hunting him down. Except outside the law."

"*Outside* the law?"

"Yep," she confirmed and coughed. "Formally, there's no charges against him, but they're acting as if there were. Doesn't that tell you anything?"

"I try to avoid guesswork in such matters."

Jola was silent for a moment, and I looked at the dark clouds obscuring the whole sky, fading only on the horizon.

"In that case, your job's going to be easier," she said.

"Oh, yeah?"

"Yeah. Because soon you'll run out of opportunities to do any guessing," added Kliza. "They're coming for him."

"What's that?"

"They found him in that hotel. Apparently, he's made the basic mistake of any fugitive. He's contacted someone in his community."

I cursed silently.

"Call him," I said without thinking. I'd have to explain it all in the evening, tell Robert every detail. And it certainly wouldn't do any good, either for me or for Reimann Investigations. "You have to warn him," I added.

"Are you crazy?"

"If they lock him up now…"

"What if they do?"

She had no idea about Damian's discoveries. She didn't know how close he'd gotten to the breakthrough. And I didn't have the time or the right to tell her.

"I know you don't trust me very much," I said.

"That's an understatement."

"But please forget about that, at least for a while. It's not about me, it's about him."

Even though I was standing with my back to the table, I could feel that Robert had finally raised his eyes and was looking at me.

"Trust me this once. And just let him know."

"No."

"Kliza, this isn't a joke."

"I know," she admitted. "And that's why I won't contact him. If they stop him, they'll check his phone and see I tried… What's the official term? Obstruction of justice?"

I wanted to smash the glass with my open hand.

"I can't afford that," she added. "Not now, when I need a clean résumé."

Before I could answer, she hung up, apparently thinking her last sentence was a sufficiently meaningful farewell. And maybe it was.

However, I had to appreciate that she gave me any information at all. The problem was how to get her to Wern in time. I felt that the slightest move on my part would attract too much interest from Robert.

I couldn't use the phone. Besides, I didn't even know Damian's number; it was only in the automatic RIC system. All I could do was log into the RIC admin panel and send the activation code, then wait for Wern to show up – if he managed to do so in time at all.

I had to take a chance.

I poured myself some Prosecco and stood behind Wojtek and Robert. I leaned over between them, putting my hand on my husband's back. It was essential to keep up appearances. And I had many years of experience in doing just that.

I made some random comments, emphasizing that it was all too difficult for me, kissed Robert and slowly walked away. The most important thing was not to make any sudden movements. It was like balancing on a tightrope.

However, all the time I had the disturbing awareness of the depth of the abyss below me.

I went into the office and turned on the computer. I entered the address, login and password, and then sent the activation code to Werner as soon as possible. I waited anxiously, tapping my fingers on the table.

I took my eyes off the monitor and glanced at the open door. Then I looked at the screen again. It felt like it was taking forever.

Damian still didn't show up. The quiet murmur of voices downstairs suggested I still had some time, but probably not much. I'd managed to keep calm so Robert wasn't immediately interested in what I was doing, but it was only a matter of minutes.

Wern finally showed up. I could breathe again.

At least for a moment.

[Werner] I don't have much time. The police are here.

"Fucking hell!" I said.

I was about to write back when I heard the sound of approaching steps. I cursed again, but this time much quieter.

Robert was climbing the last step.

[Kasandra] Run.

I didn't have time to write anything else. I turned off the RIC and then smiled at my husband, who stood in the doorway.

7

I slammed the lid on my laptop shut and put it back in my bag. I thought Kasandra had wanted to warn me, and if her warning had come just a few minutes earlier, with a bit of luck I might have escaped.

But now it was too late.

"Son?" Dad asked me, concern evident in his voice. He must have been surprised at my behaviour. As soon as he entered the room, I slammed the door behind him, but before I could explain anything, a text message had come through with an activation code. "What's going on?" he added.

"You were followed by undercover officers."

He shook his head firmly. "No one followed me. I made sure of that."

I wasn't going to debate it now. While I might have had some doubts a moment earlier – the two men stayed in the car instead of following my father – I was now sure thanks to Kasandra.

I pointed to the laptop. "I've just confirmed it."

My father went pale and turned to the window. He wanted to say something, maybe deny it, maybe apologize, but I didn't give him a chance to do either.

"It doesn't matter now," I said. "I need to get out of here as soon as possible before they send reinforcements."

He looked at me with disbelief.

"I know how it sounds," I continued. "But there's a lot more at stake here than we thought."

"Surely no one's going to organize a manhunt, son."

"No, not a manhunt. But I'm sure the cops are going to be here any minute."

"The media didn't say anything about you."

"All the worse," I said quietly. "That's how they can do more."

"Who?"

"The police, shady types… I don't know. But the answers are waiting for me on a flash drive in Wrocław."

"Where?"

"Never mind. I need to get to the car quietly, so they won't notice me."

He shook his head, which was enough to convince me that it was simply impossible. I'd never even managed to dodge ticket inspectors, let alone the police. I'd never even had an opportunity to try. And there was no point in deluding ourselves that the first attempt wouldn't be my last.

What was left for me to do? Well, I had a change of clothes and some cash. After all, I could do without a car.

All I had to do was leave the hotel unnoticed. If those officers were here for the first time, they might not be aware that it was possible to leave the lobby both from the front and from the back of the complex, where the swimming pool was, and a bit further away there were tennis courts and a forest.

They'd driven up alone; no one else was here. Or did I just think so? Maybe that's what I was supposed to think.

"What are you going to do?" Dad asked.

"I don't know."

"Maybe you should go with them?"

"And give myself up?" I interrupted him, walking up to the window. "I don't think they're going to want to talk to me about anything else."

Dad had first-hand experience of the hardships of living in the communist state. It seemed he should have at least some measure of distrust in the authorities.

I looked at the cops. They were still sitting in the car, making it look like they were waiting for someone. For a moment I was hoping irrationally that some kid with a tennis bag would run out of the main entrance and rush to the black Opel, but nothing like that happened. Those two were waiting for me. Or their friends were, who were certainly already on their way.

I had to make a decision.

"I'm going to walk out the back," I said.

Dad came up next to me and looked out of the window. "Are you sure this is a good idea?"

"I'm sure it isn't. But what else can I do?"

He turned to me. "Maybe I can help you somehow?"

"No," I replied immediately. "You'll just alert them that something's wrong. Stay in the room."

Actually, I could use a little diversion, but I didn't want Dad to take any risks. He'd already done too much. I didn't know what would happen to him and Mum when I went to Wrocław.

If I did go there.

I was still watching the officers, hoping that they'd committed the most common police sin and underestimated their opponent. That they thought I was a complete amateur who wouldn't even know they were there.

Actually, they wouldn't be too wrong.

I picked up the bag and then hugged my father, probably for the first time in fifteen years. I assured him that I would take care of myself, although in fact not much was up to me anymore.

Then I walked down the hallway towards the back exit. I didn't know the forest behind the complex very well. I'd used to ride a bike there, but I knew very well that even the residents of the surrounding villages could get lost in the trees. That had its pros and cons. With a little luck, it could help me escape. On the other side of the forest there was Niwki, and then, a little farther away, Turawa, a local hotspot for all those who liked to spend time by the water in summer.

I was convinced that somewhere there I could board a train going to Wrocław.

All I had to do was to get out of the hotel.

I stopped before the exit, peeked outside and looked around. I didn't see anyone watching the back door. I could walk from there to the swimming pool building or directly behind the restaurant.

The area was fenced off, which was a problem. Like most Opole residents, I used to play tennis there and I knew what happened if the ball went over the fence to the other side. I knew I had to walk along the forest to get past the enclosure.

I walked out of the building, still looking around. I was only visible from the car park for a moment, when I was sneaking between the hotel and the swimming pool. When I finally reached the wall, I took a deep breath. Nobody had seen me. And no one was waiting for me.

At least, that was what I thought.

When I turned to the forest, I heard a throaty male voice say, "Just take it easy, Werner."

A uniformed policeman stood a few metres away.

So they hadn't thought I was a complete novice.

I froze, not knowing what to do. The officer put his hand on his open gun holster. He looked at me with unspoken warning in his eyes, and I felt a wave of heat coming over me.

I couldn't figure out any solution. There was no point in trying to escape. A bribe? I didn't have even half the amount I'd have to give this man. A desperate attack? Even if I was a seasoned murderer, a policeman would surely be able to draw his gun.

He glanced at me with a searching, uncertain look in his eyes, as if expecting me to do something stupid. He had every reason to. I hadn't acted rationally since the beginning of the case.

"No sudden movements," he said.

I couldn't swallow and felt thick saliva collect in my throat. I stood there as if struck by a lightning, unable to move. I realized then that it was truly over, that I would be put in a small room with no windows, interrogated and then placed in police custody.

If I hadn't fled town, I might have been able to testify as a free man. But under the circumstances, the police would ask for me to be remanded in custody. And the court wouldn't need much time to think it over.

The situation was clear. All the evidence was against me, and I'd confirmed it by hiding in a suburban hotel.

So I did the best I could. I put the bag down on the ground and raised my hands, palms open.

"This is all a misunderstanding," I said.

The man moved and looked around nervously. I was not a specialist in police hierarchy, but two slanted stripes on the shoulder probably did not mean too high a rank. Nevertheless, he looked like he'd been doing his job for a long time.

He looked at the bag, and then at me.

"Pick it up," he said.

For a moment, I thought I'd misheard him. Then I realized that something was very wrong. He wasn't reaching for his radio to alert his colleagues that I was trying to escape.

"Pick it up and run."

I didn't know what to say, let alone how to react. The aggressive tone of his voice made it clear that if I did what he ordered, he would reach for his gun.

"I'm not going to," I said. "I'll do anything that—"

"You don't understand."

He got one step closer, looked around again.

"You've got to get the fuck out of here. Right now."

"What?" I blurted out.

"My CO is on the other side and he'll be here any minute."

He looked anxiously towards the forest.

"Come on, fucking come on! Put your hands down and leg it!"

"But–"

"You don't have much time," he cut me off, getting even closer. Only now did I realize that he'd taken his hand off his gun.

"I don't understand what you're saying!"

"You'll understand everything in time, Werner," he hissed. "For now, you've got to get out of here."

I opened my mouth trying to say that I didn't even know where to run, but the policeman apparently saw through me.

"The nearest railway stations are in Dębska and Chrząstowice. Do you know where that is?"

I looked at his name tag, which read *J Falkow*. Whatever was going on here, I thought I'd better remember it.

"Yeah, I think I do." I said. "But I was going to–"

"What? Go the other way and lose them in the forest?" He shook his head, and that was enough to convince me that my idea was rubbish. I remembered that there were some train tracks running through Turawa Forest, but perhaps there was no station nearby. Maybe I should really head for one of those on the other side.

But how did I even have that choice?

I looked at Falkow, and he pointed me in the right direction with a nervous gesture.

"Run, Werner! Run, while you still can."

I wasn't going to just let it go. Not when I came across a man who was apparently somehow linked to everything that was happening. I knew that time was pressing, but I couldn't afford to give up such an opportunity.

"First, explain to me what's going on here. And who are you?"

"There's no time."

"Too bad."

"Either you're gonna get out of here now, or…"

He broke off when we were heard a quiet voice calling from a distance.

"That's my supervisor," Falkow said. "You know what's going to happen when he gets here?"

"I don't care. I want to know what the fuck all this means. Who killed Blitzer? What about Ewa?"

The officer swore under his breath and wrinkled his forehead, then shot me a hostile, almost hateful look.

"I told you you'd find out everything in time."

"Well, I'm not good at waiting."

The voice reached us again. I knew Falkow would have to answer to avoid suspicion. And he did so, telling his superior where he was.

I felt hot. Only then did I realize I was a step away from getting caught.

"You have to disappear."

He was right. Although I'd missed out on the opportunity to learn something concrete, I still had the chance to listen to the recording that was waiting for me in Wrocław.

I couldn't wait any longer.

I grabbed the bag and turned around.

"Trust no one," Falkow added as I was leaving.

I stopped and looked at him.

"No one," he repeated.

8

The evening brought respite, like a wave of cool air after a sweltering day. I sat in front of the computer in my office, knowing that Werner was about to drag me into his world. And that I would stop thinking about the reality that surrounded me every day.

I checked local news websites in Opole. I knew he hadn't been caught. There wasn't a single mention in the media, and any successful police operation would have been widely reported by now. Once, it would have been possible to keep such things a secret, but these days everyone was a reporter and the whole event would have inevitably been recorded on someone's mobile phone. The police might even have bragged about it themselves. Blicki's murder was widely publicized in the local media, after all, and the police HQ needed to be able to give the press something solid as soon as possible.

Wern had somehow managed to escape. I was sure of it.

Well, no, I wasn't. But I wanted to be. Especially after the amount of effort it took me to convince Robert that I hadn't done anything wrong, sitting in my office at an unscheduled time. I didn't remember exactly what I'd said to Kliza on the phone, nor how much he'd heard. It wasn't easy to spin a matching story for him so that he'd buy it.

But in the end, I did. I convinced my husband that the conversation had nothing to do with the current case. On the contrary, it was related to another, one that was investigated by Glazur, an IT specialist Robert fired from RI some time ago. According to the story I'd spun, the husband of a woman who'd hired us to collect dirt on him for the divorce sought revenge on Glazur. It took me a while, but I explained to Robert that I felt responsible. After all, if we hadn't fired Glazur, he would have enjoyed our full protection. We made sure that our employees had nothing to be afraid of.

The latter was the result of Robert's other, less official activities. He often mixed one world with another, usually to the benefit of both. Sometimes it led to complications, but over the years those were only exceptions confirming the rule.

Eventually, I'd suggested that we call Kliza and have her verify that I was telling the truth. Robert had been willing to do it, but I knew he was just testing me. He had no intention of contacting her or anyone else.

I was safe. At least for now.

Sitting in front of the computer with a glass of sparkling wine, I sent an activation code in a text message. I felt like I was getting warmer and warmer, and it wasn't because of the booze. I was anxiously waiting for the line of text to appear on the screen, for a chance to be transported somewhere else. Words had power; they really shaped reality. Especially since there were so few of them in the world I lived in, which was dominated by fists.

I rocked a little forward and back, sipping my drink. I started to turn the glass on the counter and it struck me that I was acting like a drug addict jonesing for my next fix. Did I get into a new addiction so fast?

Before I could answer that question, Damian logged on to the RIC. I took a deep breath, realizing he must have gotten away.

[Wern] I guess this is the usual time for us now, right?
[Kas] Yes.
[Wern] When did we set it up?
[Kas] The first time I talked to you.
[Wern] I don't remember anyone asking me.
[Kas] Because you had nothing to say.

And neither had I, I added in my head. Robert was very specific in determining when I could use the computer upstairs, when I would watch TV shows with him and when I could go out on the terrace.

I'd always thought that Polish was a much richer language than English, but the phrase "control freak" was much better at conveying the meaning, sounding much more eloquent than any of its Polish equivalents, none of which communicated the essence. They didn't even come close to the heart of the problem – namely the fact that the person in question was, in fact, crazy.

[Wern] One way or another, I should probably be glad that you included me in your daily schedule.

[Kas] Maybe.

[Wern] Because you're probably like everyone who runs their own business. You work 24/7. Probably even now you're wearing a suit and sitting in some office with glass walls.

[Kas] How can you be sure I'm not sitting in the bathroom with my computer in my lap?

I'd been waiting for a chance to write that. I looked at the screen, but the reply wasn't coming. I thought, however, that Damian at least smiled slightly at the comeback.

It was only after a while that another message appeared.

[Wern] Thank you.

[Kas] For that visual?

[Wern] No, for the tip-off. If it wasn't for that, I wouldn't know how totally screwed I am.

[Kas] And are you?

[Wern] You don't even know how much.

I took another sip. The gesture was natural, unconscious. Drinking was as natural for me as breathing.

[Kas] How did you get away?
[Wern] Thanks to my own cleverness, cunning, and genius.
[Kas] So you got lucky?
[Wern] Not exactly. Somebody helped me.
[Kas] Who?

The reply took long enough to come for me to ignore it. Either something was wrong or Werner wondered if he could trust me.

After a while, I concluded I wouldn't get an answer.

I was wondering who could have helped him. According to the information Kliza had collected on him, he was the type of man who could only count on himself. At some point, he had wrapped himself in a cocoon of lonely existence – or rather, its substitute. After losing Ewa, he didn't allow anyone to come to him, withdrawing from everyone. And it was difficult for me to think of anyone who, in a crisis, would trust him enough to act against the police.

I kept looking at the blank screen.

[Kas] You there?
[Wern] Yes.
[Kas] I asked you who helped you.
[Wern] I don't know.
[Kas] I don't understand.
[Wern] That's normal for people like you.

I raised my eyebrows.

[Kas] What does that mean?
[Wern] That you grew up in a rich family, you started your
    life with the game already saved at 100% complete.
    The rest of us had to go through it from the beginning.

I didn't really know where he was going with that. I waited
some more, but he didn't say anything else.

[Kas] Are you getting somewhere specific with that?
[Wern] It's just that you don't understand certain things.
[Kas] So you're changing the subject?
[Wern] Actually, yes.

I swore quietly.

[Kas] If there's anyone you can trust, it's just me, Werner.
    You know that, don't you?
[Wern] You gave me the handle "Wern". Don't expect me
    to trust you after something like that.
[Kas] I'm serious.
[Wern] Me too.

I shook my head. Apparently, there was no way I was going
to find out who'd decided to help him. For a moment, I was
wondering if there was any other way to establish that. I could
use RI employees, but that would draw Robert's attention.

I'd find out sooner or later, I decided. Now it was time to
get down to business.

[Kas] Where are you?

[Wern] On my way to Wrocław.

[Kas] And you're writing on your laptop? Haven't you heard that one in four car accidents in Poland are caused by texting while driving?

[Wern] I'm not texting you.

[Kas] Yeah, right.

[Wern] Besides, I'm on a train. A pretty good one, too, with wifi. And this time no one's eating egg sandwiches. The last one I was on was a local connection and it reeked of them.

[Kas] Why are you going to Wrocław?

[Wern] There are answers waiting for me there.

I leaned towards the monitor.

[Kas] What are you going to do when you find them?

[Wern] I'll find the person who left them for me.

[Kas] You still assume she's alive.

[Wern] You do, too.

[Kas] How can you be so sure?

[Wern] You wouldn't be helping me, otherwise. You'd think the case was over and Reimann Investigations completed the task.

[Kas] You suspect me of acting out of purely professional motives.

[Wern] Do you have any other?

[Kas] Maybe this is my new hobby.

[Wern] Maybe. Or maybe you just like me.

[Kas] I wouldn't go that far.

Only after a while did it strike me that I was smiling at the white letters appearing and disappearing on the black screen.

I felt like a teenage schoolgirl finally getting attention from a boy in the senior year.

> [Wern] I have to go. I'll let you know as soon as I know anything else.
> [Kas] All right. Take care of yourself.
> [Wern] Sure.

After he logged out, I stayed still for a while, wondering about my motives, and then about his motives. He didn't actually need me at this point. Maybe whoever helped him even advised him to stay away from me.

I didn't have a good reputation. The public version of Kasandra Reimann did not resemble in any way the one Wojtek and Robert knew. According to the outside world, I was a cold snob who didn't care about anything or anyone, who donated to charity just to improve her image. I could imagine that someone involved in Ewa's disappearance had found out that Reimann Investigations was conducting the search and warned Damian to stay away from us.

I took a deep breath and reached for the phone. I thought it was time to find out for myself. Jola picked up after the second tone.

"I saw," she said.

"What is it that you saw?"

"What's happening in the Opole media."

I had no idea what she meant, so I quickly pulled up a local news website and looked at the homepage. It showed an official statement from the police about the body that was allegedly found on Bolko Island. They had ruled out the involvement of any third party. Ewa was said to have committed suicide using a mixture of substances that caused a cardiac arrest. They did not provide any details but the spokesman for the local police left no doubt as to the official cause of death. The victim had taken her own life.

"But given your reaction, I guess that's not why you're calling," Kliza said.

"No," I admitted.

"That's good. Because I don't want to talk about it."

I wasn't surprised. And I was wondering if Werner had already read the reports. If so, it wasn't likely to change anything – he would simply decide that this was more fake news that had nothing to do with the truth.

"I need to get in touch with your MPIS at the police HQ," I said.

"No way."

"No one–"

"I don't care if you keep it to yourself. I never disclose such things, and that's final."

I clenched my teeth and felt anger swelling inside me. Perhaps it was time I acted like the person the whole outside world thought I was – and wanted to believe I was.

"Then you're going to help me another way," I said. "You're going to call him and find out how Werner managed to sneak past the cops, right under their noses."

Kliza was silent.

"And you won't leave him alone until you figure it out," I added, as if I was still her superior. "Okay?"

She cleared her throat. "I've already done it," she said.

"Even better."

"But the MPIS has no idea how it happened. He says all the exits were covered. They questioned Werner senior, but he says he didn't see his son, that when he came to the hotel he couldn't find him there."

I brushed my hand over my hair, pulling the fringe aside and squinting.

"What happened there, Kliza?"

"I don't know," she said.

We were silent, as there was nothing to say. Asking further questions seemed pointless and depressing.

"I know that all we've discovered in this case is just the tip of the iceberg," she added. "It's more complicated than we thought."

9

Trust no one. The short phrase kept ringing in my head as I stepped off the train at Wrocław Station. Again, I felt like everyone was watching me, which made Falkow's words echo even louder.

Maybe he was right, and maybe he wasn't. I had to take into account, however, that he'd saved me from of a hopeless situation. Could he have been driven by some hidden motives? Possibly.

I thought I'd find out soon enough. Heading towards the market, I was thinking about the recent statement from the Opole police, confirming that officers were involved in the case.

The person whose body was found had nothing to do with Ewa. Suicide wasn't an option; it wouldn't make any sense. Until a few years ago I could have told myself that the cause of death was simply wrong, but these days cheating forensic technicians was virtually impossible.

Nobody manipulated the investigators. They were up to their necks in the conspiracy, which could include more people than I had previously thought. The fact that some innocent girl's death was made to look like a suicide seemed to confirm that.

I reached Solny Square in less than half an hour and headed straight for the Guinness Pub – the place Ewa had been referring to. It was there that she'd once helped me walk as I staggered, as if I'd just returned from a long period of weightlessness in space, losing the ability to function in Earth's gravity.

As I entered the pub, I was struck by how the décor and general vibe was reminiscent of the Highlander. In a way, history had come full circle, although I didn't suppose Ewa deliberately chose that as a symbol.

I greeted one of the employees with a smile and walked up to the bar, wondering how to start a conversation. I chose what I thought was the best option: simply looking at the menu. I glanced at the names of drinks. Blitzer would feel like he was in heaven. *Come As You Are*, *Du Hast*, *Ace Of Spades*, *Highway To Hell*...

"Green beer, please," I said.

"What kind?"

"Whatever."

The bartender poured from the tap, mixed it with green juice and put a frosted mug in front of me. I had no intention of drinking it all, intending to keep a sober mind, but after one sip I changed my mind.

As the bartender took orders from other customers, I looked at him, wondered if he was the one Ewa had chosen to give me the flash drive. And if so, why him?

No, I was sure there were too many people working here to find the one my fiancée had picked.

I cleared my throat to get the bartender's attention. He looked at me, then at my drink, and then turned away, evidently assuming my grunt was unintentional. When I repeated it, he changed his mind and came up to me.

"I didn't actually come here for a beer."

"In that case, I recommend the shepherd's pie. It's a kind of lamb casserole."

"I didn't come for food either."

He raised his eyebrows.

"I hear someone left a flash drive here that I'm supposed to pick up."

Even though the music was blasting from speakers, it was as if all sounds stopped suddenly. I looked at the bartender and he looked at me. We measured each other with our eyes as if we were preparing for a confrontation.

"Damian?" he finally asked.

I felt a wave of warmth down my back. "Yeah."

"You took your time."

I figured I'd have to play that game. "I couldn't get here any faster."

"Yeah, but the flash drive is safe and sound. And it's waiting for you."

"Great."

He left me for a moment, then leaned over and reached under the counter. There were some people impatient to order, and I remembered how annoying it was when I was working at the Highlander, with all those customers who came to me on weekend nights just to ask me to charge their smartphone, because it was an emergency, because it was about to shut down. All while other clients were waiting for their drinks, usually not very patiently.

Now I was the annoying one. And I wasn't going to give up fast enough.

The bartender came back with a flash drive bearing the spider symbol from Spider-Man's costume. I couldn't help but smile.

"Is it that important?" asked the man, seeing my reaction. He put the device on the countertop and I looked at it, afraid to take it in my hand, lest I accidentally wipe out the contents. I glanced up.

"Very important."

He said nothing, which made me think that they hadn't connected it to a computer and discovered that it was password-protected. That was a good decision. The flash drive could have been a breeding ground for viruses.

The bartender started to move away, but I stopped him.

"Who left it?" I asked.

"Some guy."

"Some guy?" I felt like an idiot repeating every phrase like an echo, but he nodded as if he was accustomed to interacting with people who were not in the best shape mentally. "What did he look like?"

"I don't know. I wasn't here then."

"Was he a regular?"

"No, I don't think he's even been here again after that. He'd probably pick up the flash drive himself then, wouldn't he? Now, if you'll excuse me..."

"I won't take up much of your time," I interrupted him, with an almost begging note in my voice.

He looked at the impatient customers and I came to the conclusion that I had to appeal to his professional solidarity. All I had to do was prove I worked in the same trade. And I knew exactly how to do it.

"Sorry for not being one of those people who order vodka in a large glass, straight, without ice, and a glass of mineral water," I added.

He wrinkled his forehead.

"I used to tend bar, too," I said, "and that combo was always ordered by alcoholics who hadn't drunk for years until one night they finally gave in. I knew they'd be draining both glasses in silence all night long, without bothering me."

The man smiled slightly, apparently appreciating that I had basically introduced myself as one of the annoying bastards.

"Wait a minute," he said, and then left to take some orders.

I looked at the flash drive. I wanted to plug it into my laptop, enter my password and listen to what Ewa had to say, but I couldn't miss the opportunity to learn something about the person that had left the device for me.

The bartender came back after a while. He leaned against the table and peered at me suspiciously.

"What's with the flash drive?" he asked.

"Good question."

He seemed a bit confused, so I smiled quickly and dismissed the topic with a wave of my hand.

"This is a message from a girl," I explained. "The problem is, I don't know who left it for me."

"That's a bit weird."

"But harmless. In fact, it's just an innocent game."

Nothing could have been further from the truth, but the bartender didn't seem to see it. And fortunately he decided not to dig any deeper, probably well aware that he could only spare me a moment.

"I want to get the edge over them," I added. "Which is why I asked who left it."

"Oh. Right."

"What did he look like?"

"I don't know. I didn't see him."

I looked around for the other employees, but everyone was hanging out somewhere amongst the booths occupied by the laughing, drunken young people. Wrocław had more students than any other city in Poland. If anyone wanted to verify that, all they needed was to go to any pub on a weeknight.

"And is the person who took the flash drive working today?"

"No," said the bartender.

"Could you please give me their contact information?"

"Listen…"

"It's really important. It's fun, but I really do care about this girl."

He sighed deeply. "I don't know."

"Come on, mate. I'd owe you big time."

He considered for a moment, then eventually agreed. I knew it was only because the other bartender was a man, not a woman. A woman's number would have been a lot harder to get.

I thanked him, then took a sip of my green beer. There was a slight aftertaste of something synthetic, but maybe that was just a weird impression. I put a twenty-zloty note on the table.

"Thanks," I repeated, putting the flash drive and the paper with the phone number in my pocket.

"No problem."

"Just one more thing. When did he leave it?"

The bartender thought for a moment, scratching behind his ear and squinting, as if fishing it from his memory bordered on a miracle. I wasn't surprised. So many people went through such places, so many events were held, so many things said, that everything was mixed up after a while. And yet, there were those who came once every three months and asked for "the usual", expecting the staff to remember.

"I don't know," he finally said. "A week ago, maybe two."

My mouth went dry. Whoever Ewa had sent, she'd done so relatively recently. I had the illusory feeling like I was almost close enough to touch her.

Or maybe that feeling wasn't as illusory as I thought.

I went back to the Renoma shopping centre and started looking for a hotel in the area. On Podwale Street, I found a place with a promising name. Incepcja turned out to be a small hostel that offered everything I needed.

I locked myself in the tiny room – smaller even that an average student bedsit – and lay down on the bed with my laptop on my knees, then plugged the flash drive into the USB port and took a deep breath.

A window popped up, asking for the password. I entered "Rosabelle".

Then I saw something that might as well have been the greatest mystery of the universe. I was looking at an AAC file with answers waiting for me.

It was called "Plastic bags under the sink".

It wasn't easy to open it on my old computer, but I eventually managed it, and Ewa's voice sounded from the speakers.

Plastic bags under the sink.

Years later, some children can say that the only thing their parents taught them was to collect and store plastic bags under the sink in the kitchen. I envy them.

My parents taught me a lot of things. Things I wouldn't want to know how to do.

Thanks to them, I learned how to circumvent the law to avoid paying taxes. How to run small financial pyramids to hide the origin of funds, and how that was different from a Ponzi scheme. I learned how to cover my tracks, how to launder dirty money, how to use the state to extort massive VAT write-offs…

I could go on and on.

They taught me those things no matter how I responded. And you need to know that when we started planning our own future, I made it clear to them how I was going to spend the rest of my life. With you, away from everything they'd been doing.

But in the end, their sins became mine. The shadow of their activities fell on me. And on you too, unfortunately, though I did everything I could to prevent that.

I cut myself off from them long before the accident. I call it that, but as you already know, it had nothing to do with chance. It was planned, carried out in cold blood, and then swept under the carpet.

But before it happened, I'd told my father I wasn't going to take over the firm after him. I didn't want to have anything to do with it or my parents. What still mattered to me, though, was that we should keep up appearances. For your sake, and for your parents'. Maybe a little bit for my sake, too. I don't know what my motive was. Maybe it's because I'd been keeping that façade all my life, so I couldn't imagine it just collapsing one day.

I wanted us to be different from my parents. I wanted us to have a normal, happy relationship. We wanted to have children and enjoy a peaceful, stabile, comfortable life...

I don't know why I was deluding myself that it was possible.

Maybe because my parents finally sobered up. But by then, it was too late for them to change anything.

My father worked for an organized crime group, which operated mainly in Lower Silesia. It was headed by a man nicknamed Cayman. Quite appropriate, because he really was like a powerful reptile.

He paid a lot of money to the law firm, and only a small part of it was taxed. For years, my father had no reason to complain. He earned more than he could ever spend, had no actual contact with Cayman's circle, and bribes paid to several officials kept us safe from police scrutiny.

At least, that's what they all thought.

I am convinced that if the Central Anti-Corruption Bureau hadn't followed that lead, my father would still be doing his thing, like he did in Cayman's heyday. I would still be in Opole, the incident by the Młynówka would never have happened and by now we would probably have had a bunch of children already.

But let's not get ahead of ourselves.

Agents of the CAB found out about a bribe only because one of the involved officials went too far. He worked for the tax office, held an almost entry-level position, earned little above the national average, and *yet bought some things that he shouldn't have been able to afford. That provoked typical human jealousy among his coworkers, which in turn led to suspicions. An anonymous letter from one particularly disgruntled colleague was all it took, and the CAB became interested in the official.*

A sting operation was set up. I don't think it was entirely legal. It was all so vague that the poor man didn't know who was actually offering him the bribe. Once he agreed to turn a blind eye to a small irregularity and accepted a gift in the form of several thousand zloty, agents revealed themselves.

The official fell apart quickly. He pointed his finger at Cayman, who was well known to law enforcement. All the points of contact between the official and Cayman were analyzed and the law firm that helped both of them was discovered.

I don't need to tell you that it belonged to my father.

CAB agents could have knocked on his door in the morning and pulled him out of the house by force. However, they didn't care about small fry; they wanted to get the one who threw bait into the water. They could do that by leaning on Dad, but the case was already at the official stage, when they couldn't afford any procedural missteps.

They had to act in accordance with the law, and with the Central Bureau of Investigation, because the case turned out to be much more extensive than they had initially thought. It had evolved from a small offence by a tax official into a serious operation against organized crime.

So they came to my father with an offer he couldn't refuse. They informed him that they were pursuing

Cayman and that they had enough evidence to charge him as well.

He knew what it meant. Not only would he go to jail, he'd lose everything he'd earned over the years, whether from legal or illegal sources.

He didn't have to think long about whether to become a turncoat. At the second or the third meeting, he agreed to cooperate. It was always highly beneficial to make such offers to lawyers involved in various scandals. They were well versed in rules and procedures and knew when to abandon a sinking ship.

But somebody noticed that my father was preparing a lifeboat for himself. I guess Cayman had a mole in the police, though I might be wrong. It might as well have been my father sabotaging himself – by transferring more and more money to offshore accounts to save at least a fraction of his illegal income.

Anyway, Cayman found out about everything. And he quickly did what he did best.

What was the outcome? You know very well because you came to the funeral. Because you spent weeks comforting me, helping me through that difficult time. I wasn't as close to my parents as you were to yours. But they were still my parents.

Plus I was aware of what really happened, and I felt that it could put both me and you in danger. And yet I couldn't share anything with you.

I know you. I know exactly what you'd say and what you'd persuade me to do. You wouldn't let the truth be swept under the carpet.

Or would you do that now?

You're a different man now. Life has given you a hard time. Mostly because of me – I realize that. My guilt is beyond doubt, and this recording is not an attempt at absolution.

I just want you to understand.

I've already mentioned that my parents taught me much more than just to keep plastic bags under the sink. And that's what started all my problems. Yours, too.

I knew everything. I had full knowledge of what my father was doing.

I swore I'd never make any use of it. I insisted I didn't want anything to do with his business. I promised myself I wouldn't let anything come between us.

I kept my word, in part – but only in part, I'm afraid.

You think you've guessed the ending of this story?

Think again. If everything was so obvious, I wouldn't have gone to so much trouble.

But you'll find out about it from the next recording. Trust me, I have a good reason not to tell you any more right now. Be patient for a while longer.

The recording's waiting for you somewhere else. Where I wasn't going to go, and for you it was a mandatory part of the programme.

Not far from where Blitzer dragged us.

Remember, I didn't desert you. I didn't go into a coma. I ran after you like Luxtorpeda. And you should hurry up too, because in twelve hours the file waiting for you will disappear.

The recording was over, and I sat still for a while, so confused that I couldn't process the clues Ewa had given me. I don't know how long it took for the right cogs to click in my head.

I looked at the watch and quickly remembered when Ewa's twelve-hour time limit ran out.

Absurd, I thought. She wouldn't have any way of knowing when I'd play that recording. The file wouldn't disappear; it would be waiting for me where she'd left it.

But then why would she say that?

Even though she seemed to have been hiding her true life from me, I trusted her. It didn't matter how many years had passed; my feelings were still just as strong as ever, maybe even stronger. So I believed her words without any doubt.

Because what purpose would she have in deceiving me, and after all the trouble she'd gone through with the recordings?

No, I decided, she wasn't lying. I really had just twelve hours to find the other file – the file that would give me answers to the questions that had been haunting me for a decade.

10

I rightly assumed Robert would check my phone records. He confirmed that at dinner, regardless of the presence of our son. This time Wojtek didn't have a homework assignment and he divided his attention between us and his tempura chickpea nuggets. He would eat them all the time if it wasn't for the fact that Robert only prepared them on special occasions.

My husband had been watching me closely since we'd sat down at the table. To the outside observer this would look harmless enough, like a chef trying to see if the dish he'd prepared pleased the diners, but to me it signalled another sleepless night.

"You've been talking to Kliza a lot lately," he said noncommittally.

That was all I needed to know he monitored my calls. I thanked myself silently for my caution. If it wasn't for that, sooner or later I'd have let myself call Werner and I would have been in much more trouble.

"Even though she doesn't work for us anymore," he added.

I nodded, pretending that the topic was completely irrelevant, and focused on the nuggets.

"Have you made friends with her?"

"Not really."

"Then how come there's so many calls?"

"I told you we were helping Glazur a little."

"Oh, yes."

Although there was a deeper meaning to our words, we spoke in a warm, friendly tone. I didn't know if we actually managed to fool our child and created the impression that we were a normal, happy family. There was something wrong in it, but on the other hand it was also satisfactory. And I treated that as a sacrifice on my part, too. I was ready to endure much worse degradation as long as it didn't have any negative impact on Wojtek.

"But I checked on Glazur," Robert said.

I looked up for a moment.

"You said he was threatened by the husband of a woman for whom we collected compromising evidence?"

This euphemism did not reflect in the slightest what we were trying to achieve in such pre-divorce cases. We were collecting the worst dirt we could dig up.

In any case, there wasn't a lot of dirt to pick up. It was our client who led a much wilder life outside her marriage, although her partner was hardly beyond reproach. As always, the truth lay somewhere in the middle.

Maybe that's what happened with me and Robert, too. Perhaps by gradually allowing him to do more and more, I had played my part in leading us to my current situation.

I preferred not to look for answers to those questions. Especially now, when my husband was looking at me accusingly.

"That's what you said, right?" he went on. "Or did I confuse something?"

"No, you didn't."

"But Glazur isn't in the city."

He should have added that he checked that, too. He refrained only because it might sound disturbing to Wojtek.

"We thought it would be best if he left," I said.

"Where to?"

"I don't know. Kliza took care of it."

I was heading into dangerous territory. After Jola had called, I'd made up an excuse for myself, but nothing more. It wasn't a well-planned lie that could act as a security buffer. On the contrary.

"I also checked on that husband," Robert added.

"And?"

"He doesn't look to me like he could do Glazur any harm."

Another euphemism. Robert was as good at them as he was at brutal verbal punches when the bedroom door closed behind us.

"Well," I started, trying to focus on the food. "You know how Glazur is. He's afraid of everything."

"I don't know. I don't know him that well."

"He's such a scaredy-cat, and besides..."

"I'd love to meet him."

"Yes?"

"Maybe he'd feel better if you invited him."

It was the last thing Robert would have wanted. Now I knew that there was an unspoken threat in every word. Under a veneer of appearances, we were having a completely different conversation.

"I don't know if that's a good idea," I said. "After all, we did fire him."

"Maybe you're right."

And that was where we left it – at least as far as the façade went.

Several hours later, when Wojtek was asleep and I was reading in bed, I knew that I would have to face real charges. I prepared myself as best I could. I put on the nightie that Robert liked the most. I sprinkled his favourite perfume on the inside of my thighs and between my breasts. I styled my hair the way he always wanted it to look. But I had no illusions that it would do much good.

Robert came into the bedroom angry. He slammed the door, without sparing a thought if he woke up his son or not.

He was clearly drunk. More so than usual.

I don't know how much time he'd spent trying to convince himself that this time he would be able to restrain his emotions. He certainly made an effort, but I suppose the longer he drank, the worse it was.

Without a word, he threw the duvet on the floor, and then with a violent movement of his hand he told me to get up.

I got up uncertainly and took a step towards the wall. We were on opposite sides of the bed, like fighters in the ring.

Just two, maybe three years ago I would have considered ways to save myself in such a situation, but a long time had passed since then. A lot of bruises, scratches and welts had appeared on my body. And every single one of them confirmed my conviction that I couldn't do anything that would stop Robert from getting angry.

He wasn't silent for long.

"Do you think you can fool me like that, you cunt?"

"No…"

"And you think you can lie to me and look me straight in the eye?"

"Robert…"

"Who do you think I am, huh? Some fucking idiot?"

"It's not like that."

I could have denied it. I could have tried to appeal to him. I could have begged him, showered him with compliments, expressions of love and complete devotion. But the only result would have been to delay the inevitable.

"Are you cheating on me, bitch?"

"I would never–"

"With who?" he snarled, circling the bed.

"I would never betray you." The words fell out of my mouth spontaneously. So what if I was aware of their uselessness? When you're falling into the abyss, you try to grab on to anything, even though you know how futile the effort is.

"It's unbelievable that you thought…" He broke off and laughed. "No, really, you fucking cunt. How could you even think you'd hide anything from me? You've been fucking around. But it's over, you understand? You will remember once and for all that you will never keep any secrets from me. That you can fucking fool anyone, even yourself. But not me, you fucking bitch."

I expected the first blow now, with an open hand. Usually he wasn't sure, as if he was trying to figure out how far he could go. Then it gradually started to progress.

It was different tonight, though.

Before I knew it, he swung his leg and kicked me in the knee. I fell to the floor with a moan and covered my face automatically. Robert grabbed me by the shoulders and threw me to the centre of the room uncaringly, like an airport baggage handler.

He ran straight at me and kicked me in the ribs, then the pelvis. I didn't have time to react, to say something or grab his foot. The blows were quick, deliberate, mad.

He hit me in the face with his hand.

"You whore!"

He kept slapping me for a terrifyingly long time. I felt like it would never stop, and then there would be his fists. I realized it was one of those times when he was completely out of control.

He was usually a little more careful. He was just like me in that regard when I was drinking. I knew that if I went too far, the results would force me to stop altogether. He had to be careful, too. He tried not to cause me damage that couldn't be masked.

Usually.

This time, though, he grabbed me by my throat and squeezed. I couldn't catch my breath or swallow.

"How dare you!"

I tried to say something but couldn't.

"You dirty bitch, how dare you? After everything I've done for you!"

He was clenching his hands even harder. They were as powerful as a vice, and I felt fragile and vulnerable. Still, I started defending myself, which of course only added fuel to the fire of madness burning inside him.

"You always have to fuck everything up! Not just my life, but our whole family!"

The accusations came up every time, one way or another. He blamed me not only for all his failures, but also for Wojtek's shortcomings or things completely independent of us.

In such moments, I became the source of all evil in his eyes.

I was frightened by that thought. It made me think that Robert was willing to remove me from the equation he created to make the balance positive.

The hands clenched around my neck seemed to confirm that.

I was suffocating, knowing it was getting worse. He'd never been so close to what I was most afraid of. It wasn't just the fact that he was going to kill me – at times I saw it as the only way out of this nightmare. It was devastating for me to know what would happen to Wojtek if I wasn't there. I had no doubt that Robert would direct all that violence at him. Maybe not at once, but in the end it would happen.

I stepped up my efforts to free myself, but it only made my situation worse. He clenched his fingers tighter and tighter, shaking me and shouting something. The blood stopped flowing into my brain and I couldn't understand the words.

When I felt that my eyelids were getting heavy, he hit my head on the floor several times, as if he was trying to revive me in some bizarre way.

Just as I was about to pass out, he finally let go.

Time seemed to have stopped. I panicked and tried to turn over, but Robert kept holding me down. He went still.

A moment later he shook his head, stood up and ran out of the bedroom.

I looked at the open door, afraid that I would see my son standing in the doorway, that he'd woken up when he heard the noises and decided to check what was going on. But I didn't see anyone. I was relieved, as if the fact that Wojtek was unaware was the most important thing.

I got up, wincing in pain.

Everything that followed was a more intense version of Robert's usual, simpler repentance. He cried for longer than usual. He said he'd go to the police first thing in the morning. He'd report himself, ask them to open a domestic violence file on him.

There was no end to the promises, assurances and apologies.

He didn't want to sleep with me that night. He said he didn't deserve it. He wrapped himself in a blanket in the living room. I heard him curse himself, sniff and swear. Then finally he fell asleep.

And I went quietly to the upstairs office.

I turned on the computer and sent an activation text message to Werner. I didn't know if he had his phone on, if he had internet access or whether he would ignore my message at this hour.

He showed up after less than a minute.

When I saw his IP address appear and then his username, I felt like I was taking a big sip of Prosecco. My heart was suddenly lighter.

[Damian] Shouldn't you be asleep?
[Kasandra] Tough night.
[Damian] Tell me about it.

[Kasandra] Did you find out anything?

[Damian] Actually, more than I'd like to know. And I'm not sure I want to go further.

I moved my hand over my neck and felt a sharp stab of pain in my side.

[Kasandra] I suppose you're just saying that.

[Damian] I suppose you're right.

considered it for a second.

[Kasandra] Is there anything I can do to help you?

[Damian] Not yet.

Again, I found it difficult to swallow, but this time the reason was completely different than during the incident with Robert. I realized why I was asking. And what I was getting at.

I was planning to cross the line I'd backed away from last time.

[Kasandra] Then maybe you can help me.

[Damian] How?

I drew air through my nose and stared at the open office door.

[Damian] You there?

[Kasandra] Yes.

[Damian] Are you okay?

[Kasandra] Not really. But with your help, that could change.

I glanced at the monitor and waited anxiously for his answer. Finally, it popped up.

[Damian] You can count on me.

That was all I needed to finally decide it was high time to act. Werner was the only one who could help me. He was from the outside, unrelated to Robert's business or money. Anonymous. Completely unknown to my husband. Plus, Damian was an outlaw now, prepared to do anything.

And sooner or later, he'd need help himself. Worst-case scenario, he would treat my support as a bargaining chip.

Thanks to him, I was going to do what I should have done a long time ago. I was going to break free.

11

I'd lost empathy years ago. I was completely indifferent to human hurts and worries, and I can't even remember the moment when it happened. Nevertheless, I agreed to help Kasandra Reimann – because it was in my own best interest.

Until now, she'd been interested in my case only because it was her nouveau-riche whim, maybe even a kind of a hobby. But now I had a chance to change that.

I didn't know exactly what she would require of me, but I was sure of one thing: whatever she wanted, it would become a valuable currency for me. A currency I'd use when I found Ewa.

Because I knew we'd need help. Whoever was behind her disappearance and everything that had happened afterwards had incomparably greater resources at their disposal than I did. Having an ally in the form of Kasandra Reimann could be worth a lot.

I slept for two hours before I hit the road. I would have probably left Wrocław immediately if it hadn't been for the fact that I had to wait for the night train. I didn't have much hope I'd manage to fall asleep, but apparently my body was more exhausted than I'd thought.

I took the Intercity train to Ostrów Wielkopolski, where I had to wait several hours at the station, but I still had plenty of time before Ewa's deadline. The journey from Ostrów to Witaszyce took me thirty minutes.

I was absolutely sure I was going to the right place.

Ewa claimed that it was near the village where Blitzer had dragged us. This could have referred to several points on the map of Poland, but in this case it was Jarocin – specifically, the rock festival that was held there. We were reluctant to attend any concerts, but that one time we let ourselves be convinced. And we hadn't regretted it.

I knew right away that it was a good guess because the connection with the Foo Fighters' performance was obvious. Ewa planned it so it would all start with a concert and end with a concert.

Plus, she mentioned that she hadn't deserted us. She hadn't fallen into a coma. And she'd run after us like a Luxtorpeda. All that reinforced my belief that it was Jarocin, as the names of the bands that had played there all those years age were Dezerter, Coma and Luxtorpeda.

But the actual destination was a different place, the one she didn't intend to enter – the one that was a mandatory part of the programme for me.

That could only be one place. Before the concert, we'd had some time to kill, so Blitzer had checked out the area for some points of interest. When he'd found out about the Star Wars Museum at the Witaszyce Palace, I'd decided we had to go.

A scale model of Darth Maul? A giant Jar Jar Binks I could look at and touch? Nothing could have stopped me from visiting.

While Ewa tolerated my fascination with Spider-Man, it was difficult for her to understand what I saw in Star Wars. I'd never managed to persuade her to watch more than a dozen or so minutes of *A New Hope*. With the prequel trilogy, I didn't even try. And it wasn't until much later that JJ Abrams made his gamechanger, *The Force Awakens*.

So I knew where to go.

I didn't know what was waiting for me at the museum, nor how could it disappear twelve hours after I listened to the second message Ewa left me.

More doubts came right after I bought a ticket for ten zlotys. I stood in front of miniature replicas of stormtroopers, wondering what to do next, when a man in his early thirties approached me. He had a scar under his left eye but he didn't look shady. On the contrary, he looked perfectly ordinary. At first I thought he was an employee, but he glanced around with similar curiosity to mine. Apart from us, there was no one else in the museum; in fact, the turnout was probably just about the same as on any other day.

I stared at the tourist for far too long. Finally, he met my gaze.

"What's wrong?" he asked me uncertainly.

"Nothing. I'm just waiting for someone. At least, I think I am."

His expression grew even more suspicious. I wasn't sure if I was really going to meet someone, but it seemed logical. How else would Ewa give me another file? She wouldn't risk hiding it in Obi-Wan's robe or any other place, because she'd have no way of knowing how long it would take me to get to Witaszyce. But for the same reason, she wouldn't be able to send someone to meet me. And yet, after a while I couldn't help but think that the man standing next to me was here because Ewa had asked him to come.

"I think it's you I'm waiting for," I said.

I sounded crazy, but I wasn't going to worry about it. I continued to look at the tourist, not sure how he'd act. His facial expression didn't change, which could mean anything.

It occurred to me that I might as well have talked to someone from the staff. If I was going to make a fool of myself, I could start with that.

"What do you mean?" the man asked.

He didn't sound surprised, but rather, like someone who wanted to make sure this was no mistake. Or maybe I heard what I wanted to. Maybe I wanted to get the next part of the recording so much that my mind was playing tricks on me.

Anyway, I had no choice and nothing to lose.

"That Ewa gave you something for me," I said.

"What, exactly?"

I felt a tingling sensation down my neck. His answer clearly suggested that I was not mistaken. I turned to him and gave him a long look again. "I suppose it's a flash drive."

"And you're not wrong."

I raised my eyebrows but couldn't say a word.

"But before you ask me anything, you need to know that giving it to you is the only thing I've agreed to."

"I understand."

"Don't count on anything else."

I nodded.

"No more questions, no more digging – none of that. I don't know anything about anything, anyway."

"Sure," I said. But I had no intention of letting him go. I figured as soon as he'd given me the drive, I'd press him and squeeze everything I wanted to know out of him. Who was he? How did he know Ewa? How had he found out I would be right here, right now?

Actually, I may have known the answer to that last question. Connecting the flash drive in Wrocław could have infected the hard drive of my laptop. The software could be designed so that my machine would send a signal. A short ping to the correct IP address would suffice.

The man gave me another spider-printed flash drive, and I palmed it quickly like it was a precious relic. I put it in my pocket and got down to business.

"How do you know Ewa?" I asked.

He turned away and didn't answer, but before he moved to the exit I grabbed him by the wrist. He didn't seem surprised. Had Ewa prepared him for the fact that I wouldn't give up so easily?

He gave me a hostile look and glanced at my hand. "I said no questions."

"I don't give a shit what you said," I replied, tightening my hold on him.

I thought he'd push me away and I'd see clear aggression in his eyes, but I was wrong. The man didn't seem likely to lash out, although that would be perfectly justified at the moment.

"Let go," he said.

I wanted to laugh. If he knew anything about my case, he should realize that I wouldn't give up until I got some answers from him.

There was, of course, a chance that he knew nothing about the disappearance. But he could still explain a few things to me – who he was, how he knew my fiancée and why she'd trusted him enough to hand over the flash drive.

"Let go, man!"

"No way."

He tried to pull himself free, but I wouldn't let him. It occurred to me that if we came to blows, it would be impossible to say who would have the upper hand. Neither of us was particularly muscular. But I had one strong asset.

I was desperate.

"What?" he asked, looking around anxiously. "You gonna fucking torture me?"

"I just want to know who–"

"I don't know anything, understand?"

"You must know something or you wouldn't be here!"

"I was just supposed to give you that flash drive, that's all."

"Oh, yeah? How did you know when to get here?"

"I got a message."

"What message? From who?" I asked through clenched teeth. "How? Come on. You do know something."

Suddenly I noticed profound anxiety in his eyes. He looked around and then opened his mouth a little bit. I realized he saw someone behind my back. I turned with an irrational, idiotic hope that I would see Ewa, that she had planned it all so that we would meet here and now, to make it all end here. But instead, I saw a museum employee looking at us with concern. Then I realized that I was still holding my interlocutor's wrist.

Before I could attempt to explain, though, the man took advantage of my inattention and broke away, heading for the exit. I followed him.

"Wait a minute!" the employee said, coming to stand in my way.

Ewa's messenger looked over his shoulder and ran out into the hallway.

I had no intention of explaining to the museum official that it would be best if he let me through. I just pushed him away and rushed after the man. I ran outside and looked around frantically.

The messenger was already at the gate to the palace area. I chased him, not sure if I could catch up with him. He didn't look athletic, but he was slimmer than me. He may not have worked out regularly, but he was in much better shape than I was.

I chased him towards a small square on the other side of the street, but at the last moment he turned and disappeared behind one of the crumbling buildings. When I turned the corner, I realized I'd lost him. I'd stopped just for a moment, but that had been enough for him to escape. Even if I saw him now, I'd never catch up with him.

I bent over and put my hands on my knees, thinking maybe I should go for a short run from time to time instead of playing *FIFA*. Maybe then I'd have been able to catch up with the messenger and find out who he was and why he was helping Ewa.

They must have known each other well, and she certainly trusted him. He wasn't some random guy she'd paid to appear at a certain place and at a certain time. They must have been close. Otherwise, he wouldn't have gone to so much trouble to deliver the message. He must have realized that I was going to try to get something out of him.

But really, how far was I prepared to go? I didn't know. Perhaps I should thank fate for not offering me the chance to find out. And I could still trust Ewa, like I had before.

Just like when we'd been together.

Only now this trust seemed too far-reaching. I'd lived with a person who was hiding important facts from me, who had grown up in a family of criminals – the worst kind, at that, those that wear suits and ties instead of carrying clubs and knives.

I closed my eyes and stayed still for a while. Then I wiped sweat off my forehead and straightened myself out.

I had no choice but to rent a room somewhere, sit down with my laptop and listen to the message that Ewa had prepared for me. Perhaps the last one.

I didn't really have a choice of location. As far as I knew, there was only one place around here where I could spend the night: the hotel in the palace, from which I'd run a moment ago.

Hoping not to come across the museum employee who'd seen me with the scarred man, I went to the reception desk and paid a little over a hundred zloty for a single room that had everything I needed: a bathroom and wifi access.

I sat in front of a small desk by the wall and opened my laptop. When I plugged the flash drive into the USB port, a signal sounded indicating that I had a text message. I didn't have time for Kasandra now. Whatever she wanted, it had to wait.

I entered the same password that opened all the other doors for me, and then looked at the lonely AAC file in the folder. Ewa had titled it "At the grave of those who showed us".

At the grave of those who showed us.

We shed most tears not at the graves of those we know best, but those who made us know ourselves better. Those who showed us who we really are. That's why we miss musicians and writers so much when they pass away. Both give us insight into our own souls. But this doesn't apply just to the famous and the appreciated; in my case, it also applied to my parents – even though I didn't exactly have a model relationship with either of them.

Their death made me know myself.

I re-evaluated all the assumptions that had been the foundation of my existence, with maybe one exception: you. You've always been the backbone that held together everything else in my life.

Remember that when you're judging my choices. I made them because you gave me such a strong foundation to stand on. At least for a while.

After my parents' accident, it immediately became clear what had actually happened, even though the police and the prosecutor's office kept quiet about it. This was normal procedure under such circumstances, and in the end proceedings against people responsible for the assassination were instigated.

But not only did I already know what had happened; I also had confirmation from the police.

I met a young investigating officer, Tomasz Prokocki. He told me what had happened and left no doubt as to who was involved.

My parents had been sentenced to death by Cayman. He knew that he would lose everything because of my father, but freedom was probably one of the least *important things for him. He could have continued his operation from prison – but only if he managed to save his organization. And there was no chance of that. My father knew too much and had enough documents to convict most members of that criminal enterprise.*

All of that evidence disappeared, of course, right after the accident. My parents allegedly had those papers with them in their car, which, as you know, went up in flames after the crash. It was obviously bullshit, but that didn't matter much to Prokocki. He knew there was someone who had an insight into all the material, someone who was well acquainted with the whole procedure organized by the law firm. Someone who could testify in court, not just against Cayman but against his associates, too. That person was, of course, me.

There was also something that Prokocki didn't know about.

My father had taught me more than just where to store plastic bags. He'd also taught me where to look for materials that would help me in a crisis.

He'd made copies of the most important documents, as insurance, and he'd given me everything I needed to know in case of blackmail, kidnapping or any other attempt to intimidate him or my mother.

He just hadn't anticipated the possibility that Cayman would go further and decide to remove the problem the easiest way.

Tomasz Prokocki approached me several times. He first contacted me when my parents were still alive, trying to convince me that my testimony could shed some light on what was happening in the firm. Maybe he'd known about my fraught relationship with my

parents and, together with the prosecutor, wanted to
build an alternative line of indictment against them, or
maybe he'd just thought it was good to have someone
like me as an informant. Anyway, I flat-out refused.
I was focusing on you and me, on our future. I still
didn't want to have anything to do with my father, law
enforcement agencies or the criminal world. But Prokocki
kept trying to convince me, saying that if I testified, the
prosecutor would look even more favourably on my
family. There was also a thinly veiled suggestion that I
was directly involved. I insisted, however, that I didn't
know anything, and finally I told him to leave me alone
once and for all, warning him that he was harassing
an innocent person and that I would report him to his
superiors. I don't think he cared about it too much, but at
least he let it go.

For a while.

He returned after my parents died. He probably
thought it changed everything, and that I would want to
take revenge on those who made it look like an accident.

I made it clear to him right away that it didn't change
anything because I knew nothing. For some time, I
convinced myself that I should stay away from the case
at all costs. It seemed to me that if there was nothing that
could bring my parents back to life, I wasn't obliged to do
anything.

I didn't consider all those people who might share
their fate. Or the ones Cayman and his men had killed
before them. They didn't have any scruples, as I later
found out. They trafficked girls from Ukraine, kidnapped
children, took ransoms, destroyed local businesses, broke
up families... There was nothing they wouldn't stoop to.

It took me some time to understand that I could change that.

The deaths of my parents really made me know myself.

I've changed, but only on the inside. You didn't notice anything, because I kept it under my mourning cloak. I suppose if you caught me deep in thought or worrying for no apparent reason, you assumed it was because I'd lost my parents. In reality, however, I was already planning what I would do. Once, I think after we'd watched The Illusionist, I almost told you everything. We were sitting at the Mask, drinking beer. You were eating double-tier chicken toast. I don't remember what I'd ordered. My mind was far away.

I'd already made my decision, but I still wondered when to tell you everything I'd been hiding from you. Sooner or later it had to come out. I wasn't supposed to be an anonymous informant, but to testify in court. There was no way to hide it from you, was there?

And yet you never found out about it.

And I'm sure you're wondering how that was possible. Why didn't I testify? Why did I back out at the last minute?

You'll find out everything. It's long overdue, I know, but hopefully not too late.

When I finally met with Prokocki and told him that I wanted to help him capture Cayman and his group, everything changed. Initially, the detective thought I'd present him with strong but not irrefutable evidence, that it couldn't compete with the evidence my father had collected. But I told him I had everything he needed to convict them. Copies of every document that allegedly burned in the crash.

I don't need to tell you that Prokocki was excited. It was as if he'd bought a lottery ticket to prove to someone

*how ridiculous the idea was, and then suddenly hit the
jackpot.*

*The laborious preparation of the indictment began.
I gave Prokocki all the materials, and he and the
prosecutors started to analyze them.*

*They knew they'd struck gold, and had become even
richer than they'd expected. The documents I gave them
concerned not just Cayman's organization but also people
who collaborated with it from time to time yet weren't on
the books.*

*With a little luck, the investigators would be able to
expose several crime groups. Worst-case scenario, convict
Cayman and his gang, and bring the others to justice.*

*It soon became clear that this would cause a number of
problems for me. We all understood that before long many
people would realize who was behind the conviction.*

*If it had been just about Cayman's circle, it wouldn't
have been that bad. Those people would go to jail. They
wouldn't be able to threaten me, and I could count
on the help of the police if I needed it. But under the
circumstances, the shockwave was too high. We could be
certain that somebody would finally catch my scent.*

*In addition, Prokocki found out that Cayman's shady
henchmen had attended my parents' funeral, and that
somebody'd been watching me ever since – and yes, you
too. The criminals didn't know if we were involved in my
father's dealings, but they had to assume the worst.*

*For some time we had someone tailing us, but
eventually others fell for the appearances I had created
for your sake. Including the people following us.*

*In the end, they gave up. According to Prokocki,
however, the threat still existed – and in hindsight, it's*

hardly surprising that he thought that. While nobody would be staging another accident, as it would be too suspicious, there were many ways to silence me. One of them was a kidnapping.

But was that what happened? No.

Something much worse happened. To this day, I don't know exactly how. Unfortunately, neither did Prokocki, which means that even after ten years the danger is still real.

That's why it's so crucial that you take care of yourself.

You have to stay on the move, Tiger.

I don't put each recording in a different place to make it difficult for you. It's my way of taking care of you, in fact. The best way to escape is to go where you wouldn't normally go.

That way, nobody knows where to find you.

Nobody but me.

The next recording will be the last one, I promise. It'll tell you what happened to me. It's waiting for you in another location, and this one will also disappear after twelve hours. I hope you understand that. If I hadn't told you to change your whereabouts, you would never have done it. You'd be looking for me, or maybe you'd be hiding somewhere where you think it'd be safe.

It wouldn't be. That's all I can tell you. It's not safe anywhere. And I have no doubt that somebody is following you, one way or another.

So trust me one last time and go where we never got to.

When the recording was over, I sat still, holding my breath. Then I blew the air out loudly. Ewa didn't say anything else. It sounded far too laconic.

"Go where we never got to?"

I had no idea what it meant.

12

This time I had to be patient. After sending the first text message with the code, I waited for Werner in vain. I tried again an hour later, taking advantage of Robert's absence. He'd been promising since the morning that he'd do whatever it took, that he would never raise his hand to me again and would give himself up to the police.

But it was all just for show. Did I believe him? No, of course not.

It used to be different, because the circumstances were different. What he was doing to me was progressing gradually, not exploding one day like an unexpected landmine. It had been mounting year by year, taking on a more and more dangerous form.

I should have seen the signs from the very beginning, but I'd been blinded by love.

From our first date, I'd known I was dealing with an overprotective guy. He kept filling up my wine glass, moved the chair for me, asked if the food was good, if I needed anything and if everything was okay. You don't pay attention to such things because they seem so nice.

But then there were other signs. Robert went with me to all my meetings with friends. And he always strove to be the centre of attention. More than that, in fact – he wanted to control conversations, set the tone, suggest topics. When we started to talk about something he wasn't interested in, he always found a way to move on to a different subject.

He was the one who chose what we bought at the supermarket. He was the one who decided where we went on holiday. He always drove the car, never letting me get behind the wheel.

Control freak.

I noticed he was obsessed with control much later than my friends, but isn't that what usually happens when love blurs the view of reality? And I loved Robert. I can't deny it.

Actually, I took some comfort in that awareness; because of that, I can absolve myself. After all, love is a drug. But if that is the case, people get together because they're junkies.

My addiction had stopped a long time ago, and the withdrawal had ended years ago too. Now I was just serving my sentence for what I had done.

But I wasn't going to take it anymore.

An hour after the text was sent, I went into the office. I was sore and every step took a lot of effort. I knew that, despite Robert's blatant declarations, the home security cameras were on, and one of the workers outside was still keeping an eye on me.

My husband had made sure that I wasn't going to report him.

I wasn't planning to, though. I was going to do something much more painful.

As I climbed the stairs, I looked long and hard directly at the worker outside, making it clear that his presence was the reason why I was disappearing into the office. I'd tell Robert he'd been watching me too closely, and I was afraid he'd see the marks. Plus, of course, his presence made me uncomfortable. I wanted to be alone. Every other day, that would not be enough, but after yesterday's beating the catalogue of my rights had significantly expanded. At least for a while.

I sent another code, turned on the RIC and waited. After a while, I wondered why Wern wasn't showing up.

The simplest explanation was that he didn't have internet access, but it might also mean he'd been caught by people he'd slipped away from before.

After a while, I considered another, perhaps even more disturbing possibility – that Damian might have thought it wasn't worth helping me. That I could've scared him away by asking for his assistance. Maybe he'd made a cold calculation and decided that he would lose more on that transaction than he would gain.

But he finally did show up, and I could breathe again.

We talked about inconsequential things for a while, as if we both needed that to get going. I noticed that was our tradition now. Maybe we were looking to distance ourselves from what was really important.

At some point, Damian fell silent.

[Kas] Are you alive?
[Werner] Mostly pretending. But the point is to keep up appearances.

Deep down, I knew he was right. He didn't even know how much he'd hit the nail on the head.

[Werner] It's just that I have to give them up before someone else.
[Kas] What do you mean?

Another silence.

[Werner] There are some things I'd like to tell you.
[Kas] Go ahead.

He started slowly and tentatively, line by line. He told me everything that had happened to him recently, this time without omitting anything – as far as I knew. At first, I was surprised, then increasingly less so. He gradually let me understand why he'd finally decided to tell me everything.

[Werner] As you can see, I have a problem.

[Kas] More than one.

[Werner] As if that's not enough, I just called that bartender from Wrocław.

I stared at the screen, thinking about it.

[Werner] The one I didn't find in the Guinness Pub. The one who was given the flash drive by someone.

[Kas] Yeah, I figured. He didn't answer?

[Werner] He did.

[Kas] So why is this another problem?

[Werner] Because he described to me the client who'd given him that spider-shaped flash drive. And the description matched the man I met at the museum. He also had a scar under his eye. Ewa must really trust him.

I shook my head in disbelief.

[Kas] Is that jealousy?

[Werner] More like concern, because apparently she didn't have many options when choosing her associates. This one doesn't seem like someone you can rely on.

[Kas] But his presence alone confirms Ewa is alive.

[Werner] You think so?

[Kas] Of course. You're right in assuming they must have been close. Otherwise, she would never have trusted him so much. If she was dead, this man would know about it. And he wouldn't have continued his... mission.

[Werner] Maybe you're right.

[Kas] I'm sure I am.

I tapped my fingers on the desktop, taking my hands off the keyboard for a moment. I was wondering if this was the right time to finally dispel some doubts. I finally figured it was.

[Kas] Why are you telling me all this? Especially after J Falkow told you not to trust anyone?

[Werner] Because you're out of the circle of suspicion.

[Kas] Thanks.

[Werner] It's not a compliment, just a statement of fact. Everyone else I know is somehow connected to Ewa, the city or even the region. And not knowing who my opponent is, I can't know who to avoid. Except for you.

[Kas] It's a vote of confidence, though.

[Werner] Maybe. Anyway, I need your help, and you need mine.

Although he was quite effusive, I felt that he wasn't telling me the whole truth.

[Werner] But first, I need to figure out the location of the recording.

[Kas] How did she put it? Where we never got to?

[Werner] Yes.

[Kas] And you have no idea what that would mean?

[Werner] No.

[Kas] But do you realize that this is probably the most obvious thing? Something that you should be able to remember right away?

[Werner] You're not helping. I feel the pressure.

[Kas] Think about it.

[Werner] I never stop.

[Kas] So maybe it's the wrong approach. Try not thinking.

[Werner] Oh, I'm a master at not thinking. That might help.

Apparently, it didn't, because Damian was silent. I looked at the blinking cursor and wondered if it wasn't a good time to have a little brainstorming session.

[Kas] Did your car break down on the way to your vacation? Or something like that?

[Werner] No.

[Kas] Maybe you didn't go up some summit because a storm broke out?

[Werner] Not that, either.

[Kas] So maybe it's some kind of a metaphor?

He didn't answer for a while, and then a line popped up on the screen that made me smile.

[Werner] I think I know what she meant.

[Kas] Bravo. What is it?

[Werner] About Ewa's only fixation, close to my obsession with Spider-Man.

[Kas] I don't understand.

[Werner] She was fascinated by the beginnings of settlement in Poland.

[Kas] Really?

[Werner] Everyone's got a thing. Hers was pretty cute, actually.

[Kas] I can't imagine it could be, but never mind. So what about it?

[Werner] When we were in Jarocin, Ewa pestered us to take the opportunity to go to Biskupin.

[Kas] That's not particularly close.

[Werner] It is if you live in Opole. It would have seemed quite close for us, in fact. We'd already travelled a long way, and Biskupin has all that archaeological stuff. Some prehistoric settlement – an early-Piast village, cottages, bridges, defensive walls… And in the season, they do re-enactments.

[Kas] So she wanted to go, but you and Blicki didn't let her talk you into it.

[Werner] Not for love nor money. But I promised her we'd go there someday.

[Kas] Only you never did.

[Werner] That's right.

I nodded and automatically reached for the glass of Prosecco, realizing suddenly that I'd come up completely unprepared. For the first time in a long time – actually, since I could remember – it had slipped my mind to pour myself a glass of my favourite wine. That thought shouldn't have bothered me, but it was depressing. It made me realize how natural it was for me to drink.

When was the last time I was sober?

No point in thinking about it, not in my position. I needed any tool I could use to help me survive, at least for a while, until I could get out of this hell with Werner's help.

[Kas] Then you know where you need to go to get the last recording.
[Werner] I do.
[Kas] How far are you?
[Werner] I don't know.

I quickly opened Google Maps and entered the route. If Damian had a car and drove quickly, he could be there in an hour and a half. He was less than a hundred kilometres from Biskupin as the crow flew. On the train, though, it would be different.

[Werner] I know that when I get there, I'll have all the answers.
[Kas] Are you sure about that?
[Werner] Absolutely. She promised me.

I nodded again, as if he could see it.

[Werner] And then I'm going to need your help.
[Kas] Ah.
[Werner] What's that supposed to mean?
[Kas] That now I understand why you told me everything. It was just as selfless as jalapenos are sweet.
[Werner] Hmm...
[Kas] Now you've gone all enigmatic?
[Werner] Trust me, I'm smiling.

[Kas] Then why don't you use an emoji instead of telling me about it?

[Werner] I don't know. Somehow it seems inappropriate. It's this black screen and the blinking cursor. I feel as if we're using some kind of text communicator. Or a scriptless BitchX.

[Kas] I don't know what you're talking about.

[Werner] Never mind. Let's go back to the fact that last time I checked, we made an arrangement to barter.

[Kas] Yes, we did.

I thought it was time to get down to business. If Damian was going to help me, I had to act.

[Werner] There can be no question of selflessness. Quid pro quo.

[Kas] Anything but an eye for an eye.

[Werner] Anything but that.

[Kas] Let's get to work, then, Wern. Do you have a bank around there?

[Werner] In Witaszyce? You've got to be kidding me.

I quickly checked whether there was really no bank there. It turned out that the only one was a branch of the Cooperative Bank. I didn't like the look of it much either.

[Kas] Then go to Jarocin. There are several there. Choose one, then set up an account and send me the details.

[Werner] What details?

[Kas] For the transfer, of course.

He didn't reply for a moment, and I thought that whatever he must have been expecting, it wasn't money. From my point of view, financial expenditure wasn't much of a cost. The one I bore was much worse and of a completely different kind.

> [Kas] We'll make some transfers. With one of them you will buy a car, and after you get the last recording, you will come to Pomerania.
> [Werner] To get you?
> [Kas] To get me and my son.

Again, Damian didn't reply for some time, and then wrote that he thought I should tell him a little more than that. So I did.

13

Opening an account didn't take long, but then I had to wait for the ATM card. Kasandra said that the key was to open it now, though, while I was still in Jarocin. That was how I was supposed to confuse those trailing me.

Was anyone actually chasing me? I supposed it was true. If not the police, then certainly the people I expected to hear a little more about in Ewa's next recording.

In the end, I did as Kas recommended, and then I went to Biskupin. I knew that another spider-printed flash drive was waiting for me in the museum, but it was difficult to predict where exactly Ewa had hidden it.

She had to choose a place that would be the most obvious for me. The problem was that we'd never got here, and I didn't really know what would have interested her the most.

I passed the wooden fence and entered the Archaeological Museum, then looked around. In the distance I saw a group of young people with a guide, while on the right there was a patch of land covered with grass, marked with a telling plaque: "Swamp".

Maybe that's where I should start my search. After all, it would be a fitting analogy to my situation.

I moved on along the planked path. I hung around the museum for some time, looking for anything that would trigger some association. I visited the early-Piast village under the assumption that this particular historical period would be the most interesting for Ewa.

Then I went into the museum pavilion. If we'd come here after the festival in Jarocin, I would probably have suffered unspeakable torment at this stage. I wasn't the museum visitor type, as much as anybody is.

Actually, I was only interested in animal skeletons; I paid no attention to all those bowls, ornaments and tools. I was beginning to lose hope when I saw a member of staff. I figured it couldn't hurt to ask.

The boy was a little surprised when I asked him my question.

"You're looking for something... associated with spiders?"

"Yeah," I confirmed. "Loosely."

"In what sense?"

"I've no idea."

He looked at me like I was an idiot. Not that he wasn't justified.

"It could be a cobweb or..." I stopped and shook my head. "Don't you have anything like that here?"

"Associated with spiders?"

"You've already asked."

"It's just that…"

"Never mind," I interrupted and waved him away.

Then I turned towards other exhibits, although I thought that a miniature replica of a settlement from the Lusatian era was hardly useful. It was only after a while that I realized the staff member was still looking at me. Apart from the obvious conclusion that he'd just met a moron, there was something more in his eyes.

"Why did you ask that?" he said, coming up to me.

"Because something was left for me here."

"A flash drive with a spider on it?"

I twitched. So Ewa *had* left a flash drive here for me. I felt unpleasant shivers down my back when I realized that someone had found the disk and took it from where it was supposed to wait for me.

I gave the boy a long look. "Yeah, it's about a flash drive," I confirmed. "Have you found it?"

He nodded, and then pointed to one of the mock-ups. I couldn't see from this distance what was written in the display case, but I assumed it wouldn't tell me anything anyway. Well, it should. Apparently, Ewa was trying to direct me towards that miniature.

"We found this in the temporary exhibition of–"

"Never mind the details," I cut him off, assuming that Ewa had trusted my memory too much.

I didn't even know what interested her the most. She probably told me about it once, but I evidently hadn't been paying much attention. I guess very few people could say otherwise in a similar situation.

"Do you have the drive?" I asked anxiously.

"It's at the ticket office. We thought somebody had lost it and–"

"Thank you," I cut him off, then turned around and headed for the exit.

I felt the boy's confused eyes still on me but, as I was about to find out, the reason for his confusion was not what I'd thought.

"Somebody's already asked about it," he said.

I stopped in my tracks.

"Who?"

"Some guy in his late thirties. Skinny, tall and–"

"Did he have a scar?"

The boy nodded, frowning. "Under his left eye." I felt as if I was walking down a dark alley in an abandoned city and suddenly saw someone out of the corner of my eye. The longer I thought about Ewa's messenger having been there before me, the more anxious I felt.

"When was he here?" I asked.

"This morning."

I looked around like there was a chance I'd see him somewhere.

"He asked the same question as you, but when I told him that the flash drive was waiting at the ticket office, he just walked away."

I blinked nervously.

"No, wait a minute," he added. "He wanted to know if anyone else was asking about the flash drive."

I scratched my head in thought. Maybe I didn't have anything to worry about – the man with the scar had come here to see if I'd already found the right location. He just wanted to make sure everything was going as Ewa intended.

At least, that was what I hoped.

I thanked the boy and walked quickly to the ticket office, where I collected the flash drive without any problem, apologizing for the inconvenience. Two nice attendants assured me that it was no problem and told me we'd all left something somewhere at one time or another.

"Where can I find a hotel in the area?" I asked.

"A hotel…" one of them said, giving my question some thought.

"It could be anywhere. I just need somewhere to stay for the night."

"Ah. Biskupińska Marina would be the closest, but I don't know if they offer anything to individual guests or just groups."

"They have single rooms," said the other attendant.

"Try there, then. And if they don't have anything, try Wenecka Marina."

I thanked her again and left the museum, squeezing the flash drive in my pocket in my sweaty palm. It held the answers to all the questions that plagued me. Literally. All I had to do was plug the device into my laptop and listen to what Ewa had to say to me. I would have done that right away, even sitting under the museum pavilion, but my battered ASUS's dying battery would only last for a moment.

It took me a little over a quarter of an hour to get to the Biskupińska Marina. Luckily, I had no problem with accommodation. Fifty zlotys for one night, breakfast included. That much I could afford, especially since Kasandra must have made a substantial transfer by now.

I didn't know to what extent the version she presented was true. After everything Blitzer and Kliza had told me about her, I rather expected that as far as the Reimanns went, she had the upper hand.

Apparently, though, she didn't. Under the guise of their successes and wealth, she and her husband were hiding a pathological relationship that should have been revealed long ago. Provided, of course, that Kas was telling the truth.

Anyway, I had no choice. If I wanted Kasandra to help me financially when I found Ewa, I had to help her first. And I was going to do it as soon as I found out where to look for my fiancée.

I locked the door, plugged in my laptop and sat on the bed. When the system finally booted up, I checked whether all was in order. The network was working flawlessly. Good. I needed internet access to discuss details with Kasandra tonight.

In the meantime, I was finally able to deal with what the most important thing.

Before I turned off the browser, however, I noticed that the NSI News homepage had refreshed. I raised my eyebrows because I thought for a moment that, somewhere among the latest news, the name of my hometown had flashed up.

And indeed it did.

The article wasn't in the main segment but in one of the side ones, where the latest regional headlines were displayed. This one was entitled "New facts in the Opole murder case".

I looked at the flash drive and then at the screen. I hesitated for a moment, but then, almost against my will, I clicked on the link. As I suspected, it was about Blitz.

The NSI reported that they had identified the person who was likely responsible for the murder. The police were searching but the investigators believe that the suspect had already left the city.

Below was a photo.

My photo.

Along with all the relevant information and a general description, it said that I was wanted for murder. I stared at the screen in disbelief. For some reason, I thought whoever was behind all this wouldn't go that far.

My throat went dry when I realized those people must be really desperate. And that meant I'd come close to solving the case, much more than I could have expected a few days ago.

I glanced at the flash drive and felt the blood drain from my face. I was afraid, but not because I was now being hunted across the country, and not because I could go to jail. I was afraid that I wouldn't have time to learn the story of my missing fiancée. Any moment, somebody could inform the police where I was. I'd been seen by a lot of people, though fortunately in a lot of different places, which would surely confuse the trail. Ewa had organized things well by having me run from one place to another.

The problem came down to the employees of the local museum. The boy in the pavilion may not have looked at me very closely, but the two polite women at the ticket office would certainly remember me.

I was overwhelmed by the feeling of a direct, close threat. It was as if the investigators weren't just following me but waiting in the hallway. My heart pounded like a jackhammer and I needed a moment to calm down.

I finally managed to control my shaking hands, wondering what I should do. More than anything else, I wanted to check the recording, but maybe it was more sensible to get out of here as soon as possible, to lose those trailing me while I still could.

Yeah, I guess so.

But it had been a long time since I'd listened to reason. So I plugged the spider-printed flash drive into the laptop and sat with my back against the headboard. Looking at the computer in my lap, I pressed my finger to the touchpad.

The file was called "Ice cream on a hot day". I double-clicked it gingerly, as the seemingly innocent name made me unaccountably concerned. I then took a deep breath and sat up straight.

I was ready to learn the story that had been waiting for me for ten years. The story of Ewa.

Ice cream on a hot day.

The day I was persuaded to testify against Cayman and his organization wasn't the worst day of my life, but it was certainly one of them. I made a huge mistake, and all I can say to justify it is that I was deeply convinced that I was doing what my father had wanted.

But it's not like that at all, Tiger.

I want to think that's what it was all about, but really it came down to something completely different. I was driven purely by a desire for revenge. I wanted to avenge my parents, and the only way I could do that was to hand over all the evidence to the police and take a seat in the witness box in the courtroom.

I agreed and started to testify before we all understood how far this case could go. With each new piece of evidence discovered, the circle of people involved in Cayman's activities grew.

But that wasn't the main problem. The main problem was that investigators couldn't identify some of them. They were mentioned in recorded conversations, featured in the documents, but the clues pointing to them were so vague that they stayed at large even after the gang started to break up.

My seemingly simple plan to get back at Cayman began to get complicated, even to turn against me.

You know revenge is sweet, and it's a dish best served cold, right? Of course you do. You don't have to read Mario Puzo or watch The Godfather to know that saying. After all, it's basically a description of ice cream, isn't it? And it is exceptionally fitting, especially when we eat it on a hot summer's day. Initially it brings relief, almost euphoria, but ultimately not only is it fattening and unhealthy but it rots your teeth. The decay of my life had begun much earlier, but it was that last portion of ice cream that was pivotal.

During the trial, the court granted me the status of an incognito witness. Each of the participants in the proceedings knew that if my information leaked, I would suffer severe consequences. And I wasn't the only one – you were also in danger. Perhaps even more than me, in fact, because it would be you who Cayman's people would attack in order to force me to withdraw my testimony. But nobody ever got to you. I took care of it.

That didn't mean the gang members weren't looking for me. On the contrary, the longer the trial took, the more people were detained, the more efforts were made to identify the anonymous witness who'd brought the whole group down.

In those days, criminals were still willing to turn state's evidence. They don't do that anymore because now

*they've realized how much of a problem that actually
is. They have to change their whole lives, and in return
they get just scraps from the state. They're not relocated
to well-appointed villas or provided with lavish lifestyles;
they can only count on a mere fraction of what they once
had. They should be guaranteed better conditions to
encourage them to flip and testify against other criminals,
of course, but the authorities don't want to spend money
on that. And we all suffer as a consequence.*

*My point is that they can count on quite a lot,
anyway – at least when compared to incognito witnesses
like me. When I testified, I had neither special protection
nor any guarantee that the police would take care of me
in an emergency.*

*They changed that policy a few years ago, back in
2015, passing a new law to ensure such a witness is
granted twenty-four-hour police protection. The state
offers a new place of residence and even financial
assistance to cover basic life and housing needs. It's
hardly a life of luxury, but more and more people at risk
are choosing to take advantage of the opportunity.*

I didn't have that chance – at least, not to that extent.

*It soon became clear that Cayman's men would finally
get me. They knew by then that the incognito witness
wasn't anyone from their circle, so they had to check
everyone from the outside that had worked with the
organization over the years.*

*Eventually, they found me. It was at the end of the
trial you had no idea about, and yet which cast such a
shadow all over our lives.*

*As soon as they found me, they weren't going to wait
long.*

Those guys from the Highlander were from Lower Silesia. It was their first time in Opole and they were told never to go back there again. If they'd known how much I'd brought to the case and how important I was to the police, they might have thought twice before attacking us in front of the Sneering Lodge, but they weren't aware of what I really knew. They just assumed I was the snitch and that the best solution would be to intimidate me. Once in a while, it's good to show who's in charge, who has the upper hand and who's the insignificant pawn.

How better to degrade a woman than by raping her in front of her fiancé? Perhaps they asked themselves that question at the time, laughing over a beer and watching us. I imagine their degenerate minds were ecstatic when they realized that it happened to be the day you decided to propose.

The rape and the beating were supposed to be a warning. But they became more than that: they redefined our lives, reshaped us into two completely different people.

Even after all these years, the memories of those events sometimes resurface. I try to bury them as deep as I can – I've tried a lot of drugs, and in the end I found out it's the ones you get without a prescription that work best. I know it's like running away from a burning building straight into icy water you can't get out of, but it's still some kind of rescue. Even if it only makes me delay the inevitable.

The rape went on forever, or at least it felt that way. At the beginning I was in unspeakable pain, although it was probably not just because of what was happening to my body. It was about more than that. It was about me. They destroyed all of me in the blink of an eye.

I don't want to talk about it, and you shouldn't want to hear about it. I have no doubt that you've been turning it all over in your head for the last ten years.

Anyway, you were there, you saw what happened. They destroyed the person you used to be in those first few moments.

I saw you fight for me; I saw you try your best to stop them. And I don't know whether it was more painful to know what they were doing to me, or that you couldn't help me in any way.

At some point, you lost consciousness. So did I, kind of. My eyes were open, I was looking at the night sky, but I was no longer in my body. They were hitting it like I was an empty dummy, panting like animals, grabbing my breasts and buttocks, then throttling me.

In the end, the first one came back. When he entered me again, I didn't feel anything. It felt like I was no longer a human being but a corpse.

When they finished, they warned me not to talk about Cayman or his organization anymore or they'd be back. They added something else, but I couldn't focus enough to hear what it was. I'm sure it was another pathetic threat.

In the meantime, I felt my own threats slowly rising inside me. Threats directed at them.

I didn't realize it then, but in hindsight I know that it was then that I made my decision. I was going to do everything I could to put them in jail.

I don't know how long it took me to pull my trousers up and crawl over to you. I tried to wake you up, but you were out for the count. I took your pulse, checked your breathing and reached for the phone.

I wanted to call an ambulance, but it dawned on me that if I acted like everyone else in such a situation, things would follow the usual, well-known scenario. The police would try to keep me safe, the rapists would eventually be captured and convicted, and for the rest of our lives we'd be looking over our shoulders, fearing an attack that could come any time.

I couldn't let that happen. You didn't deserve that.

Instead of an ambulance, I called Prokocki. When I told him what had happened, he wanted to send in all the squad cars in the area. I stopped him in time. Plus, I convinced him that we had a perfect opportunity to create a completely new scenario, one that would put an end to everything once and for all, and we had to seize it.

I decided to disappear. With the help of the police, I would start a new life by taking on a new identity and pretending to be missing. That's the only thing that could make Cayman's men leave me alone – me and you both.

I wasn't planning to spend ten years in hiding. I thought it would only be for a few months, maybe a year. I knew I was going to cause you a lot of pain, but there was no other way out.

And there was something else, Tiger. Something I haven't wanted to admit for a long time.

I'd say I was ashamed, but that would be an understatement. I was utterly humiliated. I felt dirty. I felt... I can't even find the right word to express how I felt in my body. I'd love to rip it off myself, to purify my soul in some way, and then begin a new life in a completely different body. It repulsed me, made me feel that there was nothing in the world as disgusting as my reflection in the mirror.

But I knew it would pass. Or, if not, that at least it would become bearable.

But at first, I couldn't stand the thought of you looking at me. It's impossible to explain it, and probably also impossible to understand it, if you haven't gone through it yourself. Nobody should ever go through that.

I thought those several months of separation would save our relationship, and that when we met again we'd be able to start building our lives anew, instead of looking at them gradually crumble and fall apart.

It was an illusion, that belief, but it only strengthened my resolve to do what I was planning. I was guided by a desire to keep us safe. And to get my revenge.

Not just for my parents now, but for myself too.

I needed to make sure that those people would suffer.

I presented my plan to Prokocki when he arrived. He didn't call for an ambulance or backup – he knew how much was at stake. By putting Cayman and his men in jail, not only would we break up the whole gang, we'd also save many lives.

It wasn't the worst day of my life, but it was the hottest. And the ice cream I got to cool me down gave me a moment's rest. But then the problems started.

Why didn't I come back after a few months? If you've looked into what happened to Cayman, I'm sure you know he was convicted. He's now serving a sentence in Strzelce Opolskie, along with most of his men. Not all of them, unfortunately.

Prokocki prepared a new life for me, as if I was a crown witness. I'm not sure how much of that was off the books, but only a few people knew about the whole thing. I could have counted them on the fingers of one hand.

I suppose the ministry agreed; politicians will accept anything if a good media narrative can be spun out of it. And the breaking-up of Cayman's gang had far-reaching consequences, and not just in Lower Silesia and the Opole region. Creating a new identity for one girl wasn't a huge cost for the state.

Especially since it was only supposed to be temporary.

As it turned out, though, things were more complicated than we'd all thought. Though perhaps we should have expected that, given how long Cayman had been able to operate with impunity.

It should have been clear to us that he had someone on the force.

But we only realized that when we had some... well, problems with detentions. Someone tipped off some of the highest-ranking people in Cayman's organization, and they not only managed to dodge arrest but to even flee the country.

Some of them are still out there to this day.

And the mole in the police that informed the criminals was never found. But one thing was certain: if that man ever learned about me, he wouldn't give up. He'd know at once that I was the nail in Cayman's coffin, and he would move heaven and earth to find me.

Eventually, my temporary scenario became permanent. And I would stay unfound.

I paused the recording for a moment and looked out the window. I thought about the policeman who'd helped me escape from Chrząstowice, the one who'd told me I shouldn't trust anyone. Could he have been Cayman's agent? No, that didn't make any sense. After what I'd just heard, I had to reevaluate my approach to the Opole police force.

Apparently, we were on the same side. And in that case, J Falkow could have been Prokocki's trusted man. Maybe that's how the commissioner had tried to help me.

But if so, why was I being pursued now?

I shook my head, recognizing that further answers were waiting for me later in the recording. There wasn't much of it left, which seemed strange because Ewa certainly had a lot more to say to me. But maybe she wanted to do it in person? Maybe I was about to hear instructions that would finally help me find her? That had to be it. The thought was as invigorating as it was terrifying.

Who was I going to meet? A fiancée I knew well, or the person she'd become after ten years? And if the former, could I even think that I really knew her?

Too many questions. Fortunately, the answers were at my fingertips. Yet someone could still prevent me from learning them at any moment.

I peered at the door, wondering how much time I had left before somebody came up with a clue. Assuming the information about Blitz's murder hadn't already alerted the public to my appearance, perhaps I had enough time to get to the end of Ewa's story.

I clicked *Play*.

I hid in Wielkopolska, although if it was up to me, I would probably have decided to go to the mountains. You know how I loved them. But maybe that's why the decision was made for me. It was all about never finding me.

And nobody ever did.

So why are you listening to this recording now? What set the whole machine in motion?

Not what but who.

I'm the one who made the decision. When we meet, I'll explain everything. For now, all you need to know is that I showed up in Wrocław for a reason. I knew that Blitzer wouldn't miss a concert by his favourite band. Although I've never really liked the Foo Fighters, they ended up changing my life with their music.

When I attended that concert, I set things in motion. More dominoes started to fall.

I thought I'd set most of them up myself, but it wasn't exactly like that. I've done everything I could to keep Cayman's people from finding out what was going on. At that stage you may have already guessed that there were some… complications. However, the consequences of my actions aren't as obvious as you might think. But I'll explain everything to you when we meet.

Are you ready for this, Tiger? If so, I'll be waiting for you. In a place that only you will recognize, and at a time only you will know.

I waited to hear the rest of it. Ewa had given me far too little to guess what she meant. I looked anxiously at the progress bar, which indicated that there were three seconds to go before the end of the recording.

"Come on," I said. "Say something more."

It felt as if time stopped.

Another second passed.

"Come on!" I pleaded.

But that was it. The recording was over; there was nothing else. I sat dumbly, feeling like Ewa had just slapped me. A place that only I would recognize? A time only I would know? What was that supposed to mean?

I had absolutely no idea.

It was all so vague, I couldn't even imagine coming up with a solution. I sat there, frozen, wondering frantically if I'd missed something.

Finally, I shook my head and decided to listen to the recording again from the beginning. I no longer thought that time was pressing and I should leave the Biskupin area as soon as possible.

I wanted to open the file, but after I double-clicked it, the window with the contents of the flash drive disappeared. I swore, not even deluding myself that it might be a coincidence. Ewa had made sure the file would self-destruct.

I put my laptop aside, got out of bed and started pacing the small room, racking my brain for a solution.

Nothing. I couldn't think of a damn thing. I stopped by the window and looked out, trying to switch off my whirling thoughts for a moment. The best ideas come to mind when you don't try to force them.

But it took the right conditions to do that – peace and calm.

Both were out of the question when I saw two police officers in front of the building talking to a restaurant employee. The waiter scratched his head, then after a while he pointed straight at my window.

14

I didn't have any problems setting up a few new bank accounts. Actually, I would have started transferring funds from the company account long ago if I'd had somewhere to put the money, but I knew that Robert would have noticed immediately if I opened an account in my own name, and it wouldn't end well for me.

At the same time, I had no one I could depend on enough to trust them with my rescue fund. That was what I called it, although in fact it was much more important that the name implies.

All the transfers I ordered were meant to ensure me and Wojtek a comfortable life for many years. Away from Robert. Away from the horror that at the moment only I had to endure, but which could also affect my child at some point in time.

I couldn't let that happen.

I knew I could trust Werner, but I held no delusions as to his impeccable character or believed that, if push came to shove, he'd never pinch even a single zloty. I expected that, if the situation forced him, he would be prepared to spend the money I had accumulated.

But he needed my help just as much as I needed his.

I was wondering how he'd managed to discover the subsequent clues that were waiting for him. Every day, I would send an activation code in a text message and then do everything I could to get into the office unnoticed, but Damian never showed up on the RIC. Not once.

At night, I started to worry more and more. I kept track of the situation and knew that the police had put out an APW for him, but I doubted they'd be able to follow his trail so quickly.

He was mainly interested in the southern part of the country, and now he was staying somewhere between Bydgoszcz and Poznań. He should be safe there, at least for a while.

The bank account he was supposed to access to buy a used car was already active. Still, no withdrawal had been made. By that evening, I was already very anxious. I realized how close my entire plan was to crashing and burning. It basically hinged on just one person.

Just before Robert had come home, I set the alert on the RIC and went downstairs. The system would notify me when there was an attempt to log in. Without the activation code it would fail, but that didn't matter. It just needed to know that Damian was trying to contact me. I hadn't used such a method before because it was too risky. A text message at the wrong time could catch Robert's attention. No, not *could*; it would for sure. And he wouldn't give up until he found out who the message was from.

I couldn't afford to make a mistake. Not at a time like this.

While I waited for my husband to come, I put the dishes in the dishwasher and cleaned the kitchen. Robert didn't like to see it in disarray when he came home after a whole day. It was rare for him to stay at work for so long, but from time to time he had no other choice. He was always irritated when it happened, and he took out his irritation not just on me but on all his subordinates as well, sometimes even on random people. It was as if the fact that he was unable to keep an eye on me stopped him from functioning normally.

For me, it meant that our clash that evening would be even worse. Fortunately, it didn't happen often, because it was usually Robert who decided who to meet and when.

But sometimes he had to replenish his stock of what he was selling, what provided us with such a lavish lifestyle – and ultimately, what allowed me to make a series of transfers to my rescue fund.

If I'd done that using only legal sources, Robert would have discovered it immediately, but since the funds came from criminal activity, I didn't have to worry. It would take several days before my husband discovered that I had taken his hard-earned dirty money.

It appeared in Robert's bank accounts because of *szaraina*. Although Robert hadn't patented the drug's name, most dealers in Poland knew who had the exclusive right to distribute it.

Szaraina. It sounded harmless, maybe even a little infantile. And that was exactly the effect Robert wanted to achieve.

In the US, the drug was known by a different name: grey death. It probably helped to market it, or maybe the opioid mixture had yet another name in the streets, one unknown to outsiders. I didn't look for more information on the subject; I didn't even know if it was the only thing Robert traded. Probably not.

There was no one recipe for *szaraina*. The ingredients differed depending on how much the customer was willing to pay. In its basic version, it was a blend of fentanyl and carfentanyl, with a splash of heroin. The effect was several times stronger than after the regular "compote" – crude heroin made from poppy straw – and it cost much less to produce.

In the US, grey death use was already taking its toll. Doctors warned that more and more people were hospitalized after overdosing on it, which was allegedly much easier than with other drugs. No great surprise, considering carfentanyl was used to put elephants to sleep. And as if that wasn't enough, it looked like manufacturers had been adding whatever they fancied into each subsequent batch. The only thing that mattered was that grey death looked right and buyers could recognize what they were buying. The effect of mixing individual ingredients was of no particular interest to anyone. Robert didn't care, either. The only thing that mattered to him was that the dealers paid on time.

He was a local tycoon, and over the years he'd built his public image in such a way as to have a number of businesses that helped him to launder his dirty money. For some time now, everything had been self-sufficient and worked like a well-oiled machine.

We'd made the most on real estate, although our operations had nothing to do with legal trade. Robert's experience of working for the Customs Service was worth a lot, and his idea was very simple – several of his companies offered low-interest loans, provided they were secured against real estate. Customers were selected on the basis of their inability to pay off their mortgages. When they missed their payments, their houses or flats were seized for next to nothing and resold at exorbitant prices.

There were many such front businesses, and Reimann Investigations was one of them. The agency wasn't bringing much profit, but it helped legalize part of the income from the sale of grey death.

I didn't feel comfortable thinking that I would be using that money to start a new life with Wojtek, but I had no choice. Anyway, things had already been set in motion. The money was in the right accounts, set up in Damian's name.

Now all I had to do was get him to withdraw everything at the right time.

Then I could run away.

I kept telling myself that, trying to lift my spirits. I needed it to get through this evening somehow. When Robert walked in, I already knew it would be bad. Mostly because I couldn't hear our son with him.

Robert peered into the kitchen and smiled softly at me. I smiled back, went up to him and kissed him.

"Where's Wojtek?" I asked.

"He's sleeping at a friend's house."

I raised my eyebrows inquiringly, trying not to show any resentment. "I didn't know anything about it."

"They came up with the idea at school."

"You could have–"

"What?" he snarled. "Called you and asked your opinion? What's the big deal? He asked me and I said yes. I don't have to consult you about everything, do I?"

I opened my mouth but he didn't give me a chance to talk.

"It's just one night at a friend's," he added. "What are you complaining about?"

"I'm not."

"And you look at me like I fucking killed your mother."

"It's just…"

"What?" he hissed, coming near me.

He didn't even take off his jacket. He'd barely had time to put the briefcase down, and he was ready to beat me up. This night would be different from any other night. I understood that already.

Just a few hours ago, I thought I was about to run away. Werner was on Ewa's trail. I'd secured the funds. All he had to do was show up here, and Wojtek and I could disappear.

I would leave no traces. None.

And Robert would never find Werner. From his perspective, it would be an anonymous, random guy I had no connection to. He'd never know he was the one who helped me get out of this living hell.

Which meant he would never be able to force me to go back.

Meanwhile, Damian went missing without a trace and the incident I was about to go through–

No, I shouldn't use euphemisms, at least not in my own mind. I was about to be tortured. I had to say it openly to myself.

And tonight it would be torture I might not survive. I saw it in my husband's eyes when he looked at me. He was angry, he had a grudge, and he needed to release all those emotions that had been building up in him throughout the day.

"What the *fuck* is your problem?" he demanded. "I can't decide for myself whether my son has a sleepover or not?"

"It's just that–"

"Just *what?*" he interrupted, grabbing my wrist.

I pretended I didn't even notice it. If I even looked at his hand or moaned in pain, he'd get angrier. He'd take that as another unfounded insult.

"No pyjamas," I said quietly. I felt pathetic. But if I ever had a good reason to be submissive, it was that night. I had to survive it in the best possible condition to be ready for Werner's arrival. "No toothbrush or–"

"Fucking hell," Robert said, letting go of my arm. He spread out his hands. "You're just unbelievable. Can't he sleep in his fucking pants for once? Or not brush his teeth? Do you even hear what you're saying?"

He hit me in the face without giving me time to react. Then he looked at his hand as if it belonged to someone else. He took a step back, looking confused. I think he was surprised himself that he'd started so early.

It was only after a while that I realized it wasn't that. He looked at the glass door to the terrace and I realized he was just worried that one of the employees could see us.

But there was no one outside. If someone did happen to notice my husband hit me, they walked away, not wanting to get into trouble. It was a common enough occurrence in our home.

It was a well-known secret what was going on here, yet none of the staff had the courage to act. Was I surprised? No. They knew exactly who they were working for, and some of them were staying in the country illegally. They had families to support and had no other options. I didn't blame them for turning a blind eye.

We didn't have any friends to alert the police. At this stage, we were only in contact with people who worked with my husband. And they knew how to keep a secret.

There was no one who could help me. No one but Werner.

Robert dropped his jacket and sat at the table. For a moment he was silent, and as usual I started deluding myself that maybe this time it would end there. But when my husband looked up, I knew I should have thought better.

"Sometimes I wonder how I can even stand you," he said.

I didn't say a word.

"I work like a motherfucker, and then I come back home and…"

He paused, shook his head, and then sighed deeply. I didn't know if this spectacle was meant for him or for me. Whenever he did that, he made it look like something switched in his head.

"You should support me."

"I support you."

"Bullshit. Instead of helping me, relieving me, taking the whole fucking burden off me, you act like you're trying to kill me."

He looked around, anxiously rubbing his neck.

"Where the fuck is the food?"

"I thought I was on my own."

"What?" he snarled. "You thought I'd be cooking after spending all day at work?"

"We can order something."

"Order yourself a fucking coffin," he murmured under his breath. He thought he was making a simple joke, but to me it sounded like a real threat, one I should take very seriously right now. He was behaving much differently than usual.

Plus, he must have known what was going on, or he wouldn't have sent Wojtek to stay with a friend.

He usually seemed surprised at how quickly the situation escalated. Most days, it was as if he really believed he could stop himself. Today, though, was not one of those days. Today, he must have known in advance that he was going to indulge himself.

Maybe he thought it was the only way he could handle the tension. Maybe he'd finally come to grips with what he was really like.

It didn't matter. What mattered was that he was ready for anything that night.

I looked for something I could defend myself with. I knew knives or other sharp objects were out of the question. I could do serious damage to him, and it would end tragically for both me and Wojtek. Robert's associates would take care of that.

"What's wrong with you?" he growled.

"Nothing."

"So what are you looking around for?"

"I was wondering what to cook for you."

"Maybe you should've thought about it earlier. To welcome your husband home the right way, just once. Eh? Don't you think I deserve that?" He stood up and looked down at me. "For all that I do for you, it's the least you could do." He paused and shook his head. "Other wives don't act like that."

Other wives don't have husbands like you, I added to myself. And even if they did, they managed to relieve all that tension in bed. I didn't have the slightest chance of that. In all our years of our marriage, we'd slept together only a few times. Robert didn't need sex. He satisfied himself in a completely different way. Sometimes I even thought he had never been attracted to me. The fact that I even got pregnant seemed like a miracle.

Initially, his asexuality was a nuisance, but ultimately it was a blessing for me. I could easily imagine what would have happened if, in addition to being beaten, there had been other forms of physical abuse.

"Get up," Robert said.

I did what he said. There was no point protesting.

Before I could say anything, he grabbed my collar and dragged me to the middle of the kitchen, ignoring my pleas, and then held my head over the sink with one hand. With the other, he reached into one of the cabinets, took out a large pot, dropped it into the sink and turned on the tap.

"I'll show you how cooking's done, you cunt."

"Robert..."

"Maybe then you'll remember something."

"Listen to me, please..."

"No. You're the one who's going to listen, you lazy bitch. And you'll learn that, instead of drinking your fucking Prosecco all day long, you could take care of your husband from time to time."

When the water started to overflow from the pot, I felt a sudden jerk, and before I knew what my husband was doing, the water had already filled my mouth. I felt my neck hit the rim of the pot.

Robert pressed harder. I tried to get away, but I couldn't get free. He was much stronger than I was, and I didn't stand a chance against him. I was running out of air and started thrashing like I was possessed.

But he kept pressing harder and harder.

I almost got a lungful of water. At the last moment Robert dragged my head up, looked at me, snorted and then slapped me hard. He was mumbling about how I looked like the most pathetic whore in the world.

I only had time to cough out water before he threw me to the floor, and I hit my head. There was ringing in my ears. Then he grabbed me by the throat and squeezed.

First, I felt a sharp pain that made me realize I'd injured myself on the rim of the pot. Then a dull ache spread across my chest and I knew I was beginning to run out of air again. Robert shook me, mumbling a litany of curses. I didn't register any of them.

At one point he let go and I turned my face to the side, coughing. He disappeared from view for a while, but came back holding a knife. He leaned over me and put the blade to my throat.

The Gerlach kit was back. As I had expected.

Robert said something about teaching me how to disembowel someone. I tried not to listen, knowing his words had about as much value as the ones I'd hear later when he apologized.

If that ever happened. I had reason to fear that this time it would be different. And after a while Robert gave me another one.

He grabbed my head with one hand, covering my eyes as if he couldn't stand my gaze. His grip was strong. It felt like my temples were clenched in the jaws of a vice.

Robert moved the blade on my neck. I felt a tearing pain, and I moaned loudly.

"Shut up! Shut up!" he roared.

I tried to get him off me, but he was far too strong.

"Calm down or I'll fucking kill you! You understand, bitch?"

He threw the knife aside, but he screamed louder and louder, spat on me and started punching me. I had a vague idea that he was waiting for that moment – the moment when he lost control and could give in to his base instincts.

I felt like there would be no end to the blows. Robert was hitting my breasts hard, which he'd never done before, and the pain was unbearable. He shook me like he was trying to expel a demon from me. Time and again I hit my head against the floor, hoping I would finally lose consciousness.

Sooner or later, I would, of course. I just hoped it would happen sooner.

At some point, he paused and I looked into his eyes, searching for his customary, pathetic repentance, but there was nothing there. He was still angry. I realized this was just an interlude.

My husband had grown tired from the effort of torturing me and needed to take a breather.

He went to the fridge, pulled out a bottle of Prosecco and then, mumbling under his breath, he swung the bottle and smashed it on the floor next to me. I felt the cool drops falling on my cheeks. Shards of glass scattered across the floor.

Then I heard a distinctive hissing: Robert had opened a bottle of beer. He turned to look out at the sea, and saw my chance. I started crawling towards the stairs, ignoring the pain in my hands and knees from the shards of broken glass. I didn't even feel that I was hurting my hands and leaving bloody marks behind. I knew I had to get to the office before it was too late.

Robert still had his back to me. He was talking to himself in a continuous murmur, drinking from the bottle. I guessed he wouldn't be interested in me until he'd finished it, though considering how quickly he drank, I didn't have much time. When I got to the stairs, I grabbed the railing and stood up.

I was dizzy so the first few steps were difficult, but then it got a little better. Upstairs, I had to hold on to the wall so I wouldn't fall over. From the corner of my eye, I saw the trail of red marks I'd left behind.

I went into the office and sent the activation code to Werner. I had to get him over here straight away. There was no time to waste; I needed help right now.

I heard a scream from downstairs. Angry as the roaring of a wounded animal. Then I heard Robert run up the stairs.

"Please…" I moaned, looking at the cursor blinking on the black background.

15

My mobile vibrated in my pocket again. I had no doubt who was trying to contact me, as only two people knew the number, and my father didn't usually send texts.

I didn't have to reach for the phone to know it was another activation code. I wasn't in a position to use it yet anyway, and besides it wasn't the most important thing right now.

I was driving down the National Road 11 in the direction of Piła, going carefully not only because of the road conditions but also to stick to the speed limit – probably for the first time in my life. It helped that I was driving an old Peugeot 206, whose one-litre engine wasn't built for racing. I'd bought it in Żnin, near Biskupin, right after I'd left the hotel room in panic. I didn't have time to take anything with me but my mobile and my money. I even left my laptop, although if I'd had a moment to think about it, I would have gone back for it.

But all that had mattered to me then was that there were no more files on the flash drives anyway – and that I had to get away as soon as possible. When the cops and the staff member approached my room, I was already gone, rushing through the courtyard towards the entrance gate. I jumped over it, turned right and just ran. I didn't know where I was going, but the destination didn't matter. I passed a red-brick primary school, which brought to mind creepy buildings in the best horror movies, and then raced along a row of identical, somewhat dilapidated detached houses.

I left Biskupin, walking along a small asphalt road between the fields and not even knowing where I would go. Eventually I found myself in the village of Gogółkowo and decided to find out where I was.

The closest bank and the nearest car dealership were in Żnin. It didn't take me long to decide that it was the right direction. I got there after an hour and a half of walking.

It took me some time to arrange the formalities and I was afraid that the police had already managed to trace me.

They couldn't have guessed where I would go, but one look too long would be enough for someone to recognize me and contact the nearest police station along the way.

The smaller the village, the safer I was. People in such places were only interested in themselves and their own affairs. They didn't really care that an alleged killer was at large in the country. So I could safely head towards the town of Piła. I planned to give the city a wide berth, as I had no intention of taking any unnecessary risks. I was on the last stretch; Ewa had to be somewhere near there.

I'd left Wielkopolska for a while, when I'd gone to Żnin, but now I was back in the region. I did not know where she was exactly, but certainly somewhere in the province. Maybe in Piła? No, that was wishful thinking. She hadn't left me any clues. All I knew was that there was a place in Wielkopolska.

A place that only I would recognize.

I still had no idea what that meant. Or why I was the only one who would know the time of the meeting. It made no sense whatsoever. It wasn't associated with any event from our life.

I'd thought about it too hard to come up with anything specific. I'd even translated it into English, and tried to match it to a song – all in vain. If I had access to Google, maybe I could have found a connection, but I was on my own. I couldn't even go to a McDonald's, sit in a corner and use the wifi, and the burner phone I'd bought wasn't a smartphone.

I took out the phone and looked at the display. I wasn't wrong about Kasandra trying to get in touch with me, and not for the first time that day, either. It occurred to me that maybe something happened that I should know about.

Maybe a change of plans? Well, if everything went according to plan, I'd be able to ask her about it shortly.

Kas had given me her address when we'd agreed on the terms of our cooperation. I was supposed to go to Rewal after I'd found the last clue – and with a little luck, after I found Ewa herself. However, the situation had changed.

I needed Kasandra's help right now. Without her, it would have been difficult for me to solve my fiancée's riddle. I needed a place where I could think calmly, without constantly looking over my shoulder. And above all, I needed a computer with internet access.

I knew I couldn't go to anyone else. Kasandra was my only salvation.

Could I really be one for her? That's what she'd said when she'd told me about the horror she'd had to endure for years. I didn't want to know the details; it was enough for me that her husband abused her, and that she and her son were finally going to get rid of him. I'd probably have helped her even if it wasn't a trade-off.

Or maybe I just wanted to think so. Perhaps in reality I would have no empathy and focus solely on solving my problems.

Anyway, we needed each other. That much was clear.

I looked at the phone again, put it back in the glove compartment and sped up a bit. Driving on Polish roads within the speed limit was actually more suspicious than exceeding it.

According to my calculations, I was more than two hundred kilometres away from Rewal. I was hoping to reach my destination in just over three hours, if I didn't come across any roadworks along the way. And unless Kasandra had sent me those messages to tell me she'd changed her mind.

16

Robert rushed into the office in a rage. I could see in his eyes that the man I'd married had completely disappeared, replaced by someone else. This stranger started to yell, insult me, threaten me and throw all my books off the shelves.

Before he pulled me out into the hallway, I had time to glance at the RIC. No sign of Werner. I was afraid the police were on his trail and he was arrested. There was no other explanation.

I would give a lot to be able to check local news from Wielkopolska and the Opole region. If I was going to be beaten up by my husband that night, I wanted to know if Damian had found his way to Ewa.

Robert beat me for an hour, pausing every now and then, as if he wanted to give me hope it was over, and then crush me like a worm. He accused me of everything under the sun, and started to hit me harder and harder.

He got excited when he saw that I was getting worse and worse. No doubt he felt like a master of life and death, drunk on knowing everything that happened to me was entirely up to him. He was far from remorseful, but I had no doubt that eventually he would feel contrition.

I just prayed that it wouldn't come too late.

During one of the interludes, I was already in so much pain I felt like I'd been hit by a car. I knew there would be no masking those wounds. It complicated my escape plan, because a battered woman would immediately draw attention.

And I had to escape unnoticed.

I pushed those thoughts away when I looked at Robert, leaning against a shelf and breathing deeply as if he'd been running. He was waving his arms around.

Could I still hope to get away? That this wasn't all going to end there and then? My husband seemed more and more angry. At this stage, I'd usually see the first signs of subsiding emotions. But not this time.

He turned around and looked at me contemptuously, then came over and kicked me in the ribs. I wriggled, cringing. I didn't know whether the pain was worse from the punches or the injuries I'd suffered so far.

"Robert..."

"Shut the fuck up!" he screamed, then kicked me again.

"Look... see what you're doing..." I said it so quietly, I didn't know if he could hear me. Even though I didn't have enough strength, I raised my hand and pointed to the corridor. He turned around for a moment and looked at the bloody stains on the walls.

He bent over and kicked me like a stray dog.

"What *I'm* doing?" he hissed "You're the one who made the whole fucking house filthy!"

He put his foot on my chest and pressed hard. It felt like I was about to hear a rib break. Robert seemed to be putting all his weight on me.

"The house," I gasped, "is full of blood."

He looked at me with rage and resentment.

"Think about what's going to happen," I said.

"Then what? Are you gonna call the police? Go ahead, call them."

He raised his leg and then reached into his pocket for his phone. He clasped it in his fist, clenching his mouth, then threw it at me. It hit me in the eye, and the pain was terrible. I felt like I was never going to be able to lift my eyelid again.

But I only let myself moan quietly.

"Wojtek."

"What about Wojtek? You're gonna hide behind a child now, you fucking cunt?"

"He'll see."

"He'll only see how they put you six feet under," Robert replied, and then grabbed my blouse, tearing the stitches as he dragged me towards the hallway. The first two buttons popped right off, but the other two were still in place when Robert threw me down to the floor, and then down the stairs, making sure that I'd crash against every hard surface on my way. My head struck the stairs, and to make it more painful, he would lift me slightly with each successive step.

When we came back downstairs, I was only half-conscious, but I was thinking about only one thing. It didn't matter what happened to me. I no longer worried if Robert would stop in time. I focused only on the fact that in the end I would be in such a state that I wouldn't be able to clean up the bloody stains and the whole mess. Wojtek would see the effects of what had happened.

I pushed that absurd thought away. I had to focus on what was happening here and now. Try to save myself. Not by physical resistance – it was too late for that. I had to try to be clever, using words as tools to dismantle my husband's madness.

"You dirty cunt," he snarled, dragging me into the living room.

There was ringing in my head, but not so loud that I couldn't hear his words, each one confirming that Robert was ready for anything. "You knew this was how it would end."

He dumped me again like a sack of garbage and I rolled over and stopped at the glass door leading out to the terrace.

I looked outside. Even though it wasn't raining, it looked like the glass was covered with droplets.

"You've worked hard for this for a long time, bitch."

He kicked me in the back and I bent double, no longer even knowing where the pain was coming from. Then he grabbed me by the shoulder, turned me around and hit me in the face with his fist. He did it with the hatred and brutality of someone who, after years of repressing his worst impulses, was finally giving vent to them.

Maybe that was what was happening right now.

"Robert, you can't…"

"I can't what?"

"Y-you'll… you'll…"

"Stop stuttering, you fucking cunt!"

He was completely out of control, beating me senselessly. He started hitting me on the ribs like I was a training bag – one, two, three, four. I thought he hesitated then, but I quickly realized that was false hope. Hope that there was still some humanity left in him.

"You're going to… kill me…" I managed to moan.

He didn't seem to hear me. He didn't even notice that I was starting to cough up blood. Red splashes appeared on his white shirt, on his rolled-up sleeves. I saw his biceps bulge and felt his muscles tense with every punch.

At some point he stopped beating me, shook his head and then grabbed my thighs. He pulled them sideways, spreading my legs. I didn't know what was happening to me anymore. I barely noticed what he was doing.

He was screaming that I was fucking others in his absence. That I brought random shitheads from the streets here. That when he finally hired people to make sure I didn't screw around, I started doing it with them.

He spread my legs even further, and then he hit me right between them. The blow was powerful, but even if it had been half as hard, it would still have taken my breath away. I felt completely paralyzed. The pain that spread between my legs seemed to go all the way to my guts.

I couldn't get a single word out. Robert picked me up, swung me and then threw me like a doll straight into the terrace door. I had just enough time to cover part of my face before the glass broke. But I didn't fall through it – my husband held me tight. If he hadn't, some glass shard would have stuck in my neck.

I wish it hadn't happened. Now I knew exactly what Edgar Allan Poe meant when he wrote about the imp of the perverse, the overwhelming feeling that you have to act against yourself, against logic.

Kill me, I said in my head, then repeated it: *Kill me.*

I knew I would be leaving my son at the mercy of this lunatic. I also knew that Robert wouldn't suffer any consequences, that my death would be completely pointless, and that there was nothing waiting for me after, only emptiness. And yet I kept repeating my silent appeal:

Kill me.

But Robert didn't need permission. He clutched my wrist and dragged me to the middle of the living room floor and then let go. My hand fell limply to the floor.

He went to the fridge to get a beer, and all I could do was turn my head. My eyes were on the iris in the pot. I'd forgotten about it completely. I hadn't watered it, and the plant was almost dead.

I closed my eyes.

I lay there, utterly powerless, drifting in and out of consciousness, unable to force myself to try to escape. I didn't know how much time had passed since my husband started beating me up.

When he came back to finish his work, he stood over me. It was like he was provoking me to make one last hopeless attempt at saving myself. I would have done so if I'd the strength to raise my hand.

I didn't know if he defeated me physically or mentally. At this stage, I couldn't understand why I was so powerless.

I was drifting away, the world becoming less and less real. So much so that, when I looked at the broken door, I thought I saw a human figure.

It took me a while to realize that someone really was standing there.

And it wasn't a random passerby.

I recognized Werner. I had no doubt it was him. At the same time, I couldn't believe he was there, thinking my brain was playing tricks on me.

Then I thought that if Damian was really here, he had to leave immediately. He wouldn't stand a chance against Robert. Before my husband had crafted his image as a serious businessman, he used to get into terrible fights in the streets. He would go to clubs just looking for trouble. I don't know why. Perhaps he just wanted to prove that, despite his upbringing in a good family, he could take care of himself on the street. Especially after all those hours spent at the gym, among other things.

Damian was no match for him in a fair fight.

I blinked cautiously, hoping that when I opened my eyes, the figure on the terrace would blend into the darkness.

The darkness. For God's sake, how long had it been since Robert had started abusing me? I only just realized how long it must have been. My mind was slowly returning to normal, my paralysis subsiding.

Unfortunately, I couldn't say the same about my body. It didn't seem to belong to me anymore.

Robert hit me in the stomach, then again, a little bit higher. All the air left my lungs.

"Hey!" I heard someone call.

My husband froze and I recognized that voice. It belonged to Werner. He was really here.

And he really should get away as soon as possible.

17

There was no time to think about it. When I drove up to the villa and heard the screams, I knew it wouldn't end well. I walked in from the back, hoping to assess the situation, but then I heard the sound of breaking glass.

What I saw was beyond my worst fears.

Admittedly, Kasandra had outlined her terrible situation to me, but she'd never said her husband abused her to such an extent. To describe this as torture was an understatement. There was no word for it in any dictionary.

My first thought was to call the police, but for obvious reasons I dismissed it immediately.

When the man turned his back on me, I realized I had a chance. I could surprise him and, with a little luck, overpower him. I just had to find something heavy and hit him on the back of the head with it.

Then he started hitting her, and I did the worst thing I could have possibly done: I gave away the element of surprise.

"Hey!" I yelled.

He froze, but only for a moment. Then he stood up and looked at me as if I had sprung from the underworld. He was breathing hard, and in his eyes I saw pure madness.

He took a step in my direction, and I stepped back, against my will. The broken glass cracked under my soles.

"Who the fuck are you?" he asked.

I took one more small step backwards. I barely realized it myself, and I was hoping that Reimann missed it. As he approached, I knew that he didn't – and that every inch mattered.

"I was walking down the beach and heard…"

"Heard what? Glass breaking?"

"Yeah."

"It's nothing," said Robert.

Only now have I realized that by coming closer to me, he wasn't trying to show who was in charge. He wanted me to get away from the broken door. From Kasandra lying on the floor, where I'd seen her a moment ago.

Now I didn't get a chance to look at her – Reimann was blocking my view – but earlier, I thought I'd seen blood. A lot of blood. In the twilight, it wasn't easy to determine Kas's condition, and when we moved away from the house, it became impossible.

The man standing in front of me suddenly smiled a little. At first I couldn't understand what he was trying to achieve. Then it occurred to me that he didn't know how long I'd been standing there. He didn't know what I'd seen and he wanted to salvage the situation.

"Thanks for your concern," he said, "but it's nothing. Really."

I looked at the broken window.

"Yeah, my wife and I were putting together a new bookcase," he explained with a shrug. "Ikea should really send their people to do things like that."

There was no Ikea in the area, but that didn't matter. Robert's offer was clear – turn a blind eye to what I might have noticed and everything would be okay.

My throat tightened. How far was he willing to go? And what could I do by myself? His broad shoulders and evident muscles left no doubt that I had no chance in a fight against him. Plus, I didn't have anything I could use as a weapon. As soon as I heard the sound of glass breaking, I'd run out of the car as if it was on fire, not thinking that I'd need not just a fire extinguisher but a whole fire brigade to deal with it.

"But thanks again for your concern," Reimann added. "If more people took notice of stuff like this, maybe there'd be a little less tragedy in the world."

"Maybe."

He smiled again. I tried to look over his shoulder, but the inside of the villa was dark.

"Where did you come from?" he asked.

I didn't know the area well enough and needed a moment to think about it. That moment raised Robert's suspicions.

"From Pobierowo," I improvised, remembering the name of one of the towns near Rewal.

"Vacation?"

"Yeah," I replied as nonchalantly as I could.

"Are you staying long?"

"Just over a week."

"Hotel or B&B?"

"B&B. Not far from here."

Luckily, he didn't ask which one it was. In case of emergency I was ready to throw the name of any species of sea birds. The area was certainly swarming with establishments called Albatross or Cormorant.

"Did you come alone?"

"Yeah. I needed to get some fresh air, have a break from the family."

"Understandable." He gave me a knowing look and I wondered if he was asking because he wanted to keep up the appearances of a normal, innocent conversation, or if he was trying to find out if anyone would notice my disappearance.

"Sometimes I walk back and forth in the evenings," I added.

"I'm not surprised. The area's great for walks."

"True."

"But be careful when entering private property."

"I didn't know this was."

"Well, we should have put up a fence," he admitted, as if he was the one to blame. "But we don't want to spoil the view."

"Quite right."

"There's a sign on the beach, by the way. You probably missed it in the dark."

I nodded, feeling saliva collecting in my throat. There was something extremely disturbing about this conversation. It was like unspeakable threats were hiding in every sentence, every word.

I got a grip on myself. I should check on Kasandra, try to help her. But how could I? I could get away and then call the police – actually, that seemed to be the only possible solution – but if I did, things would end tragically, and not just for me.

"Are you sure you're okay?" I asked. "Maybe there's something I can do to help."

"Mate," Reimann blinked and snorted. "Don't you have anything better to do?"

"Actually, no."

"Then I can recommend a great place in Pobierowo. Baltic Pipe."

"Interesting name."

"Not just the name. The whole interior design was inspired by industrial ambience. You'll like it. During the day it's a café, but in the evenings it's a cocktail bar. Tell them Robert Reimann sent you.

"That'll get me a free round?"

He laughed as if I'd said something really funny. I was starting to sweat, even though it was quite chilly after sunset.

"At least one," he said. "I'll call them right now and tell them you're coming. I might even be able to stop by as soon as my wife and I clean up a little bit."

I took a step to the right and looked towards the house. He immediately made the same move, and the smile suddenly disappeared from his face.

"Is she all right?"

"Yeah, yeah. She hurt her hand, but it's nothing serious."

We were silent for a while, looking at each other.

It's over, I thought. *The time for pretence is over. Either I act now or Reimann will take the initiative. He's already stopped testing the ground.*

"Well, anyway," he said, "thanks again."

Third time. He couldn't send me a clearer signal to go away. I nodded as if to say that I got it, and then turned towards where he'd looked.

"Baltic Pipe?" I said.

"Yeah."

"I'll be sure to drop by."

I moved on, still not having any idea of what I should do. Damn it, someone who'd been through so much in life should at least be able to make quick decisions in difficult situations, and yet I still felt like I was paralyzed.

Then I made a big mistake when I started moving away from Reimann. I turned my head towards the broken door and saw Kasandra lying in a pool of blood. I stopped in my tracks like I'd been struck by lightning – and even though I moved on a second later, it was enough for Robert to understand I'd seen too much.

He ran over to me and swung his arm. His fist landed right on my temple. The impact echoed in my ears and I felt a bolt of pain lancing through my head. I would have lost my balance if it wasn't for Reimann grabbing the bottom of my shirt. I automatically raised my hands, trying to protect my head – another mistake. Robert took advantage of the fact that I didn't counter, swinging and hitting me in the throat. The blow wasn't strong, but it was well aimed and I was suddenly unable to breathe. The pain was so excruciating I completely lost control over what was happening.

I fell to the ground, trying to shield myself. Then the kicks came. Reimann did not aim at any particular part of my body; he just rained down the blows, seeming to give vent to his anger. I got hit in the head, and another blow hit me somewhere on the torso.

Then he picked me up.

"You saw nothing, understand?"

"Y-yes..." I felt pathetic. I'd driven out here thinking I'd be rescuing Kasandra from the nightmare she'd been living for years. I was supposed to be her salvation.

Meanwhile, all I did was have an absurd, tragicomic conversation with her husband.

Reimann hit me in the stomach and I bent double, coughing. After a blow to the throat, it felt like something was broken inside. There was a metallic aftertaste in my mouth that was more paralyzing than any pain. It reminded me of what had happened at Młynówka.

"You call somebody, I'll fucking kill you, understand?"

I couldn't breathe, let alone speak, but I knew that in order to avoid further blows, I had to get something out.

"Man, what the hell are you doing?"

"Do you understand?" he yelled.

"Yeah," I answered cautiously.

"Where are you staying?"

I said nothing.

"Tell me!"

Without waiting for an answer, he hit me right in the mouth and I felt my eyeteeth move. The gums seemed to swell up immediately. He'd aimed his blow upwards, though, and I thought he'd hurt his knuckles.

"Where?"

"At the Alba... Albatross."

"Which room?"

"Number fifteen."

Reimann spat to the side and then shook me. "What's your name, motherfucker?"

I hesitated for a moment too long and Reimann realized that something was wrong. I should have answered straight away, but I knew enough not to give my real name. Robert would know all of RI's clients; he could have easily remembered me.

And he would immediately realize that my presence here was no accident.

"Tomasz Prokocki," I blurted out.

"Why the fuck are you lying?" he snarled. "You don't think I'm gonna check it?"

He hit me again, this time a little lighter, on the left. This blow was like a bell announcing the next round of a boxing match, waking up a staggering player.

I got away from him and then hit him clumsily. My right hook got him in the head, but the attack didn't have any effect. Reimann immediately recovered, grabbed my hand and twisted it. When he turned me around, I swung my other arm and hit him on the chin with my elbow. He gave a quiet groan.

I couldn't take the initiative, but I felt I could defend myself. I owed it mainly to the fact that Robert was surprised by my resistance. I was able to hit him once more before a storm of blows fell on me.

Reimann was a seasoned fighter – and he quickly proved it to me. He beat me time and time again, and I waved my hands in hopeless attempts at defence. Each of his blows reached its target. Mine mostly missed.

Finally, I rolled back, feeling like I was losing control of my own body. When he kicked me in the knee, I fell to the ground like a ragdoll.

Another blow came from above like a hammer. He hit me on the nose, and I heard something crack. I felt pain somewhere behind my eyes, so powerful that it seemed to paralyze the nerve endings.

A few more blows and I was close to passing out. I could feel the blood flowing out of my nostrils, no longer a drip but a stream. It was pouring down my mouth, down my throat. Each cough was more difficult than the last.

I felt like I was about to choke. And my face was about to become a bloody pulp.

But still Reimann didn't stop. He beat me mindlessly, as if possessed. He was screaming something, but I didn't understand what it was. His voice couldn't penetrate the buzzing in my head.

I realized it was over. After all the problems I'd managed to overcome, after coming all this way, here and now, it was all over. I would never know if Ewa was really waiting for me. I would never know what had happened to her the whole time she'd been hiding. I would never understand what she wanted to tell me.

Then the thoughts stopped making sense and I didn't understand what was going on anymore. The man who beat me up became a stranger, almost anonymous. I forgot the reason he was beating me up.

I felt completely confused. The situation seemed surreal, absurd.

Maybe that was how it always looked before death.

I was drifting away, losing consciousness, approaching a point of no return.

And then, suddenly, Reimann paused.

It was like an unexpected burst of sunshine in a thunderstorm. Time seemed to stop. The sense of the surreal intensified. There was only one thought in my head.

He killed me. He'd stopped because he'd achieved his goal and I'd just lost my life.

I managed to open one bloodstained eye. I saw Reimann breathe heavily above me.

He was lifting his clenched fist, getting ready for the final blow – a blow that would close my eyes forever.

18

The shard of glass went into my husband's neck like a knife into butter.

Robert froze with his fist raised, not making a sound. That was not what I was expecting. I was afraid one blow wouldn't be enough, that Robert would turn around, knock the broken glass out of my hand, defend himself.

This fear was also accompanied by hope – that he'd tire, bleed and suffer for a long time before he died – but it happened instantly. I'd barely crawled outside, mobilized all my strength to get up, and it was over.

All it took was a piece of glass thrust into his body.

I managed to hold him for a moment and stop him from falling onto Werner. He slipped down right next to me, and I was immediately completely, utterly exhausted. I realized how close I'd come to that stage a moment ago.

And how close Werner was to dying.

I dragged myself over to him, not sure I wasn't already too late. I saw what was going on outside and had tried to crawl there as fast as I could, but every yard required tremendous effort.

In addition, all the time I expected Robert to turn around and see me.

But he hadn't. I'd surprised him; I had the upper hand. I just hoped that in the last second of his life he would understand what had happened. And who had meted out justice.

I hadn't got that far yet. From the corner of my eye I saw Robert lying face down in the sand, not moving, but deep down I was afraid that any moment he would shake it off and stand up. And then he'd start doing all the things I hated him for.

I focused my eyes on Damian, and then I grabbed him by the wrist. I tried to feel for the pulse, but I was still numb. I couldn't feel anything.

"Wern..."

I thought I heard shallow breathing, but I wasn't sure. I felt an unpleasant chill all over my body and it occurred to me that it was too late. Not by much, but still.

I wiped the blood off his face, but he didn't even move. If he was still alive, he was already on the border. And he was about to cross it.

I knew what I had to do.

He finally deserved to hear what I wanted to say to him all those days.

I took a deep breath. This wasn't how it was supposed to be. It wasn't supposed to end like this.

I leaned over him, kissed him on the mouth. Then I straightened a little bit.

"Tiger," I said.

He twitched, as if someone had put a defibrillator to his chest. Then he opened his eyes and looked at me in disbelief.

I didn't expect him to find the strength to speak up. And yet he did.

"Ewa?" he said.

CHAPTER 3

1

Moments of awakening were like lightning illuminating the sky. Like a photographer hunting for a perfect shot, I tried to capture them, but they vanished as quickly as they appeared.

I was conscious for only a short while. Images were flashing before my eyes and I was doing everything I could to make a logical whole out of them.

Ewa couldn't be here.

And yet she leaned over me, put her hand on my cheek and asked if I could get up. I didn't have time to answer – darkness closed over me. When I opened my eyes again, I was in the living room.

Then I woke up on the couch for a moment.

I saw Ewa's battered face. I was unable to grasp what was going on and how she could be here. My mind rejected the idea of what was quite obvious.

I'd never seen Kasandra Reimann before.

I'd never heard her voice before.

She'd only contacted me through the RIC, insisting it was the only safe way. And considering the battlefield Reimann's villa had turned into, I had to conclude that she'd been right.

But if it really was Ewa, why didn't she tell me right away? What had all that been about?

And how was it possible that she'd ended up married to Robert Reimann?

How was it possible that no one had recognized her over the years? She'd made public appearances, attended events.

No, she hadn't, I corrected myself. Yes, she'd donated a lot of money to charities and supported local initiatives, but she'd never participated in lavish banquets. She'd never basked in the limelight.

For God's sake, it was really her.

Every time I woke up, I understood it better, but there were more and more questions, and no answers. It didn't make any sense at all.

Why had she showed up at that concert? And why had she chased me all over the country afterwards?

Wait a minute, I thought. It wasn't all over. She'd led me from south to north, all that time bringing me closer to Rewal, step by step.

When I finally woke up properly, she was sitting on the edge of the sofa, staring with empty eyes into the blackness outside the window. The blackness that hid Reimann's body. I shuddered at that thought, realizing that Ewa had really taken his life.

I looked at her silently, not knowing what to say. She'd changed. She looked so different, in fact, that our old friends might not have recognized her if she passed them on the street.

I'm sure that was on purpose. For years, she'd had to do everything not to remind herself of herself. Her voice had changed, too, and that was probably the most noticeable difference. Only the eyes remained the same, although somewhere deep inside them was something that squeezed my heart.

"Ewa…"

She shook her head and looked at me. "Don't move. You have cracked ribs."

I'd spent ten years picturing our meeting. These weren't the kind of words I'd expected to hear first.

"I've bandaged your chest, but you have to be careful."

"How do you…"

"I'll explain everything."

Despite her instructions, I tried to sit up. She immediately stopped me with a gentle hand on my shoulder. We looked at each other for a moment, trying to communicate things that no words could express.

Only now did I realize why we'd connected on the RIC app so quickly and effortlessly. Even though we couldn't even see each other, we'd been talking like two old friends. The conversations had flowed easily, and we could understand each other's jokes. There had been some chemistry between us from the beginning that should have made me think, considering that our entire acquaintance hadn't involved anything more than chatting.

Ewa moved her hand over my arm. Even without all the injuries visible to the naked eye, she looked like a human shadow. Blood spots and fresh bruises stood out on her pale skin. The shadows under her eyes made her look almost ghastly, and a blood vessel must have popped in one of her eyes because it was partially red.

She turned her head and again fixed her gaze on the impenetrable darkness. I felt like I'd lost her somewhere in the night abyss, not ten years ago – now. It was as if she'd left her real self out there somewhere.

She dropped her head and didn't move for a moment. I didn't even want to think how she had to be feeling. I didn't know if the first blow was fatal, and had no idea if she'd wrestled with Reimann or fought for her life – if she did what she'd done in cold blood.

I finally managed to pull myself up against the backrest. I hissed in pain, but Ewa didn't rebuke me.

"Why?" I blurted out. "What was all this for?"

"I'll explain it to you soon."

We both spoke so low that we were actually whispering, but not through fear of someone overhearing us. Neither of us had the strength to talk.

"Now we have to run, Tiger."

"Run?" I wanted to ask from whom, since Robert was lying dead in front of the house, but I bit my tongue.

"They'll be chasing us."

"Who? Those people you're hiding from? The ones from Cayman?"

"Them, too."

"Too? Who else?"

"Robert's subordinates," she replied without raising her head. "And his associates. Somebody's going to take his place and the first thing they'll do will be…" She didn't finish, just shook her head. It was clearly painful. "Everything will start all over again," she said dejectedly. Finally, she glanced up and looked at me for a moment. "I'll end up having to go through all that again, Wern."

"No, you won't." I didn't know everything, but I understood exactly what she meant. "This time you've got me. We'll be all right together."

She smiled sadly. "It must be really bad if you're resorting to clichés."

"I'm a master at that."

"True."

I turned around and lowered my legs to the floor, trying to conceal a wince of pain. But that didn't reflect the severity of my injuries.

That arsehole Reimann had to have broken a few ribs. I couldn't breathe without feeling like something was tearing my chest apart from the inside. The slightest movement caused the same.

"We have to go and get Wojtek," said Ewa. "We'll take him and leave immediately."

I looked towards the broken windows. "What about... him?"

"We're going to leave him like this."

"Are you sure? Wouldn't it be better–"

"No," she interrupted me, and got up. She lost her balance and I held her up.

She was right. We should get out of here as soon as we could. But how? We could both barely stand. Taking even a few steps seemed to be too much effort.

"We won't dispose of the body," she added. "Sooner or later they'll find it anyway, so we'd just be wasting valuable time."

"We could go a little bit out to sea with him."

"Can you paddle?"

"No," I answered without hesitation.

I wanted to ask if there was anything with an engine in the area, but then realized that if there had been, Ewa would have already considered it. A whole lot of other, more important questions filled my head, but I decided to focus on the here and now. There would be time enough later for her to tell me everything.

I got up from the couch, and we moved outside, supporting each other.

"How are you going to pick him up?" I asked.

She looked at me uncomprehendingly.

"Your son," I said. "He's sleeping at someone's, right?"

"Yes," she replied. "At a friend's."

"So you're just going to show up like this and take him away?"

"We'll think of something."

The fact that she'd used the plural had a very encouraging effect on me. I felt a surge of strength, but it was no more than an illusion. A second or two later, I was struggling to maintain my balance again.

We got into the Peugeot, me in the passenger seat, Ewa behind the wheel. She turned the key in the ignition.

"You're not taking anything?" I asked.

"No. I have everything I need."

It was difficult to decide whether she meant me or the money she'd deposited in the accounts set up in my name. For the Ewa I'd once known, the former would have probably been true. But I didn't know how much of that Ewa was left in the woman sitting next to me.

We set off along the coastal road. In my head, I heard an echo of Ewa's words, which she must have said during one of the moments I was briefly conscious.

That's not how it was supposed to go.

That was what she'd said, in an absent voice, sounding quite unlike herself. I assumed that she, too, had been picturing a lot of scenarios for our meeting, but never that one. She hadn't intended for anyone to get killed. She'd planned everything so that we would disappear without a trace – and without the shadow that followed us.

We parked under one of the houses in Rewal.

"Wait here," Ewa told me and got out of the car without waiting for an answer.

I watched her walk up to the front door and press the doorbell. I glanced at my watch. It was just past midnight – the boy was certainly asleep, as was the rest of the household. There were no lights on.

After a while, one clicked on in one of the windows. A moment later, the door opened and a sleepy-looking middle-aged woman stood at the threshold. I watched Ewa, completely ignoring the owner of the house. I was looking at my missing fiancée. And I was about to see her take her son in her arms.

What was going to happen next? Could we really fool ourselves that we could escape? And if so, what would we do next? Were we going to be a happy family, with me as a new father?

Jesus Christ, I should stop thinking like that. One thing at a time.

First we would leave the area safely, then we would think about what to do. Ewa must have had a plan, anyway. Given everything she had done in this mad endeavour, I should have expected that she'd be prepared for any contingency.

I blinked, trying to see the other woman's reaction. She retreated, clearly confused, and disappeared in the hallway. Ewa looked over her shoulder and nodded at me. Everything was fine. Maybe the woman hadn't seen the wounds, or maybe Ewa had told her some plausible story.

Wojtek showed up at the door after a while. He yawned hugely, but Ewa took his hand and led him towards the car. When he sat in the back and fastened his seat belt, he realized I was there.

"Mum? Who's that?"

The answer to that question was just as complicated as those that were still bothering me. I didn't want to face him now.

"Werner," I said, turning around with difficulty. When the boy shook my hand in greeting, sharp pain pierced the upper part of my body.

Ewa drove out of the driveway and then turned left. We took road number 102 in the direction of Trzebiatów.

We were heading towards a new life. Nobody stopped us, nobody followed us. It occurred to me that getting answers was only a matter of time, that we'd finally managed to achieve what Ewa had to have been working towards for years.

- We waited for Wojtek to fall asleep. It didn't take long; the boy was clearly exhausted. Somewhere near Kołobrzeg, he settled comfortably in the back seat. And we both sighed in relief.

"I'll start at the beginning," Ewa said.

2

I felt strange, as if I'd suddenly found myself in a completely different, foreign world. I could stop the car at the petrol station and buy whatever I wanted, without asking anyone's permission. I could turn off the main road and go in any direction I wanted. I could listen to the radio station I liked the most.

It was all up to me. Nobody was looking over my shoulder.

At first, I couldn't find myself. I felt like a prisoner released after decades behind bars.

But knowing how I'd got out almost paralyzed me. I still had a blurry image of a piece of glass piercing Robert's neck embedded in my mind. When that afterimage returned, I felt as if I was watching that scene from far away.

I saw the life drain out of my husband. I was looking at myself, grabbing his body and slipping down with it next to Werner.

I looked at him. He leaned his elbow against the window, looking ahead with unseeing eyes. I knew he was trying to put things in order in his head, but he would never manage to do that.

Not without my help.

He realized I was looking at him and gave me a fleeting smile. It vanished as soon as it appeared, probably because of the pain. His face was bruised and swollen. I was afraid he would scare Wojtek – that we both would – but my son apparently hadn't noticed the wounds in the dim light. Now he was sleeping peacefully in the back seat.

"So?" Damian urged me quietly.

"I don't know where to start."

"Mm-hmm."

"Any suggestions?" I asked.

"Start where you ended in the last recording. From 'Ice cream on a hot day'." He gave me a long look, and I tightened my hands on the steering wheel. "By the way, I didn't really like the last title very much."

"I wanted to inject some optimism into you at the finish."

"You failed," he murmured. "Maybe because, at the end, you left me with nothing."

"Nothing?"

"That last clue didn't tell me anything. It's still not telling me anything."

He looked ahead, squinting his eyes, as if he was trying to make something out of the night darkness. The road was empty. No cars had passed us for a long time.

"A place that only I was supposed to recognize? And the time I was supposed to know?" he said. "What was that all about?

"Not much."

"I figured that."

I looked in the rear-view mirror. Wojtek was still fast asleep, apparently having had a lot of excitement today, so we spoke quietly to avoid waking him up. I took a deep breath.

"I only meant that I would contact you soon, Tiger," I whispered back. "I'd give you the time and location of the meeting. And you're the only one who'd know it. That's it."

"And how were you going to do that?"

"Via the RIC," I said.

"Were you going to tell me everything? Just like that?"

"No, not just like that," I said. "I've been preparing you for this for a long time, haven't I?"

He was silent, which was probably the most painful answer. I knew that when it came down to it, I'd have to face his grievances. But it was a price I was willing to pay.

"What's all this for?" he finally asked.

"I said I'd explain everything to you."

"So start now."

"I'd rather–"

"What?" he cut in. "Stay at a motel and talk over a glass of wine? This isn't a conversation you can put off."

He was right, although I would give a lot for a drop of Prosecco. It seemed that after everything that had happened, the alcohol had stopped working. The adrenaline had boosted my metabolism and I was completely sober.

I'm sure that wasn't the case in reality. In all likelihood, I shouldn't have been driving for a good few more hours. But a possible arrest by the police would end tragically anyway.

If any uniform officer saw us, they wouldn't give up until they knew what had happened to us.

"You were hiding in Wielkopolska," Werner murmured. "That's where the last recording ended."

"Yeah."

"When was that?"

"Shortly after I'd testified against Cayman."

"Did they get a lead on you?"

"No, but…" I broke off and sighed deeply. "All the time I felt that I was only one misstep away from it."

Damian nodded, probably admitting to himself that I was right.

"There was danger hanging over me, Tiger. Constantly."

"I understand."

"And the spectre of what happened."

Werner was silent. There were the exact same dark clouds drifting in the firmament of his life. I didn't have to say anything else for him to know that it wasn't just his memory that brought up those scenes.

Nevertheless, I decided to mention something that had to be said.

"It has determined all my decisions."

He lowered his elbow and sank into the seat. He looked at me.

"What do you mean?"

"The fact that I've seen my whole life through the prism of those events… and the fear associated with them. You know what I mean?"

"Of course I do."

"Everything I've done has been caused by it. Every smallest decision was a calculation."

"Based on what?"

"To ensure your safety. I needed that, or I'd go crazy. Maybe I even did."

I was hoping he'd smile and confirm that I really had to be crazy to come up with such a plan. But Damian was silent.

"I started my studies in business psychology," I continued.

"Have you finished them?" he asked.

"Yeah."

"I dropped out. I didn't get my master's degree."

"I know. I tried to keep track of what was going on with you."

"And you didn't try to contact me even once? To let me know you're alive? That you're okay, that you're safe?"

"I thought that–"

"That what?"

Wojtek shifted in the back seat, and I realized we'd both raised our voices. Werner made an apologetic gesture and looked ahead again.

"I thought you understood that after the recordings," I said. "That's why I made them for you, Wern."

"Then they've been counterproductive, because now I'm more confused than before."

We stopped talking for a moment. I didn't need any words to know that, despite those declarations, Damian understood everything. But he had to hear some things from my mouth. And I wasn't surprised.

"I've been living with a sense of constant danger," I repeated. "And I knew Cayman's men were still after me. What's more, they were watching you, too. One wrong step on my part could have ruined everything."

Werner rubbed his temples nervously and groaned quietly in pain. "Wait, wait," he said. "Because if I understand correctly, I've misjudged the situation."

This time I didn't know what he meant.

"It wasn't the police who were my opponents," he added.
"No."

"Years ago there was no corruption, no dereliction of
duty, no cover-up and no attempt to sweep everything
under the carpet. None of those cops were guilty and none
had anything to do with your disappearance."

He was waiting for me to confirm, but I couldn't.

"Or am I wrong?" he asked.

"You're not. But there's something else."

"What?"

"There's a man in the police force who had been working
for Cayman. He's the reason they found out about me. And
I suppose the mole is still wearing the uniform. Maybe he
even got promoted. That's why I couldn't risk it, Tiger. It
would have been disastrous to contact you or Prokocki
directly."

I wanted to keep going, but I noticed that Damian was
wrinkling his brow.

"What?"

"I think I know who the mole is. Does the name Falkow
sound familiar?"

"No."

"He helped me escape from the hotel in Chrząstowice,"
he explained, then sighed loudly. "He told me I shouldn't
trust anyone."

It made sense.

"But what did he get out of it?" Damian added. "I mean…"

When he fell silent, I knew he had put it all together in a
logical whole.

"Oh, right," he murmured. "These people – they found
out what you were trying to do."

"Yes."

"And they knew that the best way to find you was to follow me. They knew I'd finally lead them to you. That's why they helped me."

I nodded and Wern turned to me. He finally looked at me the way he should have done at first – with compassion, without resentment. Finally, he took note of the fact that all that time I'd been feeling Cayman's people breathing down my neck.

"Are you all right?" he asked.

"Yes. I mean…" I paused and shook my head. My neck hurt. "I don't know. It's hard for me to hear about you being so close to those people."

He was wondering what to say.

"This is the past," he replied. "We left them behind, and you took care of it by bringing me to the seaside. Even if they'd found my trail at some point, they'll have lost it by now."

I glanced at the fuel gauge. We would have to stop and fill up soon; we couldn't risk running out of petrol somewhere between stations. But even such a mundane activity wouldn't be easy. We both looked like we'd just crawled out of a cage full of wild animals.

I realized we had a long way to go. Wherever we went, we had to be ready for complications.

Suddenly I felt Damian had put his hand on mine. I realized I was holding it on the gearstick. I glanced at Werner, but then looked back to the road.

"We'll be fine," he said.

"I know."

In the distance, dazzling car lights appeared. The driver realized that someone was coming from the opposite direction and dipped his beams, but not before I was blinded by the glare. Even after he'd passed us, I couldn't see for a moment.

"I want to hear everything," said Damian quietly. "About what happened to you, about your plan, about every move, every stage and every–"

"Give me a moment," I replied, forcing myself to smile. "I have to collect my thoughts."

"You've been collecting them for the last ten years," he said with a bite in his voice that I immediately appreciated. "And you see what came out of it."

"So I'm supposed to just spill everything now? No rhyme or reason?"

"We are going to put everything in order later," he declared. "Now I just want to know why you decided to do all this."

3

I knew Ewa well enough to realize that I couldn't get her to do what I wanted – at least, not exactly. Eventually, we reached a consensus, which boiled down to the fact that we would stop for a night somewhere near Słupsk, and there Ewa would fill in all the gaps in her story.

Along the way we had to refuel, although neither of us had a good idea how to do it without arousing suspicion. In the end, though, we both came to the conclusion that there was only one way out.

We had to make it an innocent game. Having arrived at one of the biggest petrol stations along the National 6, we woke Wojtek. I filled the tank, and he was supposed to deliver money to the cashier, pretending to be an adult. The man behind the counter gave me a long look, but from afar he couldn't see the wounds on my face. I raised my hand and nodded to him meaningfully, and he accepted the money from the boy.

Relieved, we drove on towards Słupsk.

We repeated a similar game when we paid for a room in a roadside motel, and then finally we locked ourselves inside. The car was parked in the back, although no one was likely to be looking for it. It wasn't connected in any way to the Reimann family, just a random vehicle.

It was the same with me. From this point of view, I was a perfect rescue for Ewa and Wojtek. The problem was that there was also a different perspective. The one that came down to the fact that the police were looking for me for Blitzer's murder.

I still didn't understand why he had to die. Or who had taken his life.

But I thought I'd find out everything. Here and now, in a motel room on the outskirts of Słupsk. I would have to remember this place and this time as one of the most important in my life.

Wojtek fell asleep in a flash. I envied him, thinking I wouldn't be able to sleep for the next several days. Ewa, all the more so. Even once we'd dealt with the past, we would still have to face the monsters of the present. And they seemed even more monstrous than the ones we both knew well.

We sat down at a small table in the biggest room. From the minibar, Ewa pulled out a small beer for me and two bottles of vodka for herself. She poured her first drink, closed her eyes and took a sip.

It occurred to me that I was looking at her as if she was a drug addict taking a fix. I pushed that thought away. It was just a drink, no more dangerous than my beer. But Ewa quickly deciphered the meaning behind my look.

"All things considered, it's the least of my problems," she noted.

"I wasn't going to say anything."

"You didn't have to."

We smiled briefly.

"The last time I was sober was probably the day we went to the High."

"Mm-hmm." I murmured. "So you've spent about ten years in Tipsyland."

"Was it different with you?"

"I don't know. My memories of most of that time are foggy."

"I'll take that as a no, then."

I nodded and took a sip of my beer. I shouldn't have been surprised that she had been drinking every day. Even without the baggage of experience she carried with her, living with a man like Robert Reimann justified much worse offences against herself.

I didn't want to think about it. And yet I knew I wouldn't run away from it. I was about to learn every detail of her life, every tiny aspect of what had happened to her from the moment she finished her story on the recordings.

"So you went to Wielkopolska and started studying business psychology..."

"And I met Robert there."

"I suppose you don't remember it as the best thing that ever happened to you."

I made that comment without thinking. For no sensible reason, I tried to lighten the tone. I promised to myself not to do it again. This was no laughing matter.

I expected Ewa to keep silent, but she cleared her throat meaningfully.

"I try not to remember it at all," she said. "But at that moment it was one of those things that came out of pure calculation."

I raised my brows. "In what sense?

"I was looking for a sense of security, a guarantee that nothing would happen to me if Cayman's men came after me."

"And Reimann could give you that?"

"Yes. I understood that when I discovered what he really did."

She spent some time then explaining to me that Reimann Investigations and Robert's other companies were fronts. Some had more solid façades while others were just shells that vanished as quickly as they appeared.

Reimann was rapidly developing a criminal organization, not only by selling drugs, boosters and everything that was in demand in the illegal trade, but also via scams in the real estate market. The image that emerged from Ewa's story made me think that his organization really could have protected her if Cayman's people had ever found her.

For the first time, I thought about the fact that now she'd lost her protective umbrella when she decided to break with that life and go back to the old one. The one where I was responsible for keeping her safe, or the closest thing to it.

But then I remembered the horror she had gone through. Nothing was worth putting up with that any longer, even if she had to give up her sense of security.

"When I started my relationship with him, I had no idea what kind of man he was."

"You mean…"

"I didn't expect him to do what he did to me." She wouldn't let me stop her, though I tried to do it only so that she wouldn't have to talk about things that hurt her. "I was aware of his ruthlessness and the fact that he was walking over dead bodies to achieve his goal, but... Wern, I didn't know he was going to abuse me. Nothing in his past made me even suspect him of such..."

Cruelty? I wanted to say the right word, but could think of nothing adequate. Ewa probably couldn't either, because she finally shook her head, not finishing the sentence.

"When it all started, I was already pregnant. I had no way back."

I understood that perfectly well.

"Besides, I told myself it was only temporary, that it was just some kind of psychological crisis over my pregnancy, Robert's fear that after the baby was born, all my love and attention would be focused on it."

I opened my mouth to ask one key question, but I didn't say a word. I didn't have to.

"Yes, I loved him," said Ewa. "At first it was just a matter of calculation, but then... with time..."

She broke off, adding nothing more. We sat in silence, not looking at each other, drinking slowly, but there wasn't any sluggishness in that. We were both excited, our hearts hammering.

"You understand that, don't you?" Ewa finally asked.

"Yeah."

"It was only because of the security he gave me at the time."

"I understand," I assured her once again, hoping we could drop the subject.

Ewa nodded, but I didn't think she believed me. The truth was, I didn't know if I could empathize with her situation. In theory, it shouldn't have been difficult – a raped, intimidated woman finally finds someone she can feel safe with. Under such circumstances, could anyone be surprised that she fell in love with that person?

No, probably not. Especially since she hadn't expected us to ever meet again. She had to take me out of her life for both our sakes. That was exactly what I understood.

"After graduation, we lived in Wielkopolska for a while, where he worked in the customs office," she said. "Then I went back to Rewal, his hometown, with him. At first, everything worked out. Then the problems started…"

"You don't have to talk about it."

"But I want to," she said, straightening in the chair. "You should know the whole context."

"It's okay."

"I should have picked up the first signs at the beginning. He always wanted to control the conversation, he made all decisions and he allowed me hardly any freedom. In fact, he gradually restricted it, and in the end he incapacitated me completely."

I took a drink of my beer, thinking I'd empty the bottle soon at this rate. It occurred to me to go to the nearest shop for a six-pack but I dismissed it immediately. I wanted to be sober when Ewa got to the point.

She went on to describe how Reimann restricted her freedom more and more with each passing week. At some point she wanted to leave him, but soon afterwards she found out that she was pregnant.

Then it was like a landslide. He threatened her, then hit her for the first time. It started with suffocating her, then he hit, the blows aimed carefully, so as not to leave any marks. Eventually, he started abusing her to his heart's content, especially after Wojtek was born, when Ewa couldn't leave the villa.

"I was terrified, Tiger," she whispered, fixing her absent gaze on the wall.

She seemed embarrassed, even though she didn't have the slightest reason to be. Anyone in her shoes would have been afraid.

"After what I've been through... you understand."

I nodded, sadness welling up inside me.

"With those threats, everything came back," she added, shaking off the momentary stagnation. "It seemed to me that Robert was worse than those who attacked us at the Sneering Lodge. That he was capable of much more violent things if I didn't obey him. I had been paralyzed for a long time."

Seeing her vacant gaze a moment ago, I could easily imagine that.

"At that stage, I had no one else to turn to. I'd lost all my friends," she continued. "I hardly knew anyone in Rewal. And even if I had, they were connected to Robert in one way or another. It was only when I hired employees for Reimann Investigations that I met the first people who had nothing to do with him."

Even without that information, I knew she'd nowhere to look for help. After all the horror she'd gone through, after the false hope that she would finally forget, she found herself in an even worse position.

I closed my eyes for a moment and lowered my head.

"That guy with the scar." I said. "Who is he?"

"That's Glazur."

"Who?"

"An RI employee. IT guy. I owe him everything."

"I don't understand."

"I turned to him when I thought you were my only salvation. I thought it was a safe move, but Robert started to suspect something. He fired Glazur, fortunately without digging too deep. He removed everyone who started to get too close to me."

"That's why Kliza got kicked out?"

"Yes. She and Glazur met the same fate."

"Did she know about you? About your real identity?"

"No." Ewa shook her head. "And Glazur knew only that I was in an abusive relationship and I was trying to get out of it, and that you were the only one who could help me with that."

I thought about it for a second. It all seemed logical at first, but when I started to look at the whole structure, a lot of questions arose. I assumed Ewa would soon dispel them, talking about what pushed her to make such decisions. There was one thing, however, that wouldn't leave me alone.

"But Kliza could have recognized you," I said. "When she took the case."

Ewa smiled. "That was the plan."

"And more specifically?"

"She was supposed to see the picture that Phil Braddy took at the concert. Or, if not that one, then the one you've had all these years."

I waited for further explanations, biting my tongue in order not to flood Ewa with new questions. I couldn't help myself, though.

"Who was he? Braddy?" I asked.

"He never existed. It was Glazur who posted it, setting everything in motion."

"And then he took it down?"

"No. The police did that."

I scratched my neck and leaned over the small table. "Ewa, you have to explain it to me."

"I intend to, although I was planning to tell you all about it in the order it happened. It would be easier."

"We'll get right back to that," I said. "For now, tell me, who deleted the photo?"

"Prokocki," she answered, and let out a long breath. "He had no idea I was behind everything, that I was doing everything I could to get you to find me. So he reacted as his own principles and human morality told him. He began to cover the tracks so that Cayman's men wouldn't get to me. The photos were taken down and he made sure that they wouldn't appear again."

Now I had at least a general understanding of what had happened. And how wrong we had been with Blitz. We had misread the situation, assuming it was all part of some plot concocted by the people who'd wanted to hurt Ewa.

Meanwhile, it was the police who had been trying to protect her. And they had done a pretty thorough job – a job now regulated by the law. Ewa had been an anonymous witness years ago, without any kind of legal guarantees, but since the changes in legislation had come into force, she was now entitled to full, obligatory support from the state.

Prokocki must have been terrified when he realized that somebody had tracked her down, and had been ready to do anything to prevent her from being found. And I became the victim of his endeavours.

I straightened up and put my hands on my neck. Every muscle hurt, but I tried not to show it. I felt more bruised psychologically.

"Glazur had to be careful," she added. "Or rather, I was the one who had to make sure he was careful. He didn't really know what he was getting himself into, and he was still necessary for me."

"To deliver the recordings to me?"

"That's right. And since we kept in touch via the RIC, I knew when and where you'd be."

"Hence the twelve-hour expiry for the recordings."

"Yes, although on my part it was..."

"Bluff?"

She confirmed it with a movement of her head, avoiding my gaze. "Glazur wouldn't have destroyed a flash drive even if you were late."

"So why send me on a chase like that?"

"Because you couldn't stay in one place too long. Cayman's men were tracking you down."

Ewa had no doubts about that, and neither did I. They must have been watching me for a long time, but the final confirmation they'd been following me was the fact that Falkow popped up in Chrząstowice.

Had I lost them then? Apparently I had, since none of them had found us yet. We were safe – or at least, that's what I told myself.

Ewa emptied the second bottle, draining it in one swift swallow.

"Any more questions?" she said acerbically.

"I might have a couple, actually."

"So choose one, because my mouth is getting dry and I'm afraid I won't be able to do this much longer."

"I'll get you a cure for this condition."

"If you do, I might accept more questions."

"Okay," I said, rising reluctantly, and glanced at the door. "Any preferences?"

"Prosecco," she replied without hesitation. "But, Tiger… two bottles."

I nodded and moved to leave, but she grabbed my hand. She pulled me to herself lightly, getting up from the chair. When our lips met, it felt like the whole world was spinning and we were in the eye of a hurricane, that we'd found shelter in the middle of an earthquake. It only lasted a few seconds, but it was enough for all the questions, answers, doubts and uncertainties to cease to matter anymore.

We looked at each other, and then, without saying a word, I turned around and left the room, then walked to the shop on shaking legs. I didn't think about anything; my mind was completely paralyzed. I kept glancing around, but after several hundred yards I realized I wasn't looking for a liquor store but for signs that something was wrong. A sign that we were in danger.

After all the horrors of the past hours, it was all too good to last. Were we supposed to go back to our old lives now? Build a new one together?

Both seemed equally unrealistic. I was eyeing the area as if looking for confirmation that the prospects of a happy ending to our story would soon vanish.

I would never learn what had guided Ewa, why she had done what she had, nor how she'd achieved the many things that had made her plan possible.

Any minute now, a cop would come around the corner, or I'd see a flash of moonlight on a gun held by one of Cayman's henchmen. It would all end here and now.

But I couldn't see anybody in the dark. Limping, I finally got to the petrol station. I bought two bottles of Prosecco, ignoring the apprehensive look of the employee. Then I took a four-pack of Heineken from the fridge.

On my way back to our hotel room, I felt the anxiety returning. For a moment it turned into a certainty that I wouldn't find Ewa inside.

I knocked – I don't know why – and then slowly opened the door. I took a step inside and paused. Terrified, I looked around the empty room.

"Ewa?" I asked.

4

I had an awful time waiting for Werner to come back. I tried to occupy my thoughts with something, anything, but nothing worked. They were spinning in my head like crazy. I didn't even know from which point I should continue my story.

I needed alcohol, that much was certain.

I paced the room, looking out of the window time after time, and finally I sat down with the newspaper at the table. I turned over a dozen or so pages without even knowing what I was reading. Then I went to check on Wojtek.

That was when I heard the door open.

Soon afterwards, I heard silent footsteps. Someone was walking slowly, carefully, as if in a minefield. I held my breath.

I didn't let it out until I heard Damian say my name. I left the bedroom and quietly closed the door behind me. I smiled at Werner. He looked as if he'd just faced death.

"What's wrong?" I asked.

"Nothing. You just scared the hell out of me."

"How?"

He shook his head and waved his hand, then pulled a bottle of Prosecco out of the bag, sat down at the table and started working on the cork. I sat on the other side, looking at him. He wasn't doing very well, and under different circumstances I would probably find it kind of cute, but right now I just wanted to have a drink.

When he finally opened the bottle, some wine spilled on the table. He cursed quietly and looked around.

"Don't worry about it. We'll clean up in the morning."

"I'm looking for a glass."

"Ah," I said with a smile. "No need."

I took the bottle and poured some of the drink into one of the cardboard teacups the hotel staff left for guests.

For some time, Werner drank his beer and I enjoyed my favourite drink. It made me feel better. My thoughts settled in my head so that I knew what I was supposed to say now.

Damian was tense and kept glancing at the window anxiously. I thought it was best to direct his thoughts to something other than a hypothetical threat from Robert's or Cayman's people. Yes, we'd made enemies, but no one had any idea where we were right now. No one even knew what kind of car we were driving. We were in no danger.

"Where were we?" I asked.

"You were saying that at some point you'd had enough."

"That's quite a euphemism," I admitted, putting the cup down. "I'd already gone beyond my limits."

"I see."

"And I finally decided to act."

"So why didn't you just contact me?"

"I couldn't. Robert traced every move I made. Do you know how much effort it took me to talk on the RIC? And I could only use it because tapping on the keyboard didn't arouse his suspicions – his, and those of the people he paid to keep an eye on me."

Werner raised his eyebrows.

"Gardeners, cleaners, security guards... I could go on forever. Everyone was keeping an eye on me."

"You sound like you were a prisoner in your own home."

"I was. But not just at home."

He blinked, as if this information caused him physical pain.

"I've been wondering for a long time how to contact you." I continued hurriedly. "I had to find a solution that wouldn't attract Robert's attention, and a channel of communication that I could keep secret not for a few hours or days but much longer. I didn't know how long it would take you to get there, to transfer all that money and prepare our escape."

He listened attentively, trying not to miss a word. I thought it must have been a long time since anyone had acted like that towards me. Nobody ever looked at me like that anymore.

I realized that with Werner I could enjoy a real sense of security. He didn't have to have an organization behind him that could face Cayman's mafia.

It was enough that he was willing to do anything for me.

I stared at him a little too long and he noticed that I'd drifted. He shifted anxiously and took a sip of his beer.

"I don't really understand how this solution you invented was going to help," he said.

"Because you don't know I've learned to manipulate Robert in all these years – at least to a certain extent."

"What do you mean?"

"I knew that if I made him a little more angry that night, provoked him to do worse things than usual, the following day I would be able to count on more concessions from him. He was like a pendulum, and I learned how to make it move."

"That sounds... disturbing."

I shrugged. From the outside, it really must have seemed terrible. Ultimately, the only way to influence my husband was to encourage him to beat me harder and more often. Perhaps it proved better than anything else how toxic and abusive my life had been.

"Never mind how it sounds," I said, not wanting to consider it. "One night, I started making sexual advances on him."

Damian swallowed audibly, and I realized that his imagination had to be working at full speed.

"He was asexual," I explained. "He was only satisfied by violence."

Werner inclined his head.

"I used that to make him angry when he started his daily... ritual."

"I suppose that wasn't difficult."

"No. It wasn't."

I didn't want to think back to those events. When I started accusing Robert of impotence, of not being able to make love, and finally of being attracted to men, he did everything he could to prove to me that he was none of those things.

It was just rape. Preceded by beatings and followed by beatings.

I hadn't known my husband would go that far. Sexual violence had never been his thing. It seemed like he really hadn't needed it to satisfy his degenerate desires. And yet that time I had pushed him to it.

I'd had to do it. There was no other way out.

"The next day, he did what he always did." I went on. "He didn't ask for forgiveness; he felt he didn't deserve it. He tried to beg me to repay him in kind. He expected to be able to make amends somehow. He wanted penance."

"Or he pretended to."

"No," I answered firmly. "It was true grief. True guilt."

"Somehow, he didn't look to me like he was–"

"I got to know him very well, Wern," I interrupted. "Or rather them, because there were two Roberts Reimanns. Now I'm describing the other one to you."

"Okay."

It was clear in his voice that he wasn't convinced, but that was hardly surprising. Anyone in his shoes would think they knew better than I did.

"That morning, I used what I'd worked out the previous night."

"In what way?"

"I forced him to promise to let me go on a trip. A short one, just a day trip."

Understanding dawned in Werner's eyes. "To a concert in Wrocław?"

"Yeah. I'd started planning it several months earlier, as soon as I'd found out the Foo Fighters would be performing. I knew Blitzer would be there, he wouldn't miss the opportunity." I took a deep breath and pulled my fringe aside. "And neither would I."

"You've never been a Foo Fighters fan."

I smiled briefly. "Robert didn't know that. In fact, he was convinced I loved them."

"Yeah?

"I'd been playing their albums over and over ever since I'd found out about the concert. And when the time came, Robert had no doubt that I really wanted to see them live."

Damian raised his eyebrows and let out a long breath. It was as if the knowledge of all that I'd had to do overwhelmed him.

"That day I made an order at a clothing store," I added. "I bought a grey hoodie for Robert."

"With the inscription 'There is Nothing Left to Lose' and the band's logo, right?"

"Right."

"And for yourself, the T-shirt that led me to your clues." I finally heard acknowledgement in his voice.

"It was the only way to do that without arousing suspicion," I said. "Robert rigidly controlled all my shopping. He decided what I could order."

Werner started to shudder, becoming more and more aware of how little control I'd had over my own life. I wanted him to understand that. It explained a lot, as did all the recordings I'd made for him. I was hoping they would convince him that we could get back at least some of those ten lost years. I wasn't sure if I'd achieved my goal yet.

"In the end, all I had to do was order tickets," I added.

"And count on Blitzer to see you?"

"No. I stayed out of his sight. I couldn't risk it. I was there with Robert."

"Well, yes…"

"But Glazur was there too. He had to take a picture of me, which he then posted on the *Spotted* and Foo Fighters profiles. I knew Blitz would show up in one or the other."

Werner nodded. "When it came to pick-up attempts, you could always rely on Blitzkrieg," he said in an absent voice. "Anyway…"

He broke off, but I guessed what he wanted to say – that he could also be relied on in other areas. I didn't want to think about Blitz – he was my guilty conscience. His death should never have happened. My plan shouldn't have led to that.

But I couldn't have predicted everything.

I focused back on what I was supposed to tell Damian. To make things easier, I took another sip of Prosecco. I needed at least a dozen or so more before I could continue.

Wern was looking at me expectantly.

"So this Phil Braddy was supposed to make sure Blitzer followed your lead," he said.

"Glazur."

"Well, yes... What's with the nickname, anyway?"

"That scar on his face. Gives him a glazed look."

"How appropriate."

I shrugged, wondering where to take up the story. I finally figured it was best to stick to the timeline of events. I started to talk about how I checked Blitz's progress, how I waited anxiously until there was a sign that Damian had joined the search.

And how surprised I was at the response of the police.

"Prokocki really felt responsible," I said. "He immediately made sure all the photos and clues disappeared. He meant well."

"Perhaps."

"I'm sure he did. He's the only one I don't suspect of any duplicity. He's been protecting me all these years."

"And yet there was a leak, not necessarily from Falkow," Werner murmured. "And it was that person who got Blitz killed."

I nodded sadly.

"Do you know who?" he asked.

"No," I answered. "Probably an outsider, paid for by Cayman. I doubt he'd want to use his own people or the police to do it."

"But…"

I knew exactly what he wanted to ask, but I didn't volunteer the answer. It would be better if Wern processed everything on his own.

"But they accused me," he said after a while. "Why? I mean, Prokocki must have known I didn't kill Blitz."

"I suppose so."

"But?"

"I told you, he really felt he had a duty to protect me."

"That much?"

"Are you surprised?" I asked, turning the paper cup in my hands. The bubbles rose to the surface. "He's an old-fashioned cop and he gave me his word that I'd be safe. After Cayman ordered the murder of my parents, Prokocki swore to himself that he would do anything to prevent something similar happening to me."

"So he accused me of a murder I had nothing to do with?"

"He just turned the prosecutor's attention to–"

"Come on," Damian cut me off. "I mean, it was his decision. Why would he do that?"

"To protect me," I answered in a hard voice. "He assumed you were the greatest threat to me."

Damian snorted quietly, as if what I'd said was utterly preposterous.

"He was sure that the whole thing was Cayman's doing," I added, "and that after all those years, he'd finally found a way to get to me. Because of you."

"Okay."

"Prokocki was sure you'd finally get to the truth and find me in Pomerania, and that those who'd spent years waiting to take revenge on me would follow you."

"So couldn't he just–"

"What?" I interrupted him. "Contact you when you were hiding from everyone?"

I guess it was only now that Werner realized he'd been off the grid from the moment he'd discovered his friend's body. He'd just assumed he'd been framed, and that he would be prosecuted.

And that was exactly what Cayman wanted. A desperate man on the run, searching for his missing fiancée, was much more useful to him. That was why they killed Blitzer and left Damian alive. The move was brilliant in its simplicity and gave Cayman everything he wanted – but he hadn't considered that I would lead Werner from one location to another, thus helping him lose his tail.

"Are you telling me that if I'd just talked to Prokocki, it could all have ended differently?"

"Sometimes a simple conversation is enough," I answered diplomatically and paused for a moment. "And sometimes not."

We agreed on that without saying a word. I could see that Damian felt doubly manipulated, first by me and then by the people who were after me. But I didn't think it was time to make him feel better. He had to learn about the rest.

"Prokocki finally decided that the situation was a crisis, and that Cayman was just one step away from tracking me down."

"So he pulled the trick with the body on Bolko."

"Yes," I replied and sighed.

"Who did it belong to?"

"I don't know. I suppose it was a Jane Doe, or maybe there was no body at all."

"It certainly exists in official documents."

I agreed with a quiet murmur.

"Prokocki tried to convince everyone, including you, that I was dead," I added, because I had a feeling that it had to be said outright. "But maybe he should have done it much earlier to make it work."

Werner looked outside the window at some point. I knew he'd already gathered all the elements of the puzzle into a coherent whole, at least as far as the actions of others were concerned. I wasn't sure he understood my motives.

"I had no other choice, Tiger," I added after a while.

He raised his eyebrows.

"I had to make you stay on the move all the time."

"I know."

"And I had to make sure you were the only one who could read my messages. It was absolutely crucial, because there was no doubt Cayman's men would keep an eye on you and pick up every trace I left."

Damian got up and walked to the window. For a moment he stayed motionless, not turning around. It seemed to me that there was still something that he thought was not quite right in the whole structure I had outlined for him. Just enough so he couldn't leave it be.

But I didn't know what it was.

5

A man in a baseball cap backs up two steps when he sees Damian Werner in the hotel window. His target is unlikely to notice him, but it's better to be safe than sorry.

The camouflage is quite good, given their current location. He drove up here in a lorry, a new Scania. Nobody paid any attention to him, especially not Werner.

The lorry driver wasn't surprised. Most fugitives expected to be pursued by a black SUV, not a truck. They were a constant feature on Polish roads and blended in with the surroundings.

The man knew that this was the only way he would he be able to follow Werner and Kasandra unnoticed.

He found Reimann's body moments after the two fugitives had left the villa. He didn't know what to do with it at first, but then reasoned he had plenty of time to think of something. He didn't have to drive nose-to-tail behind the blue Peugeot; he had prepared himself well in advance so as not to lose the fugitives.

Reimann was complicating things a little bit, though. The corpse could mean that the police would get involved. Investigators wouldn't wait for forensics to find out who was responsible for the murder. But was it likely anyone would get on the right track? Not really.

The driver looks at Werner and wonders how much longer he'll have to wait to take action. Actually, he's ready for it. Damian has no idea that he's being watched. When he finally realizes he and Ewa have had a tail from the beginning, it will be too late to do anything.

The man pulls his baseball cap down on his forehead and returns to the lorry. He locks the door, but he leaves the curtain open. He parked so that he has a clear view of what's going on in the hotel room, but even if he can't hear them, he's sure Kasandra is telling Werner how she's been avoiding Cayman for years. The man in the cap is convinced that he knows every detail. And that he knows each step they will make. They'll sleep, rest, and then move on. He doesn't know in which direction, but they will probably try to leave the EU. There was a reason they were heading east. In a small town just before the border, they will stop to withdraw the cash that Kasandra took from her husband's accounts. With that, they will move on to start a new life.

The driver is looking at Werner now. He sees a smile on his face, which suggests that Damian may also be thinking about that future.

Hope is the mother of fools and a treacherous mistress of lovers, the man thinks, and then settles down more comfortably and prepares for the long wait. A wait for a success that would be his crowning glory.

6

I turned away from the window and sat on the windowsill. Ewa looked at me uncertainly, as if she expected me not to understand her motives. But I understood them very well indeed. I once came across some research into domestic violence against women that made my skin crawl. I didn't remember the details, but one statistic stuck in my mind: every week, three women died at the hands of people like Robert Reimann.

Someday, Ewa could have become one of those three. Reimann's brutality had been increasing and there had been no sign of that ever changing. To escape this horror, she had to act, and with the utmost caution, not only for fear of Cayman but also of her husband. Perhaps especially because of him. If he'd known that Ewa was going to run away from him, things would have ended horribly. This explained why she'd chosen such a complex solution to the problem.

I closed my eyes for a moment, thinking about how many women there were in a similar situation. Three a week were killed by their partners, but how many more experience the same hell as Ewa? The hell that takes place behind closed doors and is therefore not included in any statistics?

"What's wrong?" Ewa spoke.

I raised my eyelids. "Nothing, I'm fine."

"You seem disturbed." She got up and approached me slowly. She stood by the window and looked around outside. "Did you see anything suspicious?"

"No," I answered, taking her hand. "Although under the circumstances a little bit of paranoia would actually be advisable."

We stood facing each other, a few inches apart, and stared at each other for so long that it felt as if the whole world stopped for a while, finally giving us an opportunity to enjoy each other's presence.

"No one is following us," said Ewa. "The police have no idea where to find us. Cayman lost our trail, and Robert's men don't know what happened yet."

"I hope so."

"I took care of it," she replied and smiled. "That's exactly why we're in no danger from them."

"But we are from others, right?"

She let go of my hand and went back to the table, then poured herself some more Prosecco and sat down so she could see me.

"That's what I'm afraid of," I said.

"What, exactly?"

It seemed to me that the three threats she'd mentioned were the entirety of our hypothetical concerns.

"I don't know if you'll be able to forgive me, Tiger."

"Forgive what?"

"Everything I've done." She paused and looked away. "I know what it must seem like."

"What?"

"As if I've been toying with you," she said, clearly embarrassed. "It's like I selfishly decided that you had to go down at least part of the road I had taken."

I frowned, considering my response. I knew her motives well enough. She should know that, although perhaps I would also have some doubts if I were in her place.

"You sound like you don't know me," I said, moving over her.

She didn't answer for a long time – too long. I knew what that meant.

I sat across from her and made myself smile. My whole face still hurt, but I thought it would be best to get used to that, given the circumstances. It didn't look like I was going to return to full health – physical or mental – anytime soon.

"And yet you know me very well," I said.

"Are you sure?"

"Yes. I'm the same guy who proposed to you at the Sneering Lodge. I may not have been him for ten years, but now I've become him again."

She was looking at me curiously. I was aware that she was going to ask the key question: *Are we still the same people we were when we got together all those years ago?* I thought we were, despite everything we'd been through.

"I didn't mean to bring down all that trouble on you, Tiger."

"I know," I answered. "And I also know that you don't realize all your own motivations."

"What's that?"

"You may not be ready to admit it, but it was all a test."

"What are you talking about?"

"About how you subconsciously wanted me to pass the test of devotion, of love. That's how you found out how much you still meant to me. And that I was willing to go through the nine circles of hell to find you."

She smiled sadly. This hadn't been her primary goal, no, but deep down she had to know it had also been part of her motivations. She had to confirm that she was dealing with the same Werner she'd known once before. She couldn't afford to repeat the mistake she'd made with Robert.

"It's not like that," she said.

"Never mind," I said. "What matters is that I showed you how much I care about you."

She acknowledged this with a slight smile. "True," she admitted.

I pulled her lightly to me and kissed her. I had a disturbing feeling that I would somehow hurt her. It was an absurd and unfounded sensation, but at the same time justified in some way. Everything Ewa had gone through had almost destroyed her, and I was afraid that with a single blunder I would be the last straw that broke her.

"You don't have to be so gentle," she said, as if she could read my mind.

"I'm not going to."

She cocked her head to the side, looking me right in the eye. "Let's do it, Tiger."

I took hold of her waist and tried to make it look like I was really going to get down to business. But I wasn't. It seemed inappropriate at the moment.

It was like I was using her, exploiting her vulnerability. There was no logic in it, but nor was anything else logical. We'd found ourselves in an impossible situation.

We were fleeing the country, being pursued by the police and Cayman's gang. In addition, as soon as Robert Reimann's men realized what was happening, they would send their own goons. And as if that wasn't enough, we had a child with us. I shook my head.

"That's not how I remember you getting down to business," she said. I looked towards the bed.

"If it weren't for Wojtek sleeping in the next room, I'd be on top of you right now and we'd be at it all night."

"Oh," she said with something akin to admiration. "Did you get gallant in your old age?"

"I've always been like this."

Instead of answering, she snuggled up to me like I was a warm blanket on a cold night. The words we exchanged had practically nothing to do with the conversation we really had – the one that didn't involve words.

We stayed still and silent for some time. Then Ewa moved away and gave me a questioning look. "What else do you want to know?" she asked.

"Everything."

"Then ask me. Let's get this over with here and now, once and for all."

"Okay," I said, letting myself be led to the table. "But I'm not interested in the past anymore."

"No?"

"I only care about what's ahead of us."

Her raised eyebrows made me think she didn't believe me. "You don't want to ask me if my culinary tastes haven't changed? Whether I suddenly developed a passion for Marvel comics, or decided to have a plastic surgery?"

"What's there to ask? I look at you and I see everything, plain and simple."

"Oh, yeah? Then go ahead, tell me what's changed." She poured herself a Prosecco, crossed her arms on her chest and waited for me to speak.

"You had a nose job, as well as fillers in your cheeks and lips."

"And?"

"That's it."

"Not exactly. I also had my receding chin corrected."

"You've never had a receding chin."

"Maybe not in your eyes," she answered with a snigger. "But ultimately, it wasn't about making myself more beautiful."

"And yet you took advantage of the opportunity."

She shrugged and smiled. I wasn't surprised she'd tried to change her appearance – if I were her, I would have done the same. Although such procedures couldn't work miracles – contrary to the claims of plastic surgeons – with a bit of luck Ewa could manage to confuse a handful of nosy people. Unless someone knew her well, they might not be able to recognize her as Kasandra Reimann. But I had no such problems.

I assumed she'd started undertaking the procedures after getting involved with Robert, as she probably hadn't had the financial means to do so earlier, but I didn't want to ask her. I wasn't interested in anything to do with that man.

Besides, I really wanted to focus on the future. There was a lot of work ahead of us.

"Perhaps I should consider having something done now," I said.

"All you have to do is grow a beard."

"You think?"

"Wherever we go, you don't need anything else, Tiger."

"Where *are* we going?"

"Into the past."

"So, Belarus?"

"Or Ukraine, or Kaliningrad," she said, and put her empty cup away. "I thought it would be best if we decided once all the accounts are cleared out."

"No one will track us down?"

"No." There was no uncertainty in her voice. She was convinced that she had taken care of everything. "Each of the accounts is set up in your name, and the deposits were just small enough for the tax office not to notice. Plus, neither I nor Robert had anything to do with them, at least on paper. Even if somebody were to... discover the body, they won't be able to freeze the accounts in time."

"I hope so."

It was our only insurance. In Belarus or Ukraine, we couldn't count on any well-paid work, but after exchanging our zlotys to roubles or hryvnias, our funds would let us live a very comfortable life. With a bit of luck, we would be able to invest them well and grow them, I thought. Anyway, Ewa probably already had a plan for that.

"The police aren't going to track me down?" I asked.

"They will, but by then we'll be far away from here."

"Are you sure?"

"Yes," she confirmed again without hesitation. "They're looking for you in Opole, maybe in other places around there. You're still safe here for a while."

She was right. Although Blitz's murder was a personal tragedy for me, for Polish law enforcement it had no priority over similar cases. In case of emergency, it was enough for Ewa to talk to Prokocki and assure him that it was pointless to continue chasing me.

"So what now?" I asked.

"First thing in the morning, we'll visit a few places, pay what we need to and then disappear."

"And the papers?"

"I've taken care of that too."

"How?"

"Do you have to be so nosy?"

"Considering you've had me running all over Poland, keeping me in the dark, I think I have–"

"Yeah, yeah," she said, cutting me off with a wave of her hand. "You have every right to know what kind of lowlifes I had to deal with."

I didn't really need to know every detail. It was obvious that Ewa used contacts she'd made through her husband. Meanwhile, she didn't ask for help from people who could report her to someone in his circle. At least not right away.

"Is Glazur still helping us?" I asked.

"No, I told him to disappear right after he gave you his last message. I couldn't risk it. He's done enough for me already. He took care of almost everything IT-related, from planting tracks in the deep web to choosing which file format to use."

"He didn't seem so resourceful to me."

"Appearances can be deceiving. He can do a lot of things."

"Should I be jealous?"

"Never," she replied snappishly. "And of nobody."

It was a good thing she had pushed him away, I thought to myself. At this stage, anyone involved in the case would only be a burden to us. I looked at Ewa and tried to gauge how confident she was that she'd be able to carry out the plan to the very end. So far, she'd been going ahead steadfastly, but how long would she be able to do that?

I didn't see any signs of doubt in her eyes. It made me believe that we were really safe.

Still, I couldn't sleep a wink when we finally went to bed. It was already dawn and it was getting lighter. The first sounds of waking birds were the ultimate confirmation that it was too late to rest.

We had an hour, maybe two. Then we unanimously decided that it was time to hit the road. Wojtek woke up only for a moment and moved from his room to the car as if in a trance. He lay down in the back seat and fell asleep again. He was a child, without a care in the world, and I envied him that.

This time, I took the wheel. I looked at the lorries parked along a small access road and stretched. It felt like my ribs were cracking.

Soon, we turned off onto a road leading east. I felt relief as if we'd left all the danger behind us. At times I wasn't even worried about what might be waiting for us at the border. At one point I almost forgot that we should still be vigilant. I lowered my guard, took the liberty of enjoying a little bit of happiness. And whenever I exchanged short glances with Ewa, I was convinced that I had every right to do so.

I drove slowly, minding the speed limit. There was a lorry dragging behind us, and had been for some time now. I think it was a Scania.

When the sun emerged from the clouds, turning the wet road into a mirror, I had the feeling that along with the dawn, our shared, joyful future was coming. I knew Ewa felt similarly. We still believed that we were immortal.

In the evening, shortly after we'd paid out all the money and eventually headed for Ukraine, life brutally made us realize how wrong we had been.

We were driving a small single-lane road, safely away from the main commuter routes. We wanted to get to the Ukraine border via provincial roads, avoiding expressways. We thought that now, when we had all our belongings in the car, all of our future ahead of us, and when we were so close to our goal, we couldn't afford even the slightest risk.

This was our mistake – the mistake that made us actually take the greatest risk.

When we were on an empty road, crossing vast fields, in the rear-view mirror I saw the same Scania that had been following us in the north. But it was too late for me to do anything. It accelerated as if the driver had fallen asleep at the wheel and the cruise control had been set so it gradually gained speed. By the time I realized the truck wouldn't have time to brake, it was already just a few metres away from our Peugeot.

7

The man in the cap is certain he's chosen the right moment. Before making the decision, he'd been following the blue car for many kilometres at the right distance. He'd studied the map in advance and prepared himself, waiting for the right moment, and it has just come. They're on a straight section of road; according to the satnav, the nearest turn is a few kilometres away.

And there's another lorry just ahead of the Peugeot. The man checked on the CB radio who was driving it, and it couldn't be better, as it turned out. The driver was a Ukrainian who didn't understand much Polish. With a bit of luck, he could be carrying some extra not-entirely-legal cargo, which would make him unlikely to alert the police.

Or maybe there won't be any reason to worry about it, the man in the cap thinks and speeds up even more. He's been watching Damian Werner closely and he knows that Kasandra's companion has no idea of the imminent threat.

Just before the front of the lorry hits the rear bumper of the Peugeot, the man steps on the brake pedal. Werner reacts exactly as he should: he accelerates.

The old 206 has maybe a hundred horse power, so it takes the car a while to accelerate. If the man hadn't braked, Damian wouldn't have stood a chance. But it wasn't about pushing them out of the way. Too risky. Although he's entirely free to make his own decisions, there is one guideline: neither Kasandra nor the child may be harmed.

Actually, he should spare Werner, too. But if it came down to it, he'd be willing to sacrifice him.

The driver picks up the radio and clears his throat. His Russian is a bit rusty – it's been a long time since he last used it – but he supposes he will be able to say as much as he needs to.

He touches a button on his side, takes a breath, and then screams to the Ukrainian driving in front of him to speed up, not to let the Peugeot behind him get ahead of the lorry.

The man doesn't know how effective his panicked screams will be, but if the other driver is actually carrying smuggled cigarettes, diesel or anything else that might upset the customs officers, he's probably not going to take any risks. In any case, the solidarity of truckers should do the job.

He is clearly accelerating, saying something on the radio, but the man in the cap isn't listening to him anymore. Now everything is up to him. He presses his foot on the accelerator again, this time with no intention of braking. The blue car is trapped.

8

"Get ahead of him!" I screamed when I knew Werner wouldn't make it in time.

All three vehicles were moving too fast, and Damian had no time to react. He could have swerved to the opposite lane, but he was aware of the double danger that would involve. It was impossible to see if anyone was coming from the opposite direction, and a head-on collision with another car would be disastrous. There was no point in deluding ourselves that any of us would survive. The Peugeot would be squished like an accordion.

And even if we were lucky enough not to run into anyone, we'd be running parallel with the lorry in front. All it would take was for the driver to turn slightly towards us and the trailer would push us off the road, which would cause us just as much damage as a head-on collision with another vehicle.

Still, I screamed as much at the top of my lungs for him to get us out of here. Fortunately, Werner ignored me and didn't even try to overtake the lorry ahead of us.

In a split second, we found ourselves in between the two vehicles.

"Mum! Mum!" Wojtek shouted from the back seat when the lorry behind us hit our bumper.

I saw Damian's knuckles whiten on the steering wheel.

"Mum! Mum!" Wojtek screamed again.

I wanted to calm him down, to tell him something, anything, but I couldn't say a word. I pressed my hands against the dashboard, even though that was probably the worst thing I could have done. If we crashed like that, my arms would snap like twigs, not to mention that it would stop the airbag from working properly – if the Peugeot even had one.

Hundreds of thoughts were flying through my head. I couldn't get a grip on myself, find the solution. I finally looked into the rear-view mirror.

"Werner!" I screamed. "He's alone!"

Damian looked at me, clearly terrified.

"The one in front of us is just a random Ukrainian!"

I could see that he didn't understand what I meant. For God's sake, we were wasting precious seconds, and I couldn't afford to waste even one more.

"Brake!"

"Are you crazy?!"

"Now!"

He finally understood – at least, I hoped so. The only way for us was to lose speed was to let the Ukrainian drive away and then accelerate rapidly. While the old 206 didn't have much power, it could accelerate quicker than the lorry.

There was no other option.

"Brake!" I screamed again.

He finally did what I asked. It all happened in a few seconds – we didn't have time to question anything. We had to save ourselves in the only possible way we could come up with.

Werner pushed the brake pedal and I stared into the mirror in horror. I was afraid Damian had overreacted and braked too suddenly.

The top of the cab behind us seemed to bend forwards as the lorry driver tried to brake. We drove for a short while bumper to bumper.

What happened next shouldn't have.

Under the pressure of the multi-tonne vehicle, Werner turned the steering wheel slightly to the right. The tyres screeched, and a split second later the Peugeot lost its grip on the road. The car pulled aside, and Wojtek let out a terrified yelp. His screaming reverberated in my head in a deafening echo.

The car swerved off the road and into a small ditch. There was a bang that sounded like an explosion, but nothing exploded. We fell into a small slope between the trees, and I quickly realized how lucky we were.

For a moment I was confused. I didn't understand what was going on. It felt so unreal that I was paralyzed, but I got over it quickly. I pulled my seatbelt, trying to turn around and check on Wojtek.

As soon I pressed the release button, the belt went back with a whistle, and I turned around. My son was fine. He was in shock, breathing unevenly and looking around anxiously, but he was fine.

I let out a long breath and noticed Damian getting out of the car. By the time I had a chance to react, he was already rushing towards the braking lorry.

He'd made the right decision. He'd seen that the driver was alone and realized that the only sensible way out was to take the initiative. The problem was, he didn't stand a chance of winning the confrontation.

I told Wojtek not to move and pushed the door open. I got out of the car like it was on fire and rushed after Werner. Suddenly, all my injuries suffered at Robert's hands seemed to disappear, or at least I no longer felt the paralyzing pain.

I was aware that it was adrenaline, and I knew the agony would return in a minute.

Werner and I ran as fast as we could. Damian realized that, for him to have any chance of overpowering the driver, he had to get to the cab before the man could react.

I couldn't catch up with him. I couldn't breathe and it felt as if something was tearing my lungs apart from the inside.

When Werner got to the lorry, I had to stop. I was in worse shape than I thought. Adrenaline or not, my body gave me a clear signal that it couldn't take any more.

I bent double, leaned on my knees and breathed loudly, looking up.

I saw the door open. The man jumped out of the cab, unaware that Damian was right next to him. As soon as he leaned out, Wern grabbed his shirt and pulled him out on the road.

Without a second thought, he kicked him right in the head.

The man didn't stand the slightest chance.

I closed my eyes for a moment, took a deep breath, and then rushed along the side of the road. From the corner of my eye, I saw a small branch that I could use. I grabbed it on the move, slowing just for a moment to bend down Then I mustered all my energy to get to the lorry as soon as possible.

Damian hit the driver again, and then suddenly froze.

I knew exactly why.

9

I acted like an automaton. I didn't think about it, I didn't calculate it, I didn't estimate my chances in a confrontation against that man. All I knew was that he was alone. That was enough for me to make a decision.

When I pulled him out of the vehicle, I didn't hesitate to hit him. Our safety was at stake – Ewa's, Wojtek's and mine. Not just safety, but our whole future.

That man could have taken her away from us.

Without a moment's notice, I hit him again and intended to continue until I was sure that he wouldn't get up. But then I looked at his face.

Blood was dripping down from the corner of his mouth and there was a cut on his temple, right next to a clear mark left by one of my blows. The red trickle was flowing down to the eye, right over a small scar underneath it.

I stood there as if struck by lightning, unable to comprehend how it was possible. Was my mind playing tricks on me? Was I dreaming? There he was, right in front of me, the man I'd met in Biskupin.

The man with a scar under his eye.

Glazur.

The one who'd been helping Ewa from the very beginning, who'd taken care of all the IT staff, who'd provided me with all those pieces of information – who had been fired for that, in fact, and had had to say goodbye to his career and was probably constantly being watched by Robert Reimann's men.

What the hell was going on here?

I took a step back, still trying to understand what had made Glazur attack us. And how he had found us.

He couldn't have had anything to do with Reimann's criminal organization, or Cayman's, or he'd have shown his true motives long ago. He'd plenty of opportunities to do that.

My head was buzzing. I heard Ewa running towards us, but I couldn't move.

"What the fuck are you…" I blurted.

The man on the ground spat out some blood and looked at me uncertainly. I couldn't see fear in his eyes, though he should have been afraid. Maybe he was working with the police? No, it didn't make any sense either.

"Who are you?" I asked.

He mumbled something incomprehensible and I took a step back. I realized he was more stunned than I was, though in his case more physically than mentally, like me. I couldn't collect my thoughts.

I turned towards where Ewa was coming from.

And that was when the blow hit me – hard and fast, sealing everything that had happened. Someone had struck me on the temple, but my mind refused to understand who it had been.

I staggered and Ewa hit me again.

There was a loud clatter in my head, as if I had been standing right next to gigantic speakers at a rock concert. Confusion gave way to utter powerlessness. I dropped to the ground, unable to cushion the fall.

Ewa stood above me, breathing hard. She lowered her hand and I saw blood dripping from the tip of the branch she was holding. I felt wetness spreading on the back of my head.

I couldn't understand anything.

Not a single thing.

Ewa walked past me without a glance. It was as if she thought I was no longer a threat and therefore not worth any attention.

She squatted by Glazur and touched his face.

She said something, but it was so quiet I couldn't make out the words.

I tried to get up, but all I could do was twitch. I realized that one of the blows must have been a lucky one, doing me more harm than Ewa had intended. At least that was what I thought, clinging to the remnants of rationality.

What had actually happened? What was *that* all about?

Had it really happened at all? Or was I asleep in a hotel room, dreaming the worst nightmare of my life?

Ewa helped Glazur get up and looked at his face. When he put his hands on her waist and spoke, he looked like a regular guy reassuring his beloved that everything was all right.

I started crawling towards them slowly, just like I had ten years ago at the Sneering Lodge.

History came full circle.

10

Glazur pulled his hands back, assured me once again that he was fine and then glanced at the Peugeot anxiously.

"Is Wojtek all right?" he asked.

"Yes, he's okay. He's a little scared, but... we'll take care of him right away."

He nodded and shifted his eyes to Werner. Glazur looked at him for a long time while I tried to assess whether he had a concussion. Realizing the reason for my concern, he embraced me and assured me that he was really fine.

"You've been hit hard," I objected.

"It could have been worse."

It was hard to disagree with that. It wasn't supposed to end like this – and most likely wouldn't have, if only Damian hadn't lost control of the car. But none of us wanted to discuss it.

There was no point now.

"You didn't have to hit him so hard," Glazur said.

I took his hand, and he pulled me to him.

"It's all right now," he said.

"I know."

He looked at Damian again.

"Is he going to make it?" he asked.

I hoped so. I never wanted to see more misfortune than absolutely necessary to carry out my plan. "Hopefully," I replied.

"You could have stopped at the first one."

"I had to make sure he wasn't going to be a danger to you anymore."

"He wouldn't be any danger. He recognized me and probably already started to understand what was going on."

I didn't think that would happen. From Damian's point of view, the situation was completely different from reality.

He deserved to know the truth. I would reveal it to him under completely different circumstances, to mitigate the blow he had received from fate.

No, not from fate. From me, Glazur and everyone else involved in this venture. It was high time I admitted it openly to myself. I took a deep breath and turned to Damian.

He was crawling towards us, leaving a red trail behind. It looked horrible, as if he was trying to cross the last yards that separated him from his own death.

I looked around anxiously.

"We don't have much time," Glazur said.

"I know."

"If you want to tell him, you have to hurry."

"I do want to, but…"

"What?" Glazur asked, and I glanced at him. He looked deep into my eyes. "He deserves to know the truth, at least."

"I know," I admitted. "But we can't afford to take any more risks."

We didn't take long to consider it. One car passing by and we would lose everything we'd been working so hard for.

We moved towards the Peugeot without a word. I knew Wojtek would be happy to see Glazur. He would probably greet him with a loud and enthusiastic "Uncle!", like he used to. Then Glazur would embrace him, take him to the driver's cab and make sure not to let Wojtek see Damian lying on the road.

We'd explain to the boy that Werner had to leave us. Wojtek wouldn't ask any questions; he hadn't had time to get to know Damian, let alone get attached to him. To my son, he was a nobody, and in a few years he wouldn't even remember having met him.

Glazur and I wouldn't be able to say the same, however.

We moved Wojtek to the lorry and then took care of what was in the Peugeot, quickly wrapping all the money in small packages and hiding it among the cargo in the trailer. Everything was ready to cross the border.

We looked at each other, satisfied, yet deep down I felt a sense of disappointment. Glazur must have seen it because his brow wrinkled with worry.

"I really wanted to explain everything to him," I said.

He looked around. "Maybe there's still time…"

"No, there isn't," I said.

Glazur nodded and got into the cab and I squatted next to Werner. He was unconscious, bleeding. In his condition, he couldn't have heard much and probably remembered even less.

"I'm sorry," I said simply.

I got up and headed for the lorry. I got inside and smiled at Glazur. He gave me a bright smile in response. I didn't need anything else to make me happy.

When we were leaving, I looked in the side mirror. I thought Werner raised his head a fraction.

11

I'd like to say I woke up in the hospital, but it wouldn't be true. I was lying in a hospital bed when I opened my eyes, but I woke up in a new reality.

It was stripped of all dreams, illusions and hopes. In the end, it became something real. A real place I'd been heading towards for some time now.

My parents were sitting by my bed. In the hallway, I saw a police officer slowly walking back and forth. From his perspective, nothing happened. He didn't have to worry about anything, especially me.

I was cleared of the charges, the search for Blitz's killer was over, and the suspect was locked up in a jail. He was a man known to the police, but unrelated to Cayman. He had been certainly hired by him, although there was no evidence of that.

The prosecution needed evidence. I didn't.

My parents had been trying to talk to me, but I wouldn't respond. At one point, they were afraid of permanent brain damage, but the doctor assured them that none of the tests showed anything disturbing.

I had a concussion, but the most severe effects had already subsided. I was fine, at least as far as ailments that an MRI could detect were concerned.

I finally spoke, just to calm my parents down. They breathed a sigh of relief, and I immediately felt guilty that I'd kept them in limbo for so long. But the truth was, I didn't know what to tell them.

Especially since they kept asking just one question. The one my father repeated when I finally spoke up.

"What happened, son?"

"I don't know."

They looked at each other.

"What do the cops say?" I asked.

"That..." Mum started, but stopped mid-sentence.

"They want to press further charges against you," Dad continued.

I felt frozen. I needed a moment to digest the information. So the cop's presence was significant, then? It seemed absurd.

Maybe I'd been hit harder than I'd thought. Maybe I didn't remember anything.

I tried to swallow, looking at my father uncertainly. "Christ," I moaned. "What charges?"

"Murder and kidnapping."

"What?"

"They say you killed someone in Rewal, son."

It dawned on me that they must have found Robert Reimann's body. And the DNA I left behind. In fact, all they needed was to check my numerous injuries.

I shifted anxiously and felt every single one of my wounds ache. I looked at my parents and tried to gauge how it all appeared from their perspective. It was obvious they didn't believe the police, but in that case what *did* they think?

"Listen..."

"You don't have to say anything," Mum interrupted.

She glanced at the door and I realized that the policeman was now standing in the doorway. I wasn't handcuffed to my bed; apparently they assumed that I wasn't in any condition to escape.

"I know," I said. "But I want to explain it to you. And I don't care if anybody's listening."

"Everything is clear to us, son."

"Not everything."

"You were framed," Dad continued. "We don't know how, but we're going to help you deal with all that."

I knew it would be like that, although I saw an unspoken question in my mother's eyes. Perhaps even more than one. I looked at her long enough to make her realize that I was waiting for her to address the subject that troubled her the most. Eventually she coughed quietly, and I nodded.

"Ask me, Mum."

"I just want to–"

"Not now," my father mumbled.

"No, now is good." I objected. "I have no reason to hide anything from the police."

They both let out a long breath without saying a word.

"Are you wondering why I went to Rewal?" I suggested, supposing that was what interested them the most. "Because Ewa was waiting for me there. That's probably what this bullshit kidnapping charge is about."

"Son…"

I raised my hand a fraction. "Wait," I said. "Let me finish."

"Ewa is dead, son."

I shook my head. "She's alive. That body they found on Bolko, it was…"

"Her," Mum interrupted. "It really was her."

Dad looked down sadly. "They ran all the tests. It's been confirmed," he added. "The police have no doubts about it."

My parents looked like they didn't have any, either. But I wasn't ready to believe it – even though, after what had happened, I should actually be open to every possibility, even the most irrational one. I should have been ready to accept anything – not just now, but much earlier.

"That's impossible," I said.

"We've seen the results ourselves, son. Commissioner Prokocki brought us to the station, showed us everything."

"Documents can be forged. And they were just trying to protect her."

"Protect her?" Mum asked. "From whom?"

"Cayman's men. The ones that chased her."

"Cayman?"

I looked at the officer like I was counting on him to explain everything to my parents. But when I met his astonished gaze, I realized one thing.

Everything I knew about Cayman came from Ewa's recordings.

The same applied to everything that had happened to her over the last decade, too. Every scrap of information about Prokocki, the witness protection programme and every move by the police had come from the same source.

Everything I knew about the situation was based on what Ewa had told me.

For God's sake, did I somehow get into one gigantic manipulation?

I felt like there was a whirlpool in my head, pulling all rational thought into the abyss. I could only watch it spin faster and faster, surrender to the current and disappear. I couldn't fish any sensible conclusions out of the maelstrom. Everything seemed both possible and impossible at the same time, feasible and nonsense. I was completely lost – and worst of all, there was no one who could answer my questions.

No one except Ewa.

"Son?"

"It's all right," I mumbled.

"Who's Cayman?"

I shook my head, squinting my eyes.

"It doesn't matter now. I'll tell the police everything I know."

Again, they looked at each other as if one was expecting the other to come up with an idea of how to help me. I expected my father to try to offer something, but before he could the officer came back into the room and we all focused our attention on him.

He pulled his mobile phone and handed it to me, as if he was pointing a gun.

"Commissioner Prokocki would like to talk to you."

I opened my mouth but said nothing. It didn't seem like standard procedure to me. If they were really going to charge me, contacting me on the phone was a bad idea.

I stretched out my hand and the officer gave me the phone.

"Yes?" I said into it.

"You've got yourself into some deep trouble," said the deputy commissioner.

"I noticed."

"But we can help you with at least some of that, if you agree to cooperate."

"To be honest, I'm not sure who I should cooperate with."

Prokocki snorted quietly. "Not the first time I've heard that," he replied. "But I always have the same answer: it's best to trust those who swear to protect the safety of citizens."

"You mean the same people who occasionally break that oath?"

"There are black sheep in every herd."

"But you're not one of them?"

"No," he said and sighed, as if annoyed at having to articulate that. "I'm your last resort, your only hope of getting out of the swamp you're sinking into."

I was silent, aware that Prokocki might actually be right. If I could believe what I'd heard on the recordings, the deputy commissioner was indeed the only person that could help me. And at this stage I no longer trusted anything I'd heard from Ewa.

"Are you still there?"

"Yes," I said.

"Okay, good. And since you haven't hung up on me, I suppose at least you're considering whether you can trust me."

"I'm considering it, yes."

Prokocki sighed again. "So let's put it this way: you have absolutely no way out, for fuck's sake," he said. "You're charged with the murder of Reimann and the kidnapping of his wife and child."

"That's absurd."

"I think so, too."

"So why–"

"Because my hunches aren't enough for my superiors or the prosecutor's office."

Neither of us said anything for a moment.

"That's why I need to know your motives. Do you understand?"

I didn't understand anything anymore, but I kept that to myself. I glanced at my parents, who were looking at me anxiously. They didn't have to say anything for me to know that, after meeting Prokocki, they trusted him for some reason.

Maybe they knew more than I did. Maybe he'd told them something and the three of them decided to keep it secret for my own good.

I shook my head and rebuked myself silently for directing those questions to myself instead of the deputy commissioner. I realized that I had made a decision. Calling me, he was in fact reaching out to me – informally, as a gesture of goodwill. I should use that.

"Kasandra Reimann is in fact Ewa, commissioner."

"Excuse me?"

"She got involved with Robert years ago to ensure her own safety, but she hadn't predicted that–"

"What the fuck are you talking about?"

A phone call wasn't the best way to tell him the whole complicated story, but I had no choice. I took a deep breath and was about to continue, but Prokocki didn't give me a chance.

"We've identified the body," he said. "This was confirmed not only by family members, but also by DNA tests. We wanted to be absolutely sure."

"That's what you say."

"Come on. What reason would I have for lying?"

"You're still trying to protect her."

"Protect who?"

"Ewa. You're afraid they'll find her."

"Who?" Prokocki demanded. "Who would be looking for her?"

"Cayman's men. The ones she testified against."

"Ewa didn't testify against anyone."

"But–"

"I don't know where you're getting this information from, but apparently you've been misled."

I tried to swallow, but my throat was dry. I coughed nervously, feeling like I was getting hot.

I clutched the phone harder, even though I didn't really have the strength. The truth was slowly beginning to dawn on me.

"But…" I started again. "She… she said…"

He finally understood who had fed me the version I was clinging to.

"Kasandra Reimann is Kasandra Reimann," he said. "We checked her as soon as her husband's body was discovered. She has nothing to do with your fiancée, except maybe some physical resemblance."

His words echoed in my head.

"You're... Are you sure?"

"Unless someone forged all her records, bribed a number of people to pretend to be her family and friends, faked photographs from the last several decades, yes. I'm sure."

I didn't know what to say.

Prokocki kept talking, assuring me he'd give me all the evidence. I would be able to see for myself that the person they'd found was my missing fiancée. Finally, he said they would show me the autopsy photos.

I lay frozen in bed. Reality seemed to form somewhere far away from me. Was it really possible that Kasandra Reimann wasn't Ewa?

At that stage, I could no longer afford to be unreasonably certain that I knew the answer. I had to admit what I'd thought was impossible not so long ago.

For God's sake, what had happened to Ewa, in that case? Where had she been for ten years? And why did she die?

More questions came to my mind as Prokocki continued to assure me that there had been no mistake. He talked for a while, but I wasn't listening to him anymore.

Then, with a shaking hand, I gave the phone to the policeman and looked at my parents.

"Where... where's my phone?" I said.

Dad pointed to one of the drawers by the bed. I assumed the phone had been checked by the police; in fact, I was surprised they hadn't taken it away. But then, maybe they assumed that I was working with someone and that they would contact me sooner or later.

In a way, she did.

When I switched on my mobile, I found an unread text message waiting for me. I opened it and saw the authorization code for the RIC.

All the blood drained from my face.

"What's going on, son?" Dad asked.

Once again, my throat was dry.

"I need a laptop," I said.

12

We were already near Łódź when the RIC system finally informed me that Wern had received the code. We didn't go to the eastern border; I had picked that direction only to confuse Damian. I had no doubt that sooner or later he would tell the police everything.

"He got the text," I said.

Glazur took his eyes off the road and looked at me. "Do you want to stop?"

"Yeah."

He nodded without trying to dissuade me from talking to Werner. He had agreed that I had to do it, even though it meant we'd waste some time. He kept pointing out that I owed it to Damian.

There was no reason I shouldn't contact him via the RIC. The connection was encrypted, which meant that any digital trail was so tangled it would be impossible to determine my location, even if someone knew where to look.

"McDonald's?" Glazur asked.

"Whatever. Anywhere they have wifi."

We didn't have to wait long to find the right place. The characteristic golden arches were visible from afar. We went down to McDonald's just behind the Skierniewice junction. Wojtek and Glazur sat down at a table near the window, and I took a seat in the corner.

I wanted to make sure no one bothered me. I ordered a large black coffee at the McCafé and logged into the RIC. Damian had been waiting for me. I took a deep breath, not knowing where I should start.

Fortunately, Werner did it for me.

[Wern] Who are you, actually?

It was not the simplest question he could have asked me, but it was a good start to a conversation. I drank a sip of coffee, regretting that I didn't have a Prosecco handy.

[Kas] Kasandra Reimann.
[Wern] And you have nothing to do with my fiancée?
[Kas] Nothing.

For a moment, there was no reply. I tried to imagine what Damian must be feeling, but I quickly pushed those thoughts away. They were too upsetting.

[Wern] Explain everything to me.
[Kas] You must understand a lot by now.
[Wern] Not enough.

I nodded, as if he could see me. I felt Glazur's gaze on me and gave him a short, reassuring look. I knew what was bothering him. He was afraid that everything we'd done over the past few years would catch up with me, that I would be tormented by remorse I couldn't cope with. I'd assured him that it wouldn't happen, that I regarded every step I'd taken as an unpleasant necessity and that I realized I'd had no choice.

I'd had to save myself. All my decisions had sprung from the need to save myself and Wojtek.

I stared at the screen and paused for a moment with my fingers over the keyboard. They were all in the right places. I slowly started to press one key after another.

[Kas] I'm sorry.

Again, I had to wait for his reply.

[Wern] I'm not interested in your apology; I'm interested in an explanation.
[Kas] I understand.
[Wern] Well, let's start with how much in those recordings was true?
[Kas] Everything I've ever told you about Robert.
[Wern] What about testifying against Cayman?
[Kas] It's also true, but... only when it comes to Ewa.
[Wern] Explain.

I looked at the blinking cursor.

[Kas] What I told you really happened. Ewa's father got involved in some shady business with Cayman and set in motion a sequence of events that ultimately led to the incident at the Sneering Lodge, and to everything else. Using the resources of Reimann Investigations, we have carefully examined each trace and gradually discovered new elements of the puzzle.

I sent the message and took a sip of my coffee.

[Wern] That's not what Prokocki says.
[Kas] He's lying. He wants you to be locked up because he thinks you're the one who killed Ewa. And Robert.

I didn't even want to think about what must be happening in Damian's head right now. He no longer knew what was true and what wasn't. He had no idea who to trust.

[Wern] But how did you find out about that case? And how did you manage to fool me? You look just like her.
[Kas] I know.
[Wern] Explain it to me.

I raked my hand through my hair, pulling on my fringe.

[Kas] You know what I've been going through for the past few years because I've told you all about it.
[Wern] Yeah.
[Kas] But you don't know how long it's been really going on. You got an edited version. But the truth is, Robert has been torturing me for many years, Wern.
[Wern] And?
[Kas] I've been looking for a way to get out of this for a long time.
[Wern] How?

[Kas] Among other things, by searching missing-persons databases. I was looking for an opportunity to use the identity of one of the missing women.

[Wern] To steal her identity. Call a spade a spade.

[Kas] All right. Initially, I only wanted to draw the police's attention after taking over the identity, so that they could help me. I thought it was the only way out of that hell.

[Wern] You could have just called them.

[Kas] No. Robert had all the people I could turn to in his pocket. Besides, he controlled me every step of the way. Even if I had managed to engage someone who was beyond his influence, he would have intervened right away. And believe me, he had the brass in his hand, too. So I finally realized that wasn't the way to go. I had to think of something else.

Damian didn't reply for some time, probably piecing together the first parts of the puzzle that would finally let him understand the whole situation.

[Wern] How did you find Ewa?

[Kas] Just like all other candidates – by browsing the database. You have no idea how long I've been waiting for someone like that. Over the years, I found a few girls I could try to impersonate, but as soon as I came across Ewa, I knew I'd finally found the right person.

[Wern] Because of the physical resemblance.

[Kas] Yes. I must have looked through hundreds, maybe thousands of different profiles. I occasionally found women who were similar to me, but I never found anyone who looked so much like me. It took some arranging on my part, and I was afraid I would arouse

Robert's suspicions, but luckily that didn't happen. The biggest problem was that I didn't know how similar my voice was to Ewa's. But in the end, I had to take that risk. And the fact that it had been a decade since you last heard it gave me confidence. Time had worked in my favour. The more years that passed, the better my chances.

Again, silence. Damian had to be slowly realizing how much effort the whole charade had cost me – effort and many years of planning. From the very beginning I knew that everything would depend on my perseverance. And finally, it had paid off.

I had to play it out psychologically, too. I was aware that Werner might have doubted whether he'd found the real Ewa. It was necessary to create the largest possible gap between what he knew and what he wanted to know.

George Loewenstein wrote about it, demonstrating that the need to bridge that gap is the driving force behind the human psyche. All I had to do was set that force in motion with the right power. That was all it took for Damian to become blinded by the need to get to the truth.

In the end, that need became so strong that it overshadowed everything else. All logic and reason vanished as I gave him more and more recordings, stoking his appetite. He didn't think rationally. He didn't even consider that it all might have been a lie.

And the longer it lasted, the greater the effect. It wasn't just about psychology; it was about physiology. Research has confirmed that waiting for a result releases dopamine in the human body – and, according to Helen Fisher, the longer we wait, the more of the neurotransmitter our brain and spinal cord produces. As a result, dopamine takes control over our decision-making process.

Ultimately, it all comes down to believing what we want to believe. We ignore facts that contradict it, and we emphasize those that confirm our expectations.

I didn't play on Damian's feelings. I played according to the universal rules of the human mind.

[Wern] When did you find her?
[Kas] A few years ago.
[Wern] And you've been preparing ever since?
[Kas] Yeah. It took a lot of sacrifices and risk, but I had no other choice.
[Wern] Yes, you did.
[Kas] No.

A short, firm response should make him realize that I had no doubts about that. But if that wasn't the case, I hoped my subsequent explanation would convince him.

[Kas] You have to understand that I couldn't turn to the law, my friends, family, or coworkers. Robert gradually eliminated all the people he couldn't control from my life. At some point, I was on my own, completely alone. The only person I could count on was Glazur, and it wasn't like he had that many options, either.
[Wern] So you got yourself an idiot to get you out of the shit.
[Kas] I knew you'd do whatever it took.

For a moment, there was no reply.

[Wern] You're sick.

I didn't know how to respond, and not just because I didn't want to argue. I just wasn't sure what my response was supposed to be.

Sometimes I thought I was living in my own distorted world shaped by violence, constant danger and alcohol. I couldn't remember the last time I'd managed to go through the day without drinking or a night without getting beaten. There were times when I thought I was crazy.

But I wasn't. I was entirely rational. I saved my child in the only way I possibly could.

I took another sip of my coffee and shook my head. I had to continue the conversation. I owed it to Werner.

[Kas] I needed someone who would do anything. And someone who I could trust with all the money in Robert's accounts. You understand that, don't you?

[Wern] No. And I doubt anyone else would, either. You should get yourself checked by a doctor.

[Kas] I had no choice, Wern.

[Wern] You could have told me the truth.

[Kas] And count on you to suddenly forget that I'd lied to you? And hope that you'd risk your life to help me, guided by your usual empathy? While Ewa was still out there somewhere?

This time he didn't know what to write back.

[Kas] I couldn't afford that kind of risk. My son's life was at stake.

[Wern] There were many other ways to get away from Robert.

If he was sitting at the table in front of me, I'd have been close to laughing in his face. He didn't know what kind of man Robert Reimann had been. He didn't realize what his men were capable of. What Robert had been capable of.

[Kas] You think?
[Wern] Yeah.
[Kas] So go ahead, tell me how I could have achieved all this. From running away to getting all the resources I needed to make sure my son has a future. Tell me how I was supposed to find someone who would not only help me get out of that hell, but wouldn't steal from me after the fact.

I wasn't expecting a response. Even if Damian had initially thought he knew the answer to my question, later he'd likely realized that there was no valid option. Eventually, I might even come to the same conclusion as me: that I had no other choice.

I kept telling myself that, but I knew that in the end I wouldn't be able to convince myself.

Besides, after all that had happened to me, could I still make any rational conclusions? After over ten years of drinking, I had long since lost sight of the line that separated what was justified by circumstances from what was unacceptable.

No. There was no point in such deliberations. Everything I'd done, I'd done to save Wojtek.

I wanted to explain that to Damian, but I felt like I didn't have to. He'd met me as a different person, but he understood my motivations. And he understood something else, something that's been haunting me and maybe would continue to for years to come.

[Wern] It was you who killed her.

[Kas] No.

[Wern] You got her killed.

[Kas] I had nothing to do with that, Wern.

[Wern] The fuck you didn't. It's because of you that Ewa either decided to reveal herself, or Cayman's men found her. Either way, you're the one who set things in motion. You've got her blood on your hands, for fuck's sake. And I won't let go until I find you. And I swear to God, you will suffer the consequences of everything you've done.

I froze for a moment. Then I looked towards the table where Wojtek and Glazur were sitting. Without a second thought, I grabbed the laptop and slammed it shut. It was like closing some door behind me, leaving not only Werner and Robert but everything that was part of my past on the other side.

I drank my coffee, staring out the window. Cars passed by on the motorway, some of them driving down to McDonald's. Life went on as usual. No one knew what I was doing.

Every year in Poland twenty thousand people went missing. More than fifty people disappeared every day. What difference did it make to them if I stole one of their identities? Even if it had led to her death, wasn't it a price worth paying to save my son from a tragic fate? A fate that Robert would eventually bring upon him?

I'd saved a lot of other people, I reassured myself. Sooner or later, my husband's organization would fall apart through internal power struggles. That would save many people whose existence I didn't even know about.

I was repeating similar conclusions to myself for some time as we drove west together – me, Wojtek and Glazur. Ultimately, though, I accepted that any such attempts to convince myself would be pointless. I had done some disgusting things and I had to face up to them. Would I ever suffer the consequences? In terms of what Wern hoped for, I certainly wouldn't.

Nobody would ever find me; nobody would track us down. We'd leave everything behind and no one would follow us.

No one but Ewa, who had become part of me.

Author's note and acknowledgements

The statistics on missing persons in Poland are alarming, but even more so are those on domestic violence against women. It is estimated that each year between 700,000 and one million Polish women experience it. Every week, three women die as a result of domestic violence.

In a way, this has contributed to the idea of this book. I wondered how far some of them would go if not only their life but also the life of their child was at stake. And if an opportunity for rescue had nothing to do with morality.

I'd assumed that searching for answers to those questions would be disturbing, and working on this book has only confirmed this. At one point I realized that I couldn't count on a happy ending to the story. I also began to wonder what it could be from the point of view of the two main characters.

Kasandra managed to save herself, but she destroyed whatever was left of Werner's life in the process. It also led to the death of an innocent person. And yet she achieved her goals, executed her entire plan. Is this a happy ending for her? I don't think the answer needs much consideration.

But can any other woman in her position count on a happy ending?

I hope so. All the more so because much depends on how we ourselves behave on a daily basis, how we react to certain events, what attitudes we promote and how we relate to what is happening in the public sphere. Physical violence is preceded by psychological abuse. And it's the result of patterns that we've been learning all our lives.

Objectivizing women – for example, by talking about a "hot piece of ass", or infantile evaluation of attractiveness on a scale from one to ten – sows a grain of disrespect in the psyche of young men. And the contempt that grows out of it is difficult to eradicate.

It's not just our problem. Globally, more women are killed by domestic violence than by car accidents, cancer or malaria.

Amnesty International says that domestic violence affects one in three women worldwide. There are still countries in which the law doesn't prohibit marital rape, such as Tunisia. Even in London, more than forty per cent of women admit to being victims of violence. How many are silent? I'm sure we'll never know.

But the question is, is that because we can't know or because we don't want to?

I hope that in this book, together we have said some important things out loud. To ourselves, perhaps, but also to others – although the former is probably the most important. For helping me with that, I would like to thank:

- you, for without you the world represented in *Never Found* would be incomplete. I only create the framework; you fill it with your imagination;
- my parents, who not only introduced me to the world of books and showed me the magic to be found therein

but also taught me how trivial things can project onto the most important ones;

- Olga, Marysia, Piotr, Mateusz, Adrian and the whole team at Filia Publishing, who had faith that that a typescript from an anonymous author could turn out to be a bestseller;
- Gabriela Niemiec and Mirosław Krzyszkowski, to whom I owe my confidence in my own literary capabilities, for there is nothing more pleasant for a writer than to hear from their editor that working with them is a pleasure;
- Michał Kramarz, whose translation of my book attracted numerous foreign publishers;
- all those who, knowing that silence is the loudest scream, speak out.

Remigiusz Mróz
Opole, May 2017

Every year in Poland, almost one million women experience various forms of violence. One in three Polish women is affected by it at least once in her lifetime. However, according to the data quoted at www.kochamszanuje.pl, only 20 per cent of perpetrators brought to trial are sentenced.

The National Competence Centre Foundation and well-known Polish women have joined forces in the public campaign "I Love. I Respect" to speak out even louder about the enormous problem of violence against women in Poland. Men have also joined the campaign. The author of this book is one of its ambassadors.

If you experience domestic violence or know of someone who does, do something. Call someone. The number of the National Domestic Abuse Helpline in the UK is 0808 2000 247.

Check out our website at
www.daturabooks.com to see our entire
catalogue.

Follow us on social media:
Twitter @daturabooks
Instagram @daturabooks
TikTok @daturabooks